STAGE FRIGHT

The firing of the blanks hit Melanie as spits of fire rather than cracks of thunder. At the first shot she clutched her chest. With the second, she rocked backwards. The last one sent her to the floor, where the carpet absorbed her fall. She rolled back and stared at the ceiling, not blinking.

The rest happened quickly. Shouts sounded. Jeramie turned on the lamp. The others gathered around. Marc knelt by her side, his face grim.

'She's dead,' he said.

Melanie closed her eyes, his pronouncement going deep inside her . . .

I am dead . . .

ABOUT THE AUTHOR

Christopher Pike was born in New York, USA but grew up in Los Angeles, where he lives to this day. Prior to becoming a writer, he worked in a factory, painted houses and programmed computers. His hobbies include astronomy, meditating, running, playing with his nieces and nephews, and making sure his books are prominently displayed in his local bookshop. He is the author of the best-selling CHAIN LETTER and SPELLBOUND which are also available from Lightning paperbacks.

CHRISTOPHER
PIKE

LAST ACT

HODDER AND STOUGHTON

FOR JENNY

First published in the USA in
1988 by Archway Paperbacks,
a division of Simon & Schuster Inc

First published in Great Britain in
1989 by Hodder and Stoughton
Second impression 1990

British Library C.I.P.

Pike, Christopher,
Last act.
I. Title
813'.54[J]

ISBN 0 340 50183 9

Printed and bound in Great Britain
for Hodder and Stoughton Paper-
backs, a division of Hodder and
Stoughton Ltd., Mill Road, Dunton
Green, Sevenoaks, Kent TN13 2YA.
(Editorial Office: 47 Bedford Square,
London WC1B 3DP) by Cox & Wyman
Ltd., Reading. Typeset by Avocet
Robinson, Buckingham.

ONE

I hate school, Melanie Martin thought as she finished the last of her trigonometry problems and sat back in her chair. The rest of the class was still busy at work on the assignment. As she had always excelled at maths, she was confident her answers were correct. At the moment, however, she couldn't have cared less. Except for the teacher, she reflected, probably not a single person in the class knew her name. It was only Friday of the second week of school and it looked as if it was going to be a long year. She had not expected to be everybody's best friend after only a few days, but she had the uneasy feeling that months could go by with her remaining a nobody.

Maybe it's my deodorant, or my shampoo. Yeah, I must have dandruff; that explains it.

Melanie was not entirely new to Care High. Her recently divorced father and she had moved to Careville—population 21,867, but only if you counted the neighbouring farmers and their prize-winning hogs—the past spring, and she'd had a good two months of school to make some kind of impression on the local crowd. She must have failed. She had spent the entire summer reading a substantial portion of Careville's closet-size library, working at an edge-of-town diner where no one under thirty or over twelve ate, wishing she were back in San Francisco, and waiting for the phone to ring and invite her into Careville's social circles, where she would be transformed into a typical teenager who had fun *all* the time. Actually, she would have been content to have fun once a week, even for a couple of hours. Perhaps today would be the day. Some gorgeous guy would approach her at lunch and say, *"Hell, you look like an intelligent and sensitive young lady. I've been watching you for some time. You've got a great body. Could I be your very closest friend?"*

But no guy would approach. Her body wasn't that great.

"Damn," the girl on her left whispered, obviously straining over a trig problem. Melanie knew her name—Susan Trels. And talk about boys chasing girls—Susan probably had the rest of September already scheduled. Melanie knew Susan was more attractive than her individual features warranted. Her eyes were a pretty blue, but her face, though tanned and unblemished, was a bit too round. Her energy was her saving grace. Watching Susan for even a minute, you could tell she got a lot out of life. Plus she was tall and blonde and nobody, male or female, could argue about that chest. Since Melanie herself was rather dainty—or flat, depending on her mood—in that area, Susan was not someone who could ordinarily arouse her sympathies.

Yet Susan really seemed to be sweating over the assignment. Melanie remembered last spring watching how effortlessly Susan had moved about campus, from one exclusive clique to another. And now she briefly wondered why someone so popular would bother taking trigonometry in her senior year. And why did Susan care if she got the problems correct anyway? It wasn't a test. On the other hand, Mr. Golden, their teacher, would probably call on a couple of them to work out the solutions on the board. Susan might be worried she would be picked.

She's trying, at least, Melanie thought.

Susan winced and mouthed another obscenity under her breath.

And if you want to be popular, you've got to know popular people.

Melanie began to check out the situation. Mr. Golden was sitting at his desk, engrossed in an astronomy book. Pale and balding, he had a bad stomach and drank Maalox as if it came from cows. He was, however, as mature a gentleman as he was a lucid instructor. She doubted he'd get angry if he saw her helping a classmate. Of course, it would be better if he didn't see her.

There were four problems. Slipping out a scratch page, Melanie hastily jotted down the solutions. Then she folded the page into a tiny square. No one was watching. A flick of the wrist and the answers would land on Susan's desk.

Susan was seated against the wall, and there was no one behind either of them. Nevertheless, Melanie hesitated, and it was just like her. She often made up her mind to do something, got all ready, and then started to worry. Maybe Mr. Golden's stomach hurt today and he was in a bad mood and would take her head off if he spotted the flying cheat sheet. Maybe Susan herself would take the assistance as a personal offence and report her. And what if she actually had the wrong answers. . . .

Just then Susan looked at her. There was something in her large blue eyes that made Melanie feel she would welcome help from any source. Susan gave a half smile, the expression slightly strained. Glancing at Mr. Golden again, Melanie took a breath and then quickly tossed the folded square onto Susan's lap. The teacher didn't raise an eyebrow. The other kids were too busy to notice. Susan unfolded the paper under her desk and then deftly slid it beneath her own papers, reaching for her eraser. Melanie felt a pleasant glow. She had conceived an out-of-the-ordinary action and had had the nerve to carry it through. There was hope for her after all.

Naturally, when Mr. Golden called for someone to work the problems out on the board, he didn't pick either Susan or Melanie. But Melanie did have the right answers, and because he collected their work at the bell, she had the satisfaction of knowing that she had been of some help.

Susan came up beside Melanie in the corridor after class as she was walking towards her locker.

"You should be a dealer in Vegas." Susan laughed.

"Pardon me?" Melanie said. The corridor was crowded. Care High had been built before World War II, when the town's population had been half of what it was now.

"The way you flicked me that paper," Susan explained, wiping strands of long blonde hair from her tanned cheeks. Melanie noted that Susan's teeth were flawlessly straight and wished again her own father had been able to get her braces a few years back. "You could be a dealer in one of the casinos."

Melanie smiled. "I used to practise card tricks." The words were no sooner past her lips than she wished she had responded differently. It had been just this past summer that she had checked a book out of the library on magic tricks. She had practised with the deck of cards only because she had had nothing else to do. Wouldn't Susan realise this and think to herself, *God, this girl sits all alone in her room playing with cards!*

But Susan appeared impressed. "When I was young, I wanted to be a magician. But my fingers were too clumsy." She giggled. "Now I have the same problem with my brain." She paused, then added quietly, "Thanks for the help."

Melanie glanced at the ground. "You looked like you were stuck."

"Your name's Melanie Martin, isn't it?"

"Oh, how did you know?" Melanie asked, pleased—then disgusted that she had shown her pleasure.

"Golden's called on you twice. Both times you had the right answers. How do you do it?"

"I study a lot." *Damn.* Another admission that she had nothing else to do.

They passed from the corridor into the courtyard. The sun was bright, the air sticky. Summer was lingering. Melanie had still to acclimatize to the midwestern humidity. The stuffy classrooms were hard on her. Oh, how she longed for a cool, salty ocean breeze! The day before she had bought two light cotton dresses out of her savings. The one she was wearing was creamy, dotted with roses that matched the red in her hair. Like most girls at Care High, Susan wasn't so formal, and wore baggy grey shorts and a loose green blouse. Susan had left the stress of the trig problem back at her desk. The confidence Melanie had previously observed and admired from afar was clear in her voice.

"I admire your discipline. My name's Susan Trels, in case you didn't know. You just moved here at the end of last year, right?"

"Yeah, I'm from San Francisco."

"Whew! Whatever made you move to this hick town?"

"It's a long story." Talking about her parents' divorce was always a drag. It reminded her of her mom. They had never got along, and Melanie wasn't exactly sure why, other than the fact that her mom—it hurt her to be this blunt with herself—simply didn't like her. And she was an only child too. Oh, well, her mom didn't like her dad, either, and she had married him.

Her dad was responsible for their move to Careville. He had grown up in the Midwest. The divorce had hurt him deeply, and he was hoping the sights and smells of his youth, so Melanie assumed, would ease his loneliness. It was strange in a way, for as a travelling salesman he was hardly ever at home.

"My dad had to change jobs," Melanie added.

"How do you like it here so far?"

"Fine."

"Ah, come on, it's the pits, isn't it? Careville's got one movie theatre, one pizza joint, one—what else? Nothing else! That's the problem."

"It's got hogs," Melanie muttered.

Susan laughed. "Really, and not all of them have four legs." And in the same breath she added, "Hey, have you met any guys since moving here?"

"A few."

"Any I know?"

"I'm—not sure." Melanie pointed towards her locker hall. "I've got to drop off my books. You're in a different locker room, aren't you?"

"I'll go with you. Where are you having lunch? Do you want to stay here or go over to McDonald's?"

Susan wanted to have lunch with her! Melanie was flattered. Usually, she never bought lunch. She brought it from home in—horror of horrors—a brown paper sack. Often, at work, they let her have the leftovers, and the turkey sandwich she had put together that morning had been made up from the diner's food.

How pathetic.

"Either place is fine with me," she said.

"Let's stay here. The snack bar is having fried chicken today. And chocolate cake, if you can believe that. Must be the mayor's birthday or something."

When Melanie deposited her books in her locker, she did so quickly, so Susan wouldn't spot her lunch sack. Susan was being friendly and casual, but Melanie couldn't help feeling that she was silently appraising her—which was not unfair; she in turn was studying Susan. Despite her complaints to the contrary, Susan appeared totally at home in Careville. Half the people who walked by said hello to her.

From Melanie's locker they went straight to the snack bar, Susan still clutching her trig text and notebook. They were served quickly. Susan was not worried about her weight. She ordered two breasts, two wings, fries, a Coke, and a piece of cake. Melanie didn't try to keep up, getting a couple of drumsticks and a milk. The cake was tempting, but chocolate carried on in her body like an acne virus.

Susan led them to the huge oak at the centre of the campus. Care High was old and ugly, but Melanie did have to admit that it had beautiful trees. The shade was refreshing. Susan casually plopped down on the thick grass, her paper plate of food resting on her legs. After a moment's hesitation, thinking of her new dress and possible stains, Melanie joined her.

"I didn't see you around town this summer," Susan said, biting into the white meat. "Did you go back to the coast, or what?"

There was no sense lying, or in telling the whole truth, for that matter. "I travelled with my dad a bit." They had gone to Chicago for a weekend. "And I worked." She smoothed her napkin across her lap and opened her milk. "What did you do?"

"Waited for school to begin so I could start waiting for it to be over."

"Oh."

"I just want to get out of this town, to either L.A. or New York." Susan flicked a fly from her bare knee. Her legs were beautifully tanned, long, and sleek. "Where did you work?"

"At a diner, out on Madison."

"You mean Sam's?"

Sam was her boss. Melanie nodded reluctantly. "I'm a waitress there. The tips are pretty good."

"I worked in the mall at JC Penney's. They made me a credit girl. The pay stunk."

"JC Penney's?" A mall in Careville?

10

"In Barters. It's thirty minutes from here. Haven't you been there?"

Melanie didn't have a car. She usually walked to school, and rode a bike to work. "I haven't been to the Penney's," she said evasively.

"You haven't missed much." Susan stuck a straw in her Coke and took a hearty drink. "Do many guys come into Sam's?"

"A few." Truck drivers, farmers, and husbands.

"Do you get hit on a lot?"

"I do my best."

Susan smiled, watching her, not fooled. "I bet you do," she said politely.

Melanie took the remark as a compliment. Despite her numerous insecurities, she had always thought she was cute. The problem was, she was never sure if anyone else her age thought so. Before the Dark Ages, her mother had said that she was a born aristocrat, and it was true her face was finely structured. The stress of the divorce had caused her to lose weight, making her cheeks somewhat hollow, and this served to emphasize her delicate appearance. Her hair was auburn, short, and shiny, cut in a fringe that almost brushed her deep-set hazel eyes. When the sun was bright, her skin dotted with freckles, and after the past summer quite a few were gathered around her nose. Her lips were her best feature. A deep rosy red and heart-shaped—she seldom used lipstick. Sadly, her teeth, particularly the bottom row, were crooked. When she smiled, she kept her mouth shut. Also, she was short, five two in heels.

"You know," Susan went on, reaching for a french fry, "at the beginning of October we're going to have the Sadie Hawkins Dance."

"Where the girl asks the guy?"

"Yeah. I'd ask my boyfriend, but he's away." She picked at her cake with a plastic fork. "Of course, he wouldn't mind if I went with someone else."

"Sounds like an understanding guy."

"He's pretty cool." Susan took a bite of the cake and nodded her approval. "How about you?"

Melanie sipped her milk. "I don't have anybody particular in mind," she said, which was quite an understatement. David was two thousand miles away, and his beat-up car had had a hard enough time reaching her house when she lived in the neighbourhood.

"It's not the engine, Melanie, it's the gas in this city!"

A dull loneliness touched Melanie. Those had been the days. David had been crazy, and so much fun. She didn't know why he hadn't written in so long.

"That's because you're new here," Susan said reasonably. "But I've lived here all my life. I could introduce you to lots of guys."

Melanie smiled, tensing inside. This girl didn't waste any time getting personal. "Do I get my pick?"

"It depends." Susan pointed to the low brick wall that enclosed the snack bar area. "You see that guy there?"

"Which?"

"The guy eating the orange. Do you know who he is?"

"No." Melanie lied. *He* was Marc Hall. *He* was the most handsome guy in the school. *He* was someone she had daydreamed about.

"His name's Marc. He's a close friend. Right now he doesn't have a girlfriend. Would you like to meet him?"

"No."

"Why not?"

"Maybe some other time." *Like tomorrow. Tomorrows are always safe.*

Susan laughed. "I knew you were shy. Don't worry. It won't come across as a set-up. I talk to Marc all the time. We're in drama together. He's starring in the play I'm going to direct."

"We never had guys like him in our drama club," Melanie said, in spite of herself. Marc was alone, looking north, in the direction of the school stadium, his strong profile striking even from across the courtyard.

Susan was amazed. "You were in drama?"

"I've done a couple of small roles." Melanie was not offended by Susan's surprise. Her acting career had started accidentally. Interior design had always interested her. At

12

Peer High, her old alma mater, she had volunteered to help put together the set for a production of *A Christmas Carol*. As luck would have it, she was backstage on opening night with her mother, when the girl who was to play the Ghost of Christmas Past had an asthma attack—an hour before curtain! Immediately the panicky drama instructor went searching for a replacement. And Melanie's mother got on her case to take the role. Melanie suspected she did it only because she knew her darling daughter would *never* go onstage. And that was precisely why Melanie took the part. There were only a few lines to memorize and she got to wear a great costume.

It was fun! Her mom said she screwed up only a couple of lines. The drama teacher thought she was wonderful, and insisted she be the ghost for the entire run—seven shows altogether. Each week she found herself looking forward to it. Nevertheless, she didn't audition for the next play. Then ten days before *Peter Pan in Kensington Gardens* was to open, Peter got appendicitis and couldn't walk, much less fly. The drama instructor cornered her. A ghost wasn't much different, he said, from a little boy who thought he was a bird. The teacher wanted her as much for her small size as her demonstrated talent. When he promised she would be wearing another imaginative costume, she said OK.

David first noticed her as Peter, and asked her out. Celebrity had its advantages.

"What did you play?" Susan asked.

"A ghost and a boy who could fly."

Susan appraised her in a serious light. "Can you do a New York accent?"

"Not me, I'm from out west," she replied in a thick East Coast accent. Then, in her own voice, "No."

Susan's eyes widened. "Hey, that was good."

"Good for what?"

"Well, like I said, our drama instructor is letting me direct the first play. I have a lot of say over who gets cast."

"I don't do accents. And I never perform without a costume that covers my face."

Susan smiled and started to get up. "Let's go talk to Marc."

"Why?"

"Why not?"

"But I really wouldn't fit in your play."

"The play has nothing to do with meeting Marc. You'll like him. There isn't a girl in Careville who doesn't."

Melanie gestured to their food. "What do we do with this?"

Susan grabbed her plate and Coke. "Melanie, in this part of the country, we take it with us."

Marc was still alone. He didn't notice them approaching until they were a few steps away. Melanie's uneasiness had switched to full-blown anxiety. She had fantasized about Marc so often that she had managed to forget that much of his attraction was because of his tough face, which was quite intimidating up close. He didn't look as if he belonged in high school. As he turned their way, she wondered whether he had flunked a grade or two and had a special distaste for chicks who got straight 'A's. His thick brown hair hung uncombed over the collar of his red shirt. He had not shaved that morning. His grey eyes were intense.

"Marc," Susan said easily. "I'd like you to meet my new friend, Melanie. We're in trig together."

He nodded slightly, a head taller than herself. "Hello, Melanie."

She blushed. "Hi." She sounded about three years old.

"Melanie's from San Francisco. She just moved here last spring."

"We've met before," Marc said, his voice soft. "When was it?"

Marc had come into the diner on July 18; she kept a diary and it had been the high point of the month. He had been alone; nevertheless, he had chosen to sit at a booth in the corner, ignoring the counter. He was polite but distant. He ordered a cheeseburger, onion rings, coffee, and a banana split. She took special care preparing his dessert, putting extra nuts and syrup on the ice cream. Several times, she swung by and asked if he wanted more coffee. Each time he nodded, barely looking up from the paper he was reading. When he left, she was disappointed to see he had scraped aside most of the peanuts. He did, however, leave a nice tip. But no slip of

14

paper saying: "Call me. I love you." It was a hard life being a waitress.

"This summer, at the diner," she answered.

"Sam's. I remember,"

"Melanie helped me cheat on a test today in Golden's," Susan said. "She's a whiz at maths." She held up a piece of chicken. "Want a bite of my breast?"

Marc finished his orange and took the whole piece of chicken. Melanie wondered about the intimate details of their friendship. Yet, if Susan was flirting with Marc, he was not reciprocating. She doubted he smiled very much.

"So will you be there after school today?" Susan asked him.

"I'm working."

"But we have to go over the script."

"Not today we don't," he said flatly, and his tone stopped even Susan.

"Where do you work?" Melanie asked, trying to establish some rapport. The top button of his red shirt lay undone. He had a great build, smooth olive skin.

"In Barters. I load freight."

"He gets union scale," Susan said. "Fifteen bucks an hour."

Marc shrugged. "When they hire me. I'm a walk-on."

"Do you often make the drive for nothing?" Melanie asked.

"Every few days, yeah. There's no predicting it."

Melanie relaxed a notch. Marc was quiet but not necessarily difficult to talk to. "So you and Susan are working on a play?"

"Yeah, it's called *Final Chance*," he said.

"What's it about?"

"It's a mystery," Susan said. "Sort of. The audience knows who the villain is, but the characters don't."

Before Melanie could ask more, they were interrupted by a stubby football player wearing a letterman's jacket and a collar of pumped-up neck muscle.

"Hey, dude!" he said, slapping Marc on the shoulder. "Coach keeps mentioning you."

"Hello, Steve," Marc said quietly.

"Yeah, every time Slater or Chet drop a pass, he curses your name! The man's worried. He's afraid we're going to get our asses kicked tomorrow night."

15

"You'll be all right," Marc said, looking away.

"But we need you!" Steve exclaimed. Marc didn't respond. "What do you say, dude? Come on, bump heads with us."

Marc was hardly listening. "I don't play football any more."

"But—"

Marc raised his hand stopping him. "You know the situation."

Steve lost his foolish grin. "Clyde?"

Marc nodded. And there was a long pause.

Who the hell is Clyde? Melanie thought.

"Well, I've got to go," Steve said finally. He patted his bulging gut. "Got to feed the machine." He touched Marc's shoulder again, lightly this time. "Take care, dude."

"Sure," Marc said.

"It was nice meeting you," Steve said to her.

"Nice meeting you," Melanie replied, trying not to smile.

When Steve was gone, Susan observed, "Steve sure makes a strong case for the relationship between football and brain damage."

"Nah, he's all right," Marc said, handing the chicken breast back to Susan. He suddenly seemed in a hurry to leave. His eye caught Melanie's. "I guess I'll be seeing you around."

"Sure," she said, remembering to smile.

Marc said good-bye to Susan and disappeared in the direction of the parking lot. "Marc has to know someone awhile before he loosens up with them," Susan said.

"I always bring out the best in guys."

"Do you like him?"

Melanie blushed. "He's a doll."

"You should see him in his shorts."

"Susan, who's Clyde?"

"A friend of Marc's. They were on the team together last year. Clyde was the quarterback. Marc was his top receiver. Then Clyde got injured, and I guess that's why Marc doesn't want to play any more."

"Is Clyde going to be all right?"

"Oh, yeah. But he won't be playing ball again." Susan

16

tossed her head in the direction Marc had headed and giggled. "So, what do you think?"

"You asked me that already."

"Come on, are you going to ask him to Sadie Hawkins?"

"I don't know him," she protested, embarrassed.

"There's only one way to fix that."

"He really doesn't have a girlfriend?"

Susan laughed. "Not yet. Just ask him. The worst that can happen is he'll laugh in your face and tell you that you're not sexy enough for him."

"You're right. I've got nothing to lose." Then Melanie added, "We'll see."

The subject was dropped for the moment, and they returned to their spot under the tree to eat their food. Eventually, Susan steered the conversation to trigonometry, hinting she wouldn't mind an occasional tutoring. "Just till I get used to Golden's idiosyncrasies." Melanie wondered if this wasn't the real reason for Susan's friendliness. But she wasn't offended, and promised Susan whatever help she could give.

When it was time for the bell to ring, Susan wanted to go in to her locker. After they went inside and turned into the dim hallway, Melanie saw someone she recognized. She turned to leave. But she was too late. She had just been introduced to the most handsome guy in the school, and perhaps it was fitting that now she had to face the most beautiful girl in the whole country. The girl glanced their way as she was removing a book from her locker. Compared to her, Susan was plain. Melanie knew her name.

"Rindy," Susan said. "Do you know Melanie?"

And, yes, Rindy knew her too.

The accident had happened last May, a month before school was let out. It was nothing really, a fender bender, and Melanie wouldn't have been so upset if she hadn't been driving her father's car—and if Rindy hadn't been so weird. As it was, when the whole thing was over, she felt awful.

The day was rainy. Her father was home, and he hadn't wanted her to walk to school that morning; he had lent her his old Pinto with its hair-trigger clutch. After school the rain started to come down in torrents and the traffic was completely backed up as Melanie was attempting to make a left turn out of Care High's parking lot. Finally, after several minutes wait, there appeared to be a break in the flow of cars. The next approaching car was slowing and had its right blinker on. Melanie naturally assumed it was pulling into the parking lot. She swung out. She was not as quick as she would have liked, but she should have had plenty of time and room to safely join the flow of traffic. The impact came as a complete surprise.

The Pinto was pushed to the right and her left elbow struck the closed window, stinging terribly. Instinctively, she slammed on the brake. The car lunged and stalled. Wincing at the pain in her arm, she pulled on the hand brake and sat back for a moment, her heart going like a pneumatic hammer.

The horns started seconds later. God, these people didn't even check to see if there was bleeding. She turned the key in the ignition, wanting to get over to the side of the road. The car took a hop and a skip and died. She had forgotten to put in the clutch. She tried again, rolling forward. Because other cars had started to go around her, she had to drive down the road before she could pull over to the kerb. Again she put on the hand brake and sat back, feeling a bruise swell under her elbow. After a moment she noticed someone standing in the rain outside her door.

She climbed out of the car slowly, feeling unsteady on her feet. She had on a jacket, but still, she was soaked in a minute. The waiting girl was even less prepared for the weather; her soggy brown dress was already turning to gravy, and her thick dark hair lay plastered in tangled lumps over her pale face. Despite this, Melanie couldn't help noticing her beauty, particularly her eyes, which were an enchanting green.

"Are you the one who hit me?" Melanie asked.

The girl did not seem to mind the rain or the question. "Are you the one who cut in front of me?" she replied calmly.

Melanie noticed she hadn't bothered to move her car—a cream-coloured Mercedes—out of the road. As a result, the northbound traffic was having to funnel across the edge of the opposite lane. "Is it so damaged you can't get it into the parking lot?"

"It's only dented. But I would like to leave it where it is until the police get here."

"The police?" Melanie said. "Is that necessary?"

"I want it made clear that you cut me off."

Melanie wiped the pelting rain from her eyes and shivered. This girl was politely putting all the blame on her. She glanced at the rear of the Pinto. The left corner had been pushed in, the bumper lifted slightly up. "But you had your right blinker on, and were slowing down. You were going to turn."

The girl didn't answer immediately, looking back the way she had come. Her face seemed to darken. She shook her head. "You made a left in front of me. Legally, you're at fault."

"But you were going to turn," Melanie repeated.

"Fine. Take me to court. You'll lose." She wiped her clinging hair, her expression vaguely flat. "Let's get this over with. I want your insurance information."

"I thought you wanted to wait for the police?"

"I've changed my mind. You have insurance, don't you?"

"My dad does." Melanie was not sure if it covered her. Fixing a new Mercedes, even one with minimal damage, would be expensive. She hated letting her dad down. The girl was not yelling at her, but was somehow making her feel unreasonably guilty.

Melanie found a couple of insurance cards inside the glove compartment. She gave one to the girl, saying, "I want the same information from you."

"What for?"

"I'm not automatically taking the responsibility."

The girl stared at her a moment, as though she were seeing her for the first time. "I understand," she said. "My name is Rindy Carpenter, One-oh-one Taff Lane. My parents are in the book. Give them a call." And with that she turned and strode back towards her Mercedes.

"Wait a second!" Melanie called.

Rindy paid her no heed.

That same night Rindy's father called her father. The exchange was cordial and businesslike. They decided to let the insurance companies handle it. A month later Melanie's dad informed her that their insurance had paid for the damage to the Carpenters' Mercedes. Her dad told her not to worry about it. Melanie was disappointed.

She avoided Rindy the last month of school. It was easy to do. Everybody seemed to avoid Rindy.

"Yes, we've met," Rindy said, closing her locker. Her voice was neither friendly nor hostile. With the poor lighting in the hallway, it was difficult to read her face. But she was still as beautiful as ever, and it seemed to Melanie that beauty always gave the advantage, no matter what the situation.

Melanie forced a smile. "In the rain, yeah. Did you get your car fixed?"

"I got a new one."

"Oh."

"What's all this?" Susan asked.

"Melanie and I were involved in a small accident last year," Rindy explained, then quickly changed the subject. "How are you, Suzy?"

"Suzy's fine. I hear you spent the summer in Switzerland."

"Austria. I was there a month."

"Must have been divine," Susan said.

"It was very pretty." She glanced past them. "If you'll excuse me, I have an appointment to keep. See you on Wednesday, Suzy."

"What is the appointment?" Susan asked.

"Nothing important. Nice seeing you again, Melanie."

"Take care," Melanie said. Watching her leave, she found her resentment towards Rindy mingled with sympathy. Something was not altogether right behind those flawless green eyes.

"Did you know the Carpenters are the richest family in Careville?" Susan said. "They have a house a couple of miles out of town that's as big as the school gymnasium."

"It doesn't surprise me, the way she switches cars."

"Yeah, what was that about an accident?"

Melanie gave Susan a quick summary of the rainy-day run-in. When she was done, Susan asked, "Why didn't you try to find a witness?"

"I didn't know anybody here. I didn't want to go up to total strangers and ask if they'd testify for me against the school's beauty queen."

"You might have found someone easier than you think. A lot of people think Rindy's a snob. She's not real popular."

"How do you get along with her?"

"Actually, not bad. But then, we've known each other since kindergarten. And I'm a snob myself."

"Is Marc friends with Rindy?"

Susan smiled. "Worried about the competition?"

"They just strike me as being similar."

"They're both reserved," Susan agreed. "To tell you the truth, I don't know how they feel about each other. Why don't you ask Marc at rehearsal next Monday?"

"You're joking."

"I'm not joking about you trying out for the play. At least take a look at the script. We have a role that must be filled soon. And the cast doesn't like the choice I originally made."

Melanie feigned disappointment. "I wasn't your first choice?"

"The first choice is not always the right choice. Please, give yourself a chance. As Melissa, you'd get to break Marc's heart."

Melanie promised her she'd think about it.

TWO

The following Monday afternoon Melanie Martin entered
Care High's theatre. The stage was lit but the auditorium
was in darkness, and she moved forward cautiously, glad for
the cool air—outside was a furnace. A scattering of people
were present, talking in hushed tones. Some were sitting in
the shadowed chairs, others standing in the corners of a richly
furnished old-fashioned living room set. Susan was nowhere
to be seen. Melanie touched the back of a chair and steered
herself into the seat.

Why am I here? she asked herself.

She came up with three reasons. They were unrelated, but
in her mind they all had a bearing on her being there. First
there was David's letter. She had been wondering why he
hadn't been writing. She should have guessed what had
happened. The letter had come Friday after school.

Dear Melanie,

*I have your last two letters sitting here on my desk. Every time
I look at them, I feel guilty. I know I haven't been writing as often
as I promised. I sort of doubt you're going to like what I have to say.*

*Last month I was down at the arcade in the mall playing
Centipede. I was having a fabulous day. I scored over a hundred
thousand three times. I was really in a groove. But who cares, right?
There was this girl standing there watching me. She looked a lot
like you. We got to talking, you know, the usual junk. Turns out
she didn't live that far from my house.*

*Are you still there? Her name's Judy and we've been going out
for the last few weeks. You'd like her—well, no, I guess you
wouldn't. But I like her, and it's not just because she resembles
you, but because she's a lot like you: sweet, quiet, considerate. I
wanted to tell you that.*

Melanie, I know before you left we discussed how we'd stay close and faithful and all that, but let's face it—you're far away. We've both got to get on with our lives. I still want to remain friends. I just don't want you counting on me.

I feel like a jerk. I'm sorry. I still think you're a great actress and a great person.

> *Take care,*
> *Dave*

She had burned the letter, all the while trying not to cry, wanting to understand why he meant so much more to her now that he belonged to someone else. She wasn't going to write him back.

Then there was reason number two. Marc Hall had come into the diner Saturday evening while she was working the three-to-nine shift. He bypassed the counter and chose the same corner booth he had before. His psychological wall, however, was not nearly so high, and he used her name twice—which she thought was a good sign—while ordering his steak and potatoes. And when she brought him a banana split minus the peanuts, he flashed her a quick smile, saying, "You remembered."

Unfortunately, he didn't ask for her number. Why should he when Rindy Carpenter was in the book?

Reason number three was almost as unpleasant as reason number one. Sunday evening her mother had called. Her dad wasn't home, so of course the two of them had got into a fight. It was all over nothing, as it always was. But one remark her mother had made stayed with her. At the end of the conversation her mom asked if she was going to take drama. "No," she had said. "It doesn't surprise me," her mother had replied.

That morning, before Mr. Golden's class, she had briefly spoken to Susan about dropping by the rehearsal. Susan had thought that would be great.

So here I am, Melanie thought. She still didn't know who she was hoping to impress: David, Judy, Marc, her mother—all of the above?

"Hello. Have you come for the audition?"

23

Standing in the aisle not far away was a dark-haired boy who looked young enough to be in junior high. He had a high-pitched voice, and his ears stuck out. Although his clothes were expensive, they were conservative. She suspected his mother had bought them.

"Sort of."

"My name's Carl. I'm the stage manager for this play. Are you Melanie?"

"Yes."

"Susan mentioned you might show up."

"Where is she?"

"Backstage. May I sit down?"

"Certainly."

He squeezed past her, taking the second seat on her left. He seemed remarkably self-possessed. "What do you think of the set?" he asked.

"I like it." The oil paintings and bookshelves matched nicely with the panelled and papered walls, showing an attention to detail she had not seen at her previous school. And the furniture was fabulous; two wooden chairs looked like genuine antiques. "What is the period of the play?" she asked.

"Immediately after World War Two. This is supposed to be a wealthy couple's country house."

"Did you help build the set, Carl?"

"I helped cut down the walls so they'd fit on our stage. We actually got the set from a junior college in Des Moines. We had to bring it to Careville on a flatbed. The thing's still too big. From where we're sitting, you can't tell, but the set walls press against the theatre walls in several places. This is a hassle because the actors need to use three different entrances. The way it is now, they'll have to go outside to get from one entrance to the other."

"They're having formal auditions this afternoon. Right?"

"For Melissa's role, yeah." Carl nodded towards the three girls who sat near the front. "There's some of your competition."

"Oh, I don't know if I'll try out."

"You should. You'd make a good Melissa."

24

"But you don't even know if I can act."

He smiled. "Can you?"

"I don't know!"

"Well, that puts you way ahead of those girls. They think they just have to get up on the stage and look pretty. They don't know how critical Susan can be. Last year I saw all of Susan's plays."

"Susan directed plays when she was a junior?"

"No, she was *in* them. Susan and Jeramie are the best actors in the school."

"That's interesting. Back where I come from, the drama instructor always directed the school plays. Why is Susan being given all this authority?"

"Starting in November, Mr. Murphy, our drama teacher, is putting on *A Streetcar Named Desire*. He wants Susan to play Blanche. No one else can, not the way she can. So she struck a deal with him. She gets to direct *Final Chance* and in return has promised to be in his play."

Melanie's confidence jumped a notch. Susan appeared to have control of the production, and Susan had given her the impression that she wanted her for Melissa. Then again, that may have just been friendly encouragement. The turmoil in her stomach warned her to be ready for rejection.

"Is that girl also auditioning?" she asked, pointing to a blonde standing on the right side of the stage.

"No, that's Tracy. She's already got a part. She's Mary, Charles's sister in the play."

"And who's Charles?"

"Marc Hall."

"Oh, is Marc here?"

"He's in the back with Susan. I could tell him you're here."

"No, don't bother."

"Marc's a great guy. My sister's playing Ronda, his wife in the play."

Melanie was disappointed Ronda was already taken. "How nice. Is she here?"

"She'll be here Wednesday."

"I hope I still am."

Carl laughed. "So you do want to try out. Just do it. I'll

25

root for you." He stood. "I've got to reroute some cables. We've got more lights on this set than we've got electricity for." He touched her on the shoulder. "Good luck."

"Thank you, Carl. I appreciate it." He was a nice guy.

She was not alone long, when a tall gangly fellow with curly black hair and a camera strung around his neck entered the theatre and plopped down beside her. He crossed his long legs, his large fingers strumming his knee. Staring straight ahead, he didn't so much as glance at her.

"Are you here to watch the auditions?" she asked tentatively.

"No," he replied curtly. "I'm here to audition."

"Which part are you trying out for?"

"The starring role, naturally."

She had assumed that must be taken by now. "Oh," she muttered.

The guy looked at her warily. With his sharp nose and pointy jaw, he reminded her of a fox. His black eyes didn't blink. "You don't think I stand much of a chance, do you?"

"Not at all." She smiled. "I think you stand a better chance than me."

He sat up. "And what do you mean by that?"

"Just that—I think you might get the part you want."

That appeared to satisfy him. He relaxed in his seat. "I better. I deserve it. I've come back a lot of times. I was here last week and they wouldn't even let me read. You'll be lucky if they let you say two words."

"I'm sure Susan will let us both read."

He laughed loudly, then cut it off suddenly. He waved a bony finger towards Tracy. "See that bleached chick? Do you know her name?"

"Yes."

"You do?" he asked suspiciously.

"She's Tracy."

"You're not friends with her, are you?"

"No. I've never met her. She was just pointed out to me." This guy was awfully uptight.

"I just like to know who I'm talking to, you understand." He paused. "What's your name?"

26

"Melanie Martin."

"I've never seen you before."

"I'm new to the area."

He thought about that a moment, then nodded to himself. "That's good, that's good." He offered his hand. "Rodney Rosenberg. Pleased to make your acquaintance."

"Pleased to make yours." Her small palm all but disappeared in his. He was quick, however, to snatch his hand back.

"Where are you from, Melanie?"

"San Francisco."

"Oh, Lord, I hate that place. It disgusts me."

She was offended. "Have you ever been there?"

He nervously smoothed the sleeves of his white silk shirt, running his hands over the thighs of his black leather trousers. "No, and don't extend me an invitation. I don't have to stick my head in the garbage can to know it stinks. Anyway, as I was saying before you interrupted me, that bleached chick is trying to keep me out of the play. See how she's talking to those other girls? Now you tell me there isn't something going on between them."

He was daring her. "But Susan's the director, not that girl."

He snorted. "Susan's a prop! Don't you see? Nothing is as it seems. How else can you explain how someone like Marc Hall, a moronic ex-jock, has been chosen to be in that play?"

"Maybe Marc has a lot of talent." Now she was mad. "Maybe he has more than you."

Rodney threw his head back and laughed. People looked over. "Talent? Hah! He just does what he's told. He plays the game." Rodney stopped smiling. "But no one tells me what to do. I've put up with this for too long. It's time I spoke my mind." He stood suddenly.

"What are you going to do?" The guy seemed capable of violence.

"What I have to do," he said gravely. He bent over and squeezed her arm. "I'm glad we met, Melanie. You're a nice kid, even though you don't know what the hell's going on."

Before she could respond, Rodney turned and strode down

the aisle, hopping onto the stage, startling Tracy and dragging her backstage by her arm. The three girls up front fell silent. Melanie began to bite her nails. She couldn't see Rodney, but she could sure *hear* him. She didn't know whether to be thankful she couldn't hear Tracy.

Rodney reappeared a minute later, stalking back up the aisle. He paused as he passed.

"I'm in," he said.

"What?"

"They want me. I'm in the play." He raised his camera. "Smile!"

The flash blinded her for a moment. When she could see again, he was gone.

Melanie spent the next twenty minutes conjuring up a half-dozen audition-related catastrophes. Indeed, she was in such a state that she was on the verge of leaving, when Susan suddenly appeared from backstage, walking casually up the aisle.

"I could kill Carl. He just told me you've been here for half an hour. I didn't expect you until later."

Melanie smiled. It was a reflex with her. "I don't have a class last period."

Wearing a white trousersuit, her blonde hair tied back in a yellow ribbon, Susan knelt in the aisle beside her. "So, do you want a script? Melissa has the first line of the play."

"Does she get to wear a bag over her head?"

Susan brushed off the remark. "I hear you met Jeramie. What did you think?"

"No, I met Carl, and this other guy—Rodney."

"What did you think of Rodney?"

"Honestly; I thought he was nuts."

"He's the best actor in the school."

Melanie sighed, feeling like an idiot. "Rodney is Jeramie, isn't he?"

"Jeramie is any number of people. Don't be embarrassed. He's always pulling stunts on the unprepared. Did you meet Tracy?"

"Carl pointed her out to me. I liked Carl a lot."

"Carl's a saint." Susan turned her head. "Hey, Tracy!

Come over here!'' As Tracy moved to obey the summons, Susan continued quietly. "Tracy's a mediocre actress, but because of certain politics, I have to have her in my play. I don't have my Ronda here today, so you'll have to read Melissa off her. Would that be OK?''

"Sure. Could I study the part before I read?'' She couldn't act while holding a script. She'd have to memorize the necessary lines.

"I'll get you a character description and some dialogue in a minute. Would you like to be last?''

"If that wouldn't upset things. How many will be before me?''

Susan glanced around. "Five so far.''

"You called?'' Tracy said, coming up behind Susan. After all the extraordinarily handsome and animated people Melanie had been encountering since meeting Susan, Tracy was something of a relief. She was decidedly plain. Even in her silver blouse and short black skirt she looked like a tomboy. Her bleached hair was short and dull, her face wide and expressionless, dominated by a huge nose. The chewing gum in her mouth appeared to be consuming the bulk of her energy. Melanie hoped Tracy was playing a bored character.

"I did,'' Susan said. "Tracy, this is Melanie. She's trying out for Melissa.''

"Hi,'' Melanie said.

"I wanted to be Melissa,'' Tracy said in place of hello.

"Well, we don't always get what we want, do we?'' Susan said with a trace of impatience. She was totally in charge. "But today you can be Ronda. We have to audition these girls.''

"Do I have to?'' Tracy asked.

"No, you don't *have* to. But if you don't, you'll piss me off.''

Tracy's gaze languished on an undistinguished point on the wall. "Oh, all right, I'll do it. But the second you see someone no good, yank her. I don't like wasting my time.''

"I know the feeling,'' Susan muttered. She again promised Melanie a script, and then left with Tracy. But it was Marc, not Susan, who passed out the sheets. He reached her last.

29

"You're going to have to move closer to the stage to read this," he said, referring to the darkness. He had on the same clothes he'd worn Friday. It was weird how he looked even better.

"I will," she said, accepting the copy. "Are you going to be one of the judges?"

"Susan will ask my opinion, I suppose, and Jeramie's, if he comes back."

"Susan told me she had already cast someone as Melissa, but that the rest of you didn't want her?"

The remark surprised Marc. He frowned. "She could have been referring to herself. She mentioned playing Melissa, but we thought that would be too much, with her directing and all."

"Oh, I see."

He turned away. "Good luck."

"Thanks!"

She moved to the fifth row, two rows behind the three girls, and tried to concentrate on the material. The character description was helpful, but unexpected: she had never seen one at the beginning of a play.

Melissa Smith: A pretty young lady in her midtwenties. Friendly and outgoing, particularly with Ronda, whom she secretly despises. Moves naturally; her actual feelings can only be guessed at by the occasional pauses she takes before speaking. People know Melissa is thinking, but not what she is thinking about.

There were three pages of dialogue—and about five minutes' worth. Melanie began to read.

ACT I
Scene I

Late afternoon in RONDA *and* CHARLES's *country house living room in upstate New York. The room is expensively furnished. Canaries can be heard chirping in an adjoining room.*

(Melissa and Ronda enter together, carrying groceries. Melissa is smiling. Ronda is more subdued.)

MELISSA: Charles has picked the perfect day to return home. I believe it was hot and humid the day he shipped out.

RONDA: But then I was with him at the station.

MELISSA: It's better that Robert went along to get him. He may be wild, but he knows how to get in and out of a crowd quickly. *(Sets down her bag on the bar top.)* Besides, the city would be oppressive today. Nothing your constitution would appreciate.

RONDA: *(Sitting wearily on the sofa with grocery bag.)* My constitution has been on the mend since Hitler shot himself. All it needs now is Charles's embrace.

MELISSA: *(Pausing.)* And his yours, I'm sure. His letter played down his injury, but I think I shall feel better when I see him all in one piece. *(Slight grimace.)* Sorry, I didn't mean to worry you.

RONDA: You're not. That he's alive is enough for me. I never told anyone this, Mellie, but before he left for Europe, I used to bargain with God. I prayed, if God would allow Charles to return alive, I wouldn't insist he go entirely unharmed. I suppose that sounds morbid, but I thought if I didn't ask too big a miracle, then perhaps it would be granted. Do you know what I mean?

MELISSA: *(With a laugh.)* Sort of like buying his fate with parts of his body? He might have thought the whole arrangement too expensive. You know how Charles is when you take him shopping.

RONDA: *(Not sure if Melissa understood her.)* Yes, I suppose I should have offered something of my own. *(Touches her chest.)* Sometimes, I think maybe I did.

MELISSA: *(Concerned.)* You poor dear. I shouldn't have kept you out so long shopping for the party. I'll get you a cool drink and then unload the car. And I'll want none of your help.

RONDA: Oh, Mellie, you're too good to me. . . .

Melanie looked up. Susan had reappeared. She wanted to begin. One of the girls in front protested; she hadn't had time to study the script. Susan replied that it didn't matter. Tracy roused herself into a semblance of life and led the first girl onto the stage. Marc reappeared and joined Susan in the last row. Just as Susan called for action, Jeramie popped in from the back and sprawled in a chair next to Marc.

The first girl was clearly experienced. She displayed no signs of nervousness and was able to give Melissa a believable personality. Yet she had a major flaw—she was hardly audible. Melanie felt sorry for her. Susan could not possibly choose her.

Playing opposite the girl, Tracy was mediocre. Melanie was glad she wasn't the real Ronda.

The next person was so bad, Melanie spent the time the girl was onstage focused on her script.

The threesome up front came next. The first two were fair. The worst that could be said about them was neither stood out. Such was not the case with the last one. She had been the individual to complain about the lack of preparation time. Her name was Heidi and she was a talent. Scarcely glancing at her lines, her voice projecting well, she acted as if she were Melissa. Melanie began to squirm in her seat. Heidi's only discernible drawback was her appearance. She was a bit chunky and had bad acne. Melanie did not know how much looks counted. Glancing over her shoulder, she saw Marc, Jeramie, and Susan whispering together. In that instant Melanie realized just how much she wanted to be in *Final Chance*.

"Excellent, Heidi," Susan called. "Melanie."

"I'm ready," she said jumping up. As she walked towards the steps at the end of the stage, suddenly, for no reason other than she was probably cursed, she got the hiccups.

"That Heidi sure has a loud voice," Tracy said as they stepped into the side entrance. Tracy still had her gum.

Melanie nodded. *Hic*. This was ridiculous. *Hic*.

"Are you scared?" Tracy asked without an iota of sympathy.

"No, are you?" *Hic*.

Tracy didn't know she was being insulted. "I work well under pressure."

Carl was waiting in the wings. "I'll let you in on a secret,

32

Melanie,'' he said. ''Susan is easily influenced by Jeramie. They date occasionally. And Jeramie has already said Heidi doesn't look like Melissa.''

''But she was so good,'' Melanie said.

''She uses her hands too much,'' Tracy said. ''Just like Meryl Streep. It gets annoying.''

Swell, you're comparing her to the best actress in the world.

''Ready?'' Susan called out.

''Yeah!'' Tracy yelled, nodding towards the living room set. ''You go first, Melanie.''

The Ghost of Christmas Past and Peter Pan couldn't help her now. Thought was her worst enemy. If she could keep her mind blank and stay out of her own way, she might pull it off with whatever innate talent she supposedly possessed. Sucking in a breath, she strode out under the lights and opened her mouth to speak.

Hic!

There, the worst had happened, and with it came a revelation of sorts. So Melissa had the hiccups. So what? Lots of people must have had the hiccups immediately after World War II. She carried on.

''Charles has picked the perfect day to return home. I believe it was hot and humid the day he shipped out.''

''But then I was with him at the station,'' Tracy said.

''It's better that Robert went alone . . . ''

The three pages of dialogue were spoken and done within what seemed only a moment. Suddenly standing there with no lines left, Melanie had absolutely no idea how she had done. All she remembered was having glanced at her script a few times, and having hiccuped twice. Surely that wouldn't be grounds for the thumbs-down. What reassured her most was that she *felt* like a mid-century young lady from New York who secretly hated her best friend. Hopefully, her judges had felt she acted it.

''That was nice, Melanie,'' Susan said, coming down the aisle. ''Very nice.'' She looked at Heidi, who was again sitting with her friends. ''Could you and Melanie please wait outside while we have a quick conference?'' She raised her voice, taking in all the girls. ''And the rest of you, what can I say?

You tried your best. Thanks for your time."

One of Heidi's friends' faces crumpled. And all the rejects left without a word and in a hurry. Once outside, Melanie found herself alone with Heidi. They lingered beside the school's peeling yellow plaster walls, staying in the shade. It was after three, but the sun was putting in a full day's work.

"Have you ever been to New York?" Heidi asked casually.

"No. I hope it didn't show?"

"Not at all. You could have gone to the same elementary school I did."

Melanie smiled. "So that's where you got all the practice with the accent."

"I don't think it gives me much of an advantage. I liked your naturalness. You know how to stay out of your character's way."

"I use astral projection."

Heidi thought that was funny. The next ten minutes were spent talking about different plays, favourite actors. Heidi seemed to be a nice girl. Too bad they both couldn't win.

Melanie wasn't to keep that opinion.

When Susan finally appeared, she had a script in one hand, and Tracy in tow. She didn't appear worried about breaking someone's heart. Melanie leaned against the wall, wanting the support. Heidi stood tightly erect.

"The verdict, please," Heidi giggled nervously.

"I'm sorry, Heidi," Susan said.

A tremor went through Heidi. "What do you mean?"

"We feel Melanie will make a better Melissa," Susan said. "But you made it tough for us to choose."

A soothing warmth spread through Melanie's chest, as if her heart had been given a blissful elixir to pump. It was a shame Heidi had to spoil the sensation.

"This is some kind of joke," Heidi said coldly.

"You do too many funny things with your hands," Tracy said.

"Hush," Susan said. "Heidi, you know how I hate turning you down."

"No, I don't think that's true," Heidi said, her rage

34

barely concealed. "You insisted I come to this audition. I think you were looking forward to turning me down."

"Heidi," Susan began.

"How could you choose this amateur over me?" Tears formed at the corners of her eyes. "She's obviously never been on a stage in her life!"

"Melanie has experience," Susan said. "Don't take it so hard. Murphy wants us both for *A Streetcar Named Desire*. That role will be much more important."

"I won't play it!" Heidi swore. "I'll just be there to make you look good. You can get this *hack* here to perform with you."

"If it means that much to you," Melanie said quietly, "I'll withdraw."

"You'll do no such thing," Susan said, angry now. "Some people are just sore losers. And you're one of them, Heidi. You should congratulate Melanie, not insult her."

Melanie expected another torrent of abuse. Heidi surprised her by suddenly regaining control of herself. Wiping the tears from her cheeks, she said, "Congratulations, Melanie, I'm sure you'll enjoy being Melissa."

"The next play sounds like it'll be a lot of fun," Melanie said.

"I'll have fun," Heidi assured her. She looked at Susan. "Am I invited to opening night?"

"You can have all the free tickets you want," Susan said.

"Let's not go overboard," Tracy said.

"I'll be there." Heidi nodded, turning to leave. "You can bet I'll be there."

They stood in silence, watching as Heidi vanished around the corner of the building. "That girl's got no class," Tracy said finally, yawning like a sleepy bear. "Hey, Susan, I'm going to split. I've had enough for one day. See you in rehearsal, Melanie."

When they were alone, Susan said, "Ain't I a genius? You really do make a great Melissa."

"I do? How did you know I would last Friday?"

"Instinct. Actually, though, I wasn't sure until I saw you onstage."

"Was I the unanimous choice?"

Susan laughed. "That's confidential. But before we go any further, I have to be sure you can come to each rehearsal. They'll be after school Monday, Wednesday, and Friday. Count on about two or three hours each day."

"That's no problem. During the week I usually don't start work till five." Now she could feel the celebration starting inside. She was going to be working with interesting people. She would have friends. She would get to look at Marc—a lot.

Susan handed her the script. "Here's a copy of the play, minus the last act. You'll get that later. Study hard."

"I will." The manuscript was a photocopy contained in a looseleaf notebook. Melanie wondered if *Final Chance* had ever been published in book form. She glanced at the first page: By Stan Russel, Copyright 1949, All Rights Reserved. "Where did you get this?" she asked.

"Marc, Jeramie, and I were prowling around this second-hand bookstore in Kansas City. Jeramie found it in some dusty corner. I suspect it's seldom performed, even though it's a neat story. I was thinking of writing to the author and inviting him to our opening night. But for all I know, he's dead."

"I'm eager to see how the plot goes."

"He's a good writer. I hope I won't spoil it for you by telling you that Melissa comes to a bad end."

Melanie made a face. "Does she get murdered?"

"Worse."

That evening at work Melanie kept expecting Marc to come in. She even checked the refrigerator to be sure they had fresh bananas and whipped cream just in case. But he never showed, and she wondered why she had thought he would.

Sam was pleased to hear she'd be in a play. Whatever hours she needed off were fine with him. He even told her to invite the whole cast by after any performance and the desserts would be on the house.

When she rode into her dark driveway that night on her trusty Schwinn ten-speed, she was delighted to see her father was home. He had been gone since the day before school started.

Inside, she found him asleep in his favourite chair, a cup of cold tea nearby, the TV on low. For a minute she knelt silently on the floor at his feet, sighing as she saw the tiredness in his face. He was a small person, like herself, with the same delicate features that were incongruous with his career as a salesman. That was the reason, really, that they had no money, and was perhaps one of the reasons her mother had split. He was not suited for his job. He lacked aggressiveness, energy.

He would want to hear about the audition. Also, it was never good for him to pass an entire night in the chair; he would always wake with a stiff neck. She shook him gently. He opened his brown eyes slowly. "I was just dreaming about you, Melanie," he said softly.

"You're wrong, you're still dreaming." She leaned forward and hugged him. "What was I doing?"

For a moment a shadow crossed his face. Then he smiled. "I don't remember." He sat up. "Tell me how you've been? When did we last talk?"

"A couple of weeks ago. Oh, so much has happened since then! I've been having the neatest time. . . . " She told him about meeting Susan and Marc, and winning the Melissa role. He listened attentively, asking several questions about the audition and the play. Yet it was obvious he was exhausted. When she was through rattling on, he kissed her good night and went straight to bed. Her offer of a cooked dinner had been politely refused. Minutes later she could hear him snoring. It was then she realised she hadn't asked a word about his trip.

The house was fairly tidy, but she gave it a quick going-over each night before bed. A shower and assorted odds and ends added to the time; it was after ten before she was under the covers. With school the next day, homework to catch up on, and work in the evening, prudence dictated lights out. Had she not—accidentally?—left the manuscript on her bedstand, she probably wouldn't have been tempted to discover Melissa's fate that night. She intended to read for only five minutes. As a quick aid, she jotted down on the first page who was playing whom.

Melanie didn't put down the play until she had finished
Act II.

*Melissa and Ronda return home to Ronda's country house after an
afternoon of shopping in preparation for a party. The party is being
given in honour of Charles—Ronda's husband, who is returning home,
wounded and decorated, after World War II. The extent of his injury
is not known. Melissa and Ronda are old friends who went to school
together, along with Mary and Robert. Mary is Charles's younger sister.
She is very devoted to him. Robert and Charles are also friends, or were
until they entered the service. During basic training Robert began to
show signs of instability, and once on the battlefields of Europe his
condition deteriorated. He would point his unloaded rifle at others in
his battalion and pretend he was killing them. Charles was never sure
if Robert was only faking his craziness to avoid combat. Eventually,
Charles did report Robert to their superior officer. Not long after that,
Robert was sent home and discharged. Whether he was anagry at Charles
for reporting him is not clear. Like Melissa, it's hard to tell how Robert
feels.*

*Alone in the country house, Melissa and Ronda discuss Robert and
Charles's history. Melissa also inquires, in passing, if Ronda has been
seeing Robert since his discharge. Melissa, in fact, does know that Ronda
has been spending a great deal of time with Robert, and doesn't approve.
Ronda is sensitive to her unspoken accusation. Nevertheless, Ronda
admits to visiting Robert. The whole group, including Charles and
Mary, have always known that Robert loves Ronda. Because of his
unstable condition, Ronda feels it's her responsibility to help Robert
get back on his feet. She tells Melissa this, who doesn't openly question
her motivation. Indeed, Melissa says she wished Charles had also played
the crazy man, and returned home before being injured. There seems
to be some confusion as to the exact extent of Charles's injury.*

*Robert has gone to fetch Charles at the railway station. Anxious to
have the house spotless before they arrive, the ladies start clearing up.
While attending to the bar, Melissa finds a handgun in a cabinet.*

"What is this?" she asks. "It belongs to Robert," Ronda explains. "Or rather, it's something he stole from the army." Because of the way Robert had carried on with guns in Europe, Ronda has taken it away from him. Melissa also finds a box of shells in the cabinet. She leaves the gun on top of the bar while they finish cleaning the house.

While Melissa is downstairs checking the wine cellar, Mary arrives. Mary doesn't like Ronda. She feels Ronda isn't good enough for Charles. Mary also knows Ronda has been seeing Robert during Charles's absence. With Melissa out of sight, she unfairly accuses Ronda of being unfaithful to Charles. A fight ensues, during which Mary's jealousy of the rich and beautiful Ronda becomes apparent. Coming back up the stairs, Melissa catches the tail end of the argument. But the two settle down when Melissa re-enters the living room. Mary also notices the gun, and picks it up before setting it back on the bar.

Thinking the men won't be back for a while, the three ladies run out to do some last-minute shopping. Harmony has been momentarily restored. Or so it seems. Unknown to Ronda and Mary, Melissa has slipped the gun into her bag.

Robert and Charles arrive at an empty house. It is immediately obvious Charles is hurt far worse than the others think. He has lost his right arm. Fidgeting, as is his habit, Robert says he doesn't believe Ronda knows about the amputation. Charles insists she must; in the second letter, he said, he had specifically talked about his arm. Unless, of course, the letter got lost in the mail.

Robert and Charles talk about the war, and about their childhood, jumping back and forth, weaving Ronda into everything. Robert is so erratic, it's hard to tell whether he loves or hates Charles. But it's clear he's fascinated with Ronda.

Eventually, the ladies return. The reunion has its joy and its sorrow. Both Melissa and Mary are upset to see that Charles has lost a limb. On the other hand, Ronda doesn't seem surprised, although she denies having received Charles's last letter. Ronda is just overjoyed to see her husband alive and breathing. Mary starts to fight with Ronda again, but Melissa stops her. Standing apart from the others, Robert watches and says nothing.

The party begins but the festive spirit is missing. Charles is tired from his travels and Ronda also pleads exhaustion. After a while, everyone retires to his or her bed, each enjoying a room alone, except for Charles and Ronda, who sleep together.

In the middle of the night Ronda gets up to use the bathroom. She has weak kidneys. It has been a habit throughout her life to use the bathroom two or three times a night. Compounding this physical problem is another habit of hers; she likes to hit the bottle, particularly when no one's around. Before returning to her bed, she stops at the bar and opens the small icebox underneath. It is then Ronda notices Melissa sitting quietly on the couch.

They begin to talk. Melissa's voice is dreamlike, as if she could be sleepwalking. She tells Ronda how much she loves Charles, and how much she hates her. By her silence Ronda encourages Melissa to continue. Melissa, it seems, even blames Ronda for the loss of Charles's arm. Melissa feels it had been Ronda's responsibility to keep Charles out of the war. While talking, Melissa stands and opens the back door. Ronda notices she is wearing gloves. When Ronda asks why, Melissa removes Robert's gun from a desk drawer and points it at her. Startled, Ronda backs towards the bar. Melissa shoots her three times in the chest.

Before hurrying back to her bedroom, Melissa drops the gun beside the body and shuts the icebox door, turning off the only light. In the dark, the voices of Mary, Robert, and Charles can be heard. What has happened?

Melanie set down the play. End of Act II. Her eyes were heavy. She glanced at the clock. Five after twelve.

Melanie was both impressed with and confused by *Final Chance*. The dialogue was clever. She liked the sense of not being sure what was going to happen. In every relationship there was the possibility of an explosion. But the conclusion of Act II was a disappointment. It violated every rule of a mystery by revealing the culprit at the same time as the crime. What was left to learn?

It's a mystery. Sort of. The audience knows who the villain is, but the characters don't.

Turning off the light, laying her head down to sleep, Melanie wondered what would happen in the last act.

THREE

The first rehearsal for *Final Chance* took place Wednesday afternoon, two days after Melanie's successful audition. Susan had promised it would be a long one. Nobody in the cast had to work that day, and Susan wanted to run through Acts I and II, and Melanie had already memorized many of Melissa's lines. She carried the script wherever she went.

Melanie was making good on her promise to help Susan with trigonometry. Before the rehearsal began, they worked on Mr. Golden's latest assignment on the set sofa. They were making slow progress.

"I'll give you a hint," Melanie said, pointing to the expensive calculator—which was capable of performing every imaginable trig function—balanced on Susan's knee. "Get rid of that thing. It makes it too easy. You don't have to think."

Susan scratched her head. "But I don't want to think. That's why I'm bugging you."

"You're not bugging me. One good turn deserves another."

Susan spoke seriously. "I would've asked for your help even if I'd picked Heidi."

"Really?"

"I'm like everyone else our age. I have no scruples about using people." She glanced at her textbook with distaste and shut it. "Can we continue another time? The others will be here soon."

"Sure."

Susan leaned back in the luxurious couch, regarding Melanie thoughtfully. "What's your opinion of the story?"

"I like it. What happens at the end?"

"Melissa gets caught."

"Darn. I was hoping to get away with it."

41

"Act Three starts a month after Act Two. There's a twist at the end that's a lot of fun. From what I remember. Do you know Jeramie has the only copy of the whole play?"

"How's that?"

"I don't know, he's the one who bought it. I think he's going to charge me for the rest."

Was Susan being serious? "But how can you direct it without having the entire script?"

Susan chuckled. "This is Careville. The mayor doesn't even have his own phone." She sat up suddenly, her tone changing. "Melanie, I have a confession to make."

Melanie had a moment of panic. "Do you have someone else in mind to play Melissa?"

Susan saw her concern and laughed. "No, that's not it at all. But I have something to say I don't think you're going to like. I would have told you earlier, but I was afraid you wouldn't take the part. Actually, it's a small miracle you haven't already heard."

"I have to do a nude scene?"

"No. Rindy is playing Ronda."

"I see," Melanie said automatically. The news took a moment to penetrate. She had to reassess how she felt about Rindy. There was still some resentment inside, nothing deep, but enough to make her lose her enthusiasm for the afternoon's rehearsal. "Does Rindy know about me?"

"Yes. She doesn't mind."

Melanie swallowed. "If she doesn't mind, I don't mind."

"Honestly?"

Bitterness had never been her strong suit. "Sure."

"Are you mad at me for not telling you earlier?"

"No. Oh! Carl is Rindy's younger brother!"

Susan's mouth suddenly dropped.

"You speak my darling's name much too casually," a silky voice whispered in Melanie's ear. Cold metal touched her ear. She had heard no one approach. Her heart skipped a beat. Susan laughed, getting over her surprise.

"Jeramie, you cat!" Susan said. "Where did you come from?"

Melanie found she was trembling and fought to stop it.

42

Jeramie—she had forgotten how tall and thin he was—swept from around the back of the couch, his black hair flowing over his silky green shirt. He wore a maniacal grin that went uncomfortably well with the revolver he was carrying. A 35mm camera hung around his neck.

"I didn't scare you, Melanie, did I?" he asked.

"Yes. No! A little."

Jeramie nodded gravely. "I understand answers like that."

Susan stood, grabbing her trig text and papers. "Jeramie, be so kind as to amuse Melanie until I return from my locker. Teach her how to use your gun. That'll be one less thing we'll have to do in rehearsal. And, Melanie, make sure it's not loaded."

When Susan was gone, Jeramie sat on the couch beside her and stared. Melanie stared back. "You have beautiful eyes," he said finally. "I can see my own in them."

"Mine are hazel. Yours are black. What are you talking about?" She decided she had better assert herself around Jeramie.

Jeramie smiled and relaxed back into the sofa, crossing his beanpole legs. "You must think I'm weird. But you're only half right."

"You're a perfect Robert."

He surprised her. "I'd rather play Charles," he said seriously. "He's a good guy. Bad people bore me." He looked at her. "Do I bore you?"

"You're one of the most interesting people I've ever met," she said honestly. "Do you really hate San Francisco?"

"It disgusts me." He spun the bullet chambers. "So you're going to be our murderess. I don't envy you."

"I don't understand?"

He smiled again. "Most people have given up trying to understand me. You'll learn." He put the gun to his forehead, pulled the trigger. The noise of the falling hammer made her jump slightly. He continued in a softer tone. "You'll also learn it's never good to play a character you wouldn't want to be. When you get off the stage, it can follow you."

"Why did you pick this play if you didn't want to be Robert?"

"I didn't *pick* the play. I found it. The others wanted me to play Robert. That's how they see me." He handed her the gun, changing the subject. "This is a Smith and Wesson thirty-eight, model ten, with a four-inch barrel. It was a popular gun after World War Two. It's still popular. Robert couldn't have stolen this particular weapon from the army, but we can't get the right one, so it all evens out. Notice there isn't a safety."

"Why is that?" She'd never realised guns were so heavy. She'd never handled one before. Her father hated them. She shared his feelings.

"Revolvers seldom have safeties. Cock it."

"What?"

"Pull the hammer back." He helped her. "*Now* pull the trigger." Pointing at the floor, she did so. The hammer fell with a sharp click. He continued. "When the hammer's cocked, the trigger has to go through only one pressure point. That's called single action. But this is a double-action gun. When the hammer is not cocked, you have to pull the trigger back far to get it to fire."

"Is all this important? I'll just be using blanks."

Jeramie pulled a handful of shells from his pocket, the brass cartridges bright in his palm. "Most people don't realise that a blank, except for having wax and no lead pellet at the tip, is identical to a real bullet. At extremely close range a blank's dangerous. It could blind you."

"Wasn't an actor killed by a blank?"

Jeramie paused. "You haven't read Act Three, have you?"

"No. Could you give me a copy of it?"

"Susan has a copy. Get it from her. Mine's covered with doodles."

"She says she doesn't."

"Well, she must have lost it then. Anyway, you're right, an actor was killed by a blank. His shells were of high calibre and he happened to place the nozzle here—" Jeramie touched a spot just above his ear. "Probably the weakest part of the skull. Someone should have told him what I'm telling you now."

"I'll be careful," she promised. Her opinion of Jeramie was changing. She had a feeling it would constantly be changing. "Isn't it illegal to use a real gun in a school play?"

"Was it illegal in San Francisco?"

"Yes."

"Then it's probably illegal here. But who's going to tell?" He took the gun back and began to load it.

"Why do I have to shoot Ronda three times?"

"In case you miss." He gave her the gun back. "Come on, let's do it. You can shoot me."

Reluctantly, Melanie got to her feet. She would have preferred practising with the others around. "Where should I stand?" she said.

Jeramie checked the film in his camera, nodded towards a spot at the end of the sofa. "Over there, on the right. No, you're going the wrong way. When we say right, we mean *stage* right, right from the point of view of the actors. Remember that or you'll get confused during rehearsal."

"I did know it. I just forgot."

Jeramie moved into position. "I'll be backing away from the couch towards the cabinet and bar. By the way, that's my mommy's china cabinet."

"It's very pretty." Made of polished walnut, a head taller than Jeramie and stocked with cups and plates—his mother must have been enthusiastic about her son's career to risk lending it. A mirror glittered behind the china. Looking at Jeramie, she could see herself.

"Point the gun at me, please," he said, focusing his lens on her. She did so. "Excellent! Smile, Melissa!" The flash made her jump. "Caught you in the act," he said.

"What are you doing?"

"Posterity. The yearbook." He let his camera dangle. "What does Ronda say before Melissa murders her?"

" 'But we were friends.' "

"You've been studying. Very good." He took a step closer, grinning. "Are you ready?"

"Should I cock it?"

"For the first shot? Yes, it's always dramatic. Ready?"

"No. Are you sure these are blanks?"

"I'd stake my life on it."

That wasn't the answer she'd wanted to hear. Her fragmented reflection in the cabinet mirror was disturbing. She was shooting herself. "I'm going to aim a bit to the right."

"No." Jeramie was firm. "This is why we are practising. It's hard for most people to aim and fire even an empty gun at someone. You have to get over that. Ready?"

"You're absolutely positive they're blanks?"

"I bought them this afternoon in Barters at Arnie's Arsenal. Arnie has nothing against me."

"All right. Should I open the yard door like it says in the script?"

"Do you know why Melissa does it in the play? Remember, the door's supposed to be locked from the inside."

"So the others might think someone entered from the outside and killed Ronda?"

"Exactly. For now, though, leave the door alone." He showed a trace of impatience. "Come on, make me immortal. Kill me."

Melanie raised the gun, moved slowly towards Jeramie, summoning her accent. "You're a thorn. I have to pull you out. And throw you away."

Horror spread across Jeramie's face—so real, her trigger finger trembled. "But we were friends," he moaned.

She cocked the hammer. "I'm no one's friend." She fired. *Bang!*

The noise was deafening. Startled, she almost dropped the gun. But there was hardly any recoil. Jeramie sagged back, touching the corner of the icebox at the base of the bar. In quick succession she shot him twice more. He dropped to the floor, rolling on his side.

"It's loud," she gasped. "How did I do? Jeramie? Jeramie?" He didn't move. "You're not dead, Robert," she said, stopping herself from panicking.

He looked up at her with one eye, half his face pressed against the floor. "Not yet." Then he was on his feet in seemingly one movement. "I have to go."

"Why?"

"I have to go get Rindy."

"You have to pick her up somewhere?"

Jeramie leapt off the stage. His agility was remarkable. "I have to find my beloved. I can't live without her now that I've died for her."

Melanie sat back down, placing the gun beside her on the couch. She picked up her notebook, planning to do more homework. She ended up starting a letter to David. She didn't know why she was writing it. Revenge?

Dear David,

You were right, I didn't enjoy reading your last letter. I felt betrayed, and was mad. But after thinking about it awhile, I realise everything you said is true. Two thousand miles is a long way, especially when neither of us has an American Express Card for airplane tickets. And as the song says, "Don't feel so down and out, I've found someone of my own." I'd like to tell you he's a lot like you, but the truth is, you have nothing in common. He's strong, quiet, and handsome. I won't bore you with a lot of details.

I'm in a play. It's called Final Chance, *by a Stan Russel. In it I get to kill that awful girl who whacked my car last spring. I can hardly wait.*

Melanie put down her pen. Marc and Tracy were just coming in. She stood to greet them, but they went into the Green Room, stage left, without looking her way, and shut the door. Boy, they really seemed absorbed in each other. Leaving her notebook behind, she crept down the hall towards the door. Not wishing to pry, she still wanted to know what it was they felt they needed privacy to discuss. She was awful. David's new girlfriend would never do this. Leaning against the wall next to the Green Room door, she tilted her head at a favourable angle. Marc and Tracy were arguing. Unfortunately, she couldn't hear exactly what they were arguing about. But she did catch her name once, and another name, Clyde.

"Melanie?"

"Yes?" she gasped, standing so straight so suddenly, she

47

probably gained a permanent inch. It was Carl. Inside the Green Room, Marc and Tracy had fallen silent.

Carl smiled. "How are you doing?"

"Nothing."

"Huh?"

"Fine."

"I wanted to congratulate you." He stuck out his hand. She shook it mechanically. Still silence in the Green Room.

"Thank you." She started back towards the stage. "For what?"

He laughed. "Getting the part, of course." He nodded towards the Green Room, which she was trying to get away from as quickly as possible. "Is Marc in there?"

"I wouldn't know." She added quickly, "I just learned Rindy's your sister."

"You don't mind? With what happened with your cars and all?"

"Accidents happen."

He looked at her. "Rindy will be here in a few minutes. She's a good actress. You'll enjoy working with her."

"I'm sure I will."

"Would you like a tour of the stage?" he asked as he gestured about.

"Sure."

A tour it was. Leading her from one corner to the other, he bombarded her with more information than she wanted. She half listened. He finished with an explanation of a dusty fire-escape door on the far left—stage right, Melanie reminded herself—of the set, opposite the hallway leading to the Green Room.

"This door has a history at Careville. It's an emergency exit. Never open it. If you do, an alarm will go off here and at the fire department. At least twice in the last five years some actor has forgotten that and accidentally leaned against the handle in the middle of a play. You can imagine how a bunch of men bursting in with hoses can wreck a show."

Melanie assured him she'd keep her hands off. She noticed Susan had returned and was standing in the doorway of the

Green Room, presumably talking to Marc and Tracy. Melanie excused herself from Carl and returned to the sofa to collect her books. Carl, meanwhile, noticing an overhead light was loose, left through a back door to find a ladder. Only when Melanie had her things in her hands did she spot the girl sitting alone in the dark in the centre of the auditorium. *Rindy*.

Better to clear up any bad feelings before rehearsal began. Melanie took the steps down off the stage and moved slowly up the aisle. Rindy did not turn to follow her approach. Melanie realised Rindy's eyes were shut. She coughed discreetly. Rindy looked over.

"Hello, Melanie," she said softly.

"Am I disturbing you?"

"No. The word is you're Melissa." Rindy's long black hair and equally dark emotional distance cloaked her with double layers of mystery. Melanie decided to get straight to the point.

"I hope we can be friends."

Rindy smiled faintly. "As long as we stay out of the rain, we should be fine."

"Well, it shouldn't rain in here," Melanie said gamely. "Did you see Jeramie?"

"No."

"He left a little while ago, looking for you." Rindy was not impressed. Melanie added, "He showed me how to use his gun."

"Really?" Rindy showed signs of life. "And did he show you his camera?"

"Yeah. He took my picture. At the weirdest time."

Rindy chuckled quietly. "You have to learn when he has film in that thing and when he doesn't. You're never safe until you do."

"Are you close friends?"

"Friends?" Rindy had wandered off for a moment. "We go way back. We dance together a lot, sometimes at a club in Barters, other times in my basement. It's cool down there in the summer. He likes the music so loud, it hurts." She chuckled again. "With him, dancing is like a mating rite.

Every time we finish, he proposes. I have to keep turning him down."

"He's an unusual guy," Melanie said.

"He's stark raving mad."

"I'm looking forward to this play."

Rindy took a cigarette and lighter from her purse and yawned. "It should be one fireball of fun."

The rehearsal got under way shortly afterwards. The object of the day, Susan said when they were all gathered together, was to get a feel for what it would take to keep them from embarrassing themselves in front of the student body. She was being silly. Melanie knew Susan intended *Final Chance* to be the best play Care High had ever put on.

They started with the beginning of Act I, so Rindy and Melanie were on the stage first, the others sitting halfway up the rows. Rindy had done her homework too; she hardly needed the script. Melanie was impressed with and slightly taken aback by her skill. Rindy gave Ronda a life all her own, particularly conveying the hidden fragility Stan Russel had embodied in his character. She made Ronda hard to hate.

Susan, however, interrupted them constantly. Should Ronda look happy here? she would ask. Should Melissa fix her hat? Should Melissa touch Ronda at this point? Mr. Russel had left a lot to the director's discretion.

When Melissa went down to the wine cellar, Melanie retired to the audience, purposely sitting next to Marc. Did he know she'd been eavesdropping earlier? He was more friendly than usual.

"I noticed you riding a bike to school this morning," he said.

"I don't usually," she said, embarrassed. Yeah, usually she walked.

"If it's getting dark when we leave, I can give you a ride home. I've got a truck."

She recited a quick silent prayer for an early sunset. "That would be nice. Do you think we'll get to the end of Act Two today?"

"That's the plan. I guess you know you're going to kill my wife."

"You won't hold it against me?"

He smiled. She wished he did it more often. "I'm afraid you'll have to pay."

Susan hushed them. Tracy was just starting her entrance. Melanie watched and listened closely. Tracy was a far better Mary than Ronda. But that wasn't saying a lot. Melanie found the moments when Tracy and Rindy weren't acting more interesting. Tracy was being so artificial in her politeness, it was obvious she didn't like Rindy. This disdain carried over into the story and gave Tracy's performance what edge of realism it did possess, and which it did not deserve. In both roles, real and imagined, Rindy handled Tracy carefully.

When it was time for Melissa to return from the wine cellar, Susan told Melanie to wait inside the stage right entrance, visible to part of the audience but not to the arguing girls. Then when the three of them left to go shopping, Susan had her secretly slip the gun in her bag.

"Only the most observant audience members will see this," Susan explained. "But in the next scene, the majority may notice the gun is missing."

"Why is Melissa taking it?" Melanie asked.

"In the last act," Susan said, "it's implied she must have an outsider handle the gun. We learn when the police dusted the gun that they found prints belonging to Robert, Mary, Ronda, and one unidentified person."

Before the guys got up for their scene, the group had a discussion. Charles no longer had his right arm. How were they supposed to hide Marc's? Wearing a coat slung over his right shoulder seemed so cliché, but after numerous experiments, they discovered no alternative solution. Susan told Marc he would have to get the arm taped down for the opening night because it kept popping out.

Marc was a fine actor. Melanie could see him going to Hollywood and becoming a heartthrob on a major soap. He had a certain squint like Clint Eastwood that worked well in almost any situation. Jeramie, however, was in a class by himself. Had this been Broadway, he still would have stolen the show. Of course he could imitate Robert's brooding twitches, but it was his control, his downplaying of Robert's instability, that impressed her most. He only suggested Robert's internal turmoil, leaving you unsure.

They skipped the scene in which all the characters were at the party. It was complicated, and it was getting late. And Susan wanted to run through the murder.

"This is the only other scene where Rindy and Melanie are alone," she said. "If we work it out, you can rehearse alone."

As they started, the cast all raised a question. When Ronda first notices Melissa on the couch, Ronda had been going through the icebox. Then when she goes to sit with Melissa, she leaves the door slightly ajar. Now why, they all asked Susan, would anyone leave the icebox open?

"I think it's because she's startled," Susan said. "And the open door makes the audience tense by distracting them. I believe Stan Russel's using psychology here. Remember, the only light we'll have is from the icebox. When Ronda falls dead next to it, think how neat it'll look having just the slit of cold white light shining over her bloody body. I definitely want the icebox open."

"But then I'll shut it?" Melanie asked.

"Yes," Susan said. "You'll drop the gun next to Rindy, shut the fridge, and then walk off in the direction of the Green Room, which is the direction to Melissa's bedroom."

"It'll be dark at that point," Rindy said.

"I like the dark," Jeramie said.

Jeramie gave Melanie a box of spare blanks and again showed her how to load the revolver. When the moment came to shoot Rindy, she didn't hesitate. Maybe she still harboured resentment towards her. But she doubted it.

Jeramie took a picture of Rindy lying dead on the floor. Rindy smiled at the click of the camera.

Finally, the rehearsal was finished. Tired and hungry, Melanie was relieved, and yet, when she got outside, and saw there was enough light left to ride her bike home, she wished Susan had kept them longer. Susan left with Jeramie,

Rindy with Carl, and Marc went off with Tracy. Sniff.

No one loves me.

Undoing the chain that tied her bike to a fence far from the parking lot, Melanie felt pretty low.

She was a quarter of a mile down the road, when a white Ford pickup pulled alongside her.

"Hey, wasn't I supposed to give you a ride?" Marc asked, matching her speed, his elbow leaning out of his open window. Tracy sat beside him—not close enough to put an arm around, thank God—looking straight ahead.

"I thought you meant if it was dark," she said.

"It's up to you."

"I am a bit tired," she said, stopping. Marc gunned the engine briefly, pulled up to the kerb, and climbed out. He had undone the buttons on his shirt and rolled the sleeves up over his biceps; his muscles literally bulged through the material. He picked up the bike with one hand. Tracy hadn't even turned around.

"With all this riding," he said, "you must be in good shape."

She smiled. "I can eat what I want and not get fat."

He swung the bike into the back. "Hop in. Where do you live?"

Melanie hurried around to the passenger side. Tracy, chewing a jaw-busting wad, glanced at her. "Fancy meeting you here," Tracy said, lazily scooting over.

"Amazing, isn't it," Melanie agreed. Marc put the truck in gear. "My address is Nine-oh-one East Monroe," she said. "Do you know where it is?"

"Yeah," Marc said.

Tracy snorted. "When you grow up in this town, you know every house. That's the grey one with the awful picket fence, isn't it?"

"We're fixing it," she replied quietly. She was very self-conscious about her house. She worked on it when she could. Unfortunately, her father couldn't afford the twenty gallons of paint it would take to do the exterior, which was what it needed the most.

"I have a buddy who can get you a deal on the wood

you need to repair it,'' Marc said, turning onto another road, accelerating. The breeze through the open windows felt good. He was no longer heading towards Monroe.

"Great." She doubted they could afford the deal.

"Where are you going?" Tracy asked.

"To your house."

"Ain't you going to drop Melanie off first?"

"Nope."

Apparently, Tracy knew not to argue with Marc. "So how did you like working with Rindy?" she asked Melanie.

"It was fun," Melanie said. "She's so beautiful."

"And she knows it," Tracy said. "Sometimes Rindy—"

"Don't start," Marc said.

"I was just going to say how Rindy sometimes reminds me of Genevieve Bujold when she was young."

I'm sure that's what was on the tip of your tongue.

"I liked your Mary," Melanie said diplomatically.

"Thanks, but I think the role is somewhat limiting. I don't get to demonstrate all the facets of my personality."

Melanie almost gagged. Marc kept a straight face. He probably wasn't listening.

Tracy's house had a tacky front porch, and the lawn needed to be cut; it didn't even have a fence. Tracy left her gum in the ashtray of the truck as she got out. Melanie was glad to be rid of her.

"I really appreciate the ride," she said as they set off again.

"It's no problem."

"Are you working tonight?"

"Nah. Too late. They hire at three and six. I'm just going to get something to eat."

"Do you eat out a lot?"

"Yeah, usually. Once a day."

"Your mom doesn't like to cook?"

"My parents are dead."

"Oh, I'm sorry." *Idiot!*

He shrugged. "It happened when I was small. We were camping about a hundred miles from here. There was a tornado." He paused. "I hardly think about it any more. I live with my uncle. He's never at home."

54

"My dad's never home either. And my mom still lives in San Francisco. They just went through a divorce."

"Doesn't sound like fun."

"It's for the best. My mom never liked either of us."

"My mom and dad couldn't bear to be apart."

"That's terrible that happened to them."

She must have sounded upset. Marc smiled reassuringly. "Don't hassle it. They were happy. They left together. I don't feel sorry for them."

Time to change the subject. "Where are you going to eat?"

"Probably the Pizza Hut."

She nodded, remaining quiet, waiting, praying. . . .

"Would you like to join me?" he asked.

"Sounds like fun," she said casually.

The Pizza Hut was at the far end of town adjacent to a farm. The waitress seated them at a booth by the window. One thing Melanie had to give Iowa—it had beautiful sunsets. The sun settling on the distant horizon set the ocean of cornstalks on fire. The orange light softened Marc's face.

"Are you ready to order?" the waitress asked. She was an elderly lady, wrinkled but erect. Melanie wondered what she made in tips.

"What would you like?" Marc asked her.

"What are you having?"

"Pepperoni."

"That sounds good."

"We'll have a medium-size pepperoni, thin crust," Marc said. "Thirsty?"

"I'd like some milk," Melanie said.

"And a milk and a coffee," Marc said, handing back the unused menus. The waitress made a note on her pad and left. Marc sipped his water and remarked, "A friend of mine always used to do what you just did."

"What was that?"

"Whatever the other person ordered, he always had the same thing. Didn't matter what it was."

Melanie smiled. "I guess some of us just can't make up our own minds."

"Oh, Clyde had a mind of his own." Marc was quiet for a moment. "Yeah, he was his own person, that's for sure."

There was a nostalgic note in his voice. "He was the friend you played football with?" Melanie asked.

"Yeah."

"I hear you were pretty good."

"Clyde made me look good."

"Where is he? I don't think I've met him."

Marc hesitated. "He graduated."

"Do you still see him?"

"Off and on." Marc glanced out the window, the final rays of the sun slipping from his face.

"I always wondered how football players could stand getting hit all the time," she said.

Marc nodded. "Yeah. Sometimes I used to feel like my spine was going to snap." He fiddled with the silverware, seesawing the fork with the help of the knife. "I'm glad it's over."

She started to ask what attracted him to acting, when a most incredible idea hit her. It was so amazing it could hardly fit inside her head. *I could ask Marc to Sadie Hawkins this very instant!* She could blurt out the question and save herself the hour of sleep she lost every night worrying about it. But she had to do it quick before she—

But what if he says no?

"Marc?"

"Hmmm?" He was looking down.

"I—I heard Jeramie's a great dancer."

"He's got double-jointed hips."

She laughed. "Rindy told me they dance together at her house a lot."

"Not any more."

"Really? Why not?"

"I don't know."

"Do you like to dance?"

"Not at all." He picked up the knife, testing its sharpness on his thumb. "The last dance I went to was a year ago. They have one around this time each year. I forget what it's called."

"Sadie Hawkins?"

"Yeah, that's the one. I couldn't wait till it was over."

God, this was hopeless. "Why did you go?"

"This girl asked me."

"Rindy?"

He frowned. "No. Her name was— I've forgotten her name. She moved away."

It must have been an awful night.

"You went because you didn't want to disappoint her?"

Marc nodded. "She was a nice kid. Debbie, that was her name."

Melanie summoned her courage. "Has anyone asked you this year?"

He raised his head, catching on. "No. All the girls at school know I hate dances. Debbie told them."

Melanie forced a smile. "She didn't tell me." He didn't answer, studying her in that oddly penetrating way he had. "Would you disappoint me?" she asked meekly.

He put down the knife. The waitress arrived with their coffee and milk. Waiting for her to leave, Melanie aged a lifetime. Marc thanked the lady, and when they were finally alone again, he looked her in the eye and said, "I suppose I could ask Jeramie for a few dance lessons."

"Oh, neat!" she said, unable to hide her joy.

Marc leaned back and grinned. "And I promise I'll remember your name a year from now."

FOUR

Susan laughed when Melanie came out of her bedroom wearing the cowboy outfit. Her black leather boots were years old, and the two-gallon hat she had on was pretty standard as far as Texan hats went. It was the shirt Susan found funny. Melanie had made it herself. The style was more suitable for Elvis Presley than John Wayne. The material was the shiniest satin blend of blue plaid imaginable. The light from the nearby lamp kept bouncing off her as if she were a giant Christmas tree ornament.

"Too bright, huh?" Melanie said.

Susan squinted. "It wouldn't be so bad if I were wearing sunglasses. Just kidding! Marc's going to be wearing the same shirt?"

"Let's hope so," Melanie said, shivering with anticipation. She had given Marc his shirt that afternoon at lunch in a box securely taped shut. "You can try it on when you get home," she had told him, afraid to see his face when he did. He had assured her he would like it. He had seemed surprised that she'd go to all that trouble for him.

Susan winked. "I wish I'd been there when you measured him for it."

"It was a very stimulating experience," Melanie assured her. In reality, Marc had simply given her a shirt that "was OK" to use as a model.

Susan picked at the sleeve of her own red and black Pendleton. "Jeramie and I are going to look ordinary next to you two."

"I can't imagine Jeramie ever coming across as ordinary." Melanie nodded towards Susan's blue denim miniskirt, her long legs bare. "And if you bend over, you won't be lacking for attention."

"I'm wearing a leotard underneath this."

Melanie hesitated before asking, "So, you and Jeramie are just going as friends?"

"Oh, yeah. It's funny, I'm not sure who asked who."

During rehearsals Rindy had mentioned she wouldn't be attending the dance. Melanie wondered if this was a major disappointment to Jeramie. Around Rindy he still acted crazy, but there was a trying-to-please element in his madness. Despite the hours they had spent together working on Ronda and Melissa—many of them alone—Melanie continued to feel she didn't understand Rindy. The girl lived in another world. It didn't seem a happy one.

Melanie no longer felt the least resentment towards her.

She heard a car pull into the driveway. "That's them!" She jumped.

Susan laughed. "Calm down. We see these guys every day."

I feel this way every day.

Her father came out of his bedroom as she ran for the door. He hooted at her outfit. Laughing and reaching for the doorknob, she hushed him. Then it occurred to her that she should at least wait until they knocked before opening the door. She should've known better. Jeramie didn't knock. He just walked in.

"My obsession," he whispered, embracing her, kissing her hard on the lips before she could get out of the way. He had on the same coloured Pendleton shirt as Susan, but his Abraham Lincoln hat was definitely a unique touch. "Are you ready?" He breathed in her ear.

"She's in the other room," Melanie said.

"My obsession," he whispered, letting her go, walking right past her dad without turning his head.

"That's the Jeramie you told me about?" her father asked.

"There's only one of them." She spotted Marc coming up the steps. If nothing else, the shirt fitted. "Hi, Marc."

"Hello," he said softly, stepping inside.

She put her hand to her mouth. "You don't like it?"

"The shirt?" He glanced down, and she wasn't sure if he'd ever seen it in the light. He cleared his throat. "It's

comfortable.'' He noticed her father, offered his hand.
''Mr. Martin?''

''Dad, this is Marc.''

They shook hands. ''Melanie's told me a lot about you,
Marc.''

Dammit, Dad!

''We've been spending a lot of time together working on
the play,'' Marc said. ''I hope to see you opening night.''

''He can't be there,'' Melanie said quickly. ''He has to
be in Chicago in a couple of weeks.'' The news didn't depress
her though. Actually, she preferred to have a couple of
performances under her belt before he saw her.

''I'll catch it when I get back.'' Her dad gave her a quick
glance as he spoke. He approved of Marc. She'd known he
would.

''Mr. Martin!'' Jeramie exclaimed, striding back into the
hall, removing his tall black hat and pumping Melanie's
dad's hand. ''How are you this fine evening, sir? I am
Jeramie. I am an important person.''

Her dad chuckled. ''You're in the play too?''

Jeramie spoke confidentially. ''Sir, we're *all* in the play.
It goes on *all* the time. You'll see.''

''He was dropped as a child,'' Susan explained, coming
up behind Jeramie.

''Every child should be,'' Jeramie said.

''We better go,'' Melanie said.

They went in Marc's truck. No one seemed to mind being
jammed together in the front seat. As they parked and walked
towards the brightly lit gym, Marc took Melanie's hand.
The moment would have been just perfect if Jeramie hadn't
decided to take her other hand.

Naturally, Jeramie had his camera with him. He took their
picture as they handed in their tickets at the door. For once
Melanie was glad of his flashbulbs. She wanted to remember
this night.

''Are you sure I can't help you with those?'' Marc asked
as she pocketed the stubs. The tickets had cost ten dollars
apiece.

"You can come into Sam's tomorrow evening and leave me a big tip," she said.

The gym looked like a barn: there was straw all over the floor and haystacks were holding down the four corners of the basketball court. They even had a hog on a platform near the bleachers. It was disgustingly fat and looked none the prettier for the colourful county fair ribbons pinned on its hide. Its master was having a hard time keeping it in place. Perhaps Porky could smell the ham being laid out, besides the rolls and fixings, on the long aluminium foil-covered tables running lengthwise beneath the backboards. Seeing the beast, Jeramie immediately grabbed Susan, saying there was nothing like rapping with a pig before a dance. Melanie suddenly found herself alone with Marc.

In a room full of people. Sigh.

"Want to dance?" he asked.

The band was still setting up. She laughed. "Shouldn't we wait for the music to start?"

"Jeramie didn't give me that tip."

"Did you really take lessons from him?"

"One. He said he was glad I wasn't his date."

She was feeling brave. "Well, *I'm* glad."

He nodded. "We'll have fun. Would you like something to drink?"

"Sure."

As Marc was preparing their drinks at the punch bowl, she noticed he held the cups in his right hand as he poured.

"You're not left-handed, are you?" she asked.

Her observation seemed to catch him off guard. "Uh, yeah, I am, actually." He handed her a glass. "Is that bad?"

I find it very sexy.

"No, it's good. I was feeling bad about Charles having lost his right arm. But since you're left-handed, you'll be able to get around."

Heading for the food tables, they ran into Mr. Golden, the trig teacher. He was chaperoning the dance. After meeting Marc, Mr. Golden said, "You did very well on your exam today, Melanie."

With rehearsals and work, she hadn't had the time to study

properly; she'd found the test difficult. "You graded them already? How many did I miss?"

"Six. That's a B plus."

"That's not bad," she said, pleased.

"Second best grade in the class. Your friend, Susan, missed only five."

"She did!"

"Susan's a hard worker," Mr. Golden said.

"She sure is." *I taught her everything she knows*, Melanie thought. Yet she wasn't jealous. Wasn't it the highest compliment a teacher could receive to be excelled by his or her student?

They got some punch and food—Melanie passed on the ham out of respect for the dance mascot—and sat in the bleachers, watching the couples come in. Most of the people were still strangers to her. Marc pointed out several, giving brief biographical information and calling a few over to meet her. Marc's friends held him in high esteem; it was nothing they said, just the way they treated him—guys and girls both. She felt fortunate.

The band finally finished tuning up and launched into their first number. Marc led her onto the jammed floor. Normally, she was a better than average dancer. She must have been nervous; she couldn't find her rhythm. Plus, Marc was as bad as he had led her to believe. For someone who'd been a star athlete, he was awfully stiff. At the conclusion of the first song, she suggested they take a break. But he'd have none of it. He was determined to improve upon last year.

"Debbie wanted to take a break after the first song too," he warned.

The band went on to Neil Young's "Are you Ready for the Country". Maybe the older songs were easier to let go with. Both of them began to loosen up. Marc stopped stepping on her feet. Floating like Michael Jackson, Jeramie swung by.

"I ditched Susan!" he exclaimed proudly, popping another flash in their eyes before disappearing into the crowd.

After the seventh song they were both hot and sweaty.

They decided to take a break and get in line for pictures. All photos were to be taken on a haystack. The company of the award-winning hog was optional.

They got flagged down before they could reach the line. "Marc! Over here! How are ya?"

It was Tracy, toting the stubby football player Melanie had met the same day she'd met Susan and Marc.

"Hi, Tracy," Melanie said.

"Hi," Tracy quipped, not even glancing at her. "Marc, I've got to talk to you. I've got to tell you about this complete bitch we just ran into. She—"

Melanie immediately tuned out. Tracy was continually encountering *complete* bitches and *complete* bastards. They chased her throughout the universe. Too bad Melissa didn't murder Mary instead of poor Ronda.

Stubby noticed her wandering eyes. He stuck out his hand. "I'm Steven Fisher. Five-six- two hundred and ten pounds of all-American beef."

"I'm Melanie." He crushed her fingers. "I'm a vegetarian."

Steve grinned. He wasn't a bad sort. "I've got them bullets you need."

With all the rehearsing, she was low on blanks. Jeramie said he was out. Tracy must have told Steve this. "I could buy them from you?"

"From the store where I work—Arnie's Arsenal, in Barters. I'm there evenings after football practice. But give a call before you come, ask for me. Old Arnie don't know where nothing is."

"I'll do that." It was a detail she preferred attending to herself. Steve interrupted Tracy's caviling.

"Hey, dude, did you see what Garh High did to us last week?"

"And she just freaked—" Tracy was saying.

"I wasn't there," Marc said, looking disinterested.

"My man! Don't you even go to the games?"

"Dammit, Steve," Tracy said. "You're always bothering Marc and interrupting me."

But All-American Beef wasn't easily insulted. "Coach

wanted me to talk to you again. Coach told me to tell you we *really* miss you, dude."

"You tell Coach, if he wants to tell me something, he has my phone number." Marc took her arm. "Now Melanie and I have to get in line for pictures. Goodbye."

"I'll tell you later what happened with that bitch," Tracy said, reassuring him.

"I'm saving a place on the bench for you at tomorrow's game!" Steve called.

When they were out of earshot, Melanie said, "It's great being popular, isn't it?"

Marc shrugged. "Steve told you where to get the blanks?"

"Yeah."

"Good. Be sure to give him a call."

The remainder of the dance passed quickly. Once rid of Tracy and the other distractions, Melanie began to enjoy herself again, and time took on the quality of a succession of delightful moments. The photos were only five dollars. Marc insisted on paying. The gross hog was not the only model available. There was a baby pig and, except for his bad breath, this little stinker was very cute. Piggy stuck his snout in her ear just as the camera flashed. She couldn't wait to see the print.

They danced and danced. Debbie from last year wouldn't have recognized her date. Marc seemed to enjoy whirling her, so much so that she started to get dizzy. Of course she didn't have the heart to tell him to slow down.

The later it got, the louder it got, and the band hadn't turned up its amps. Everybody on the floor seemed to be chattering at the top of their lungs. There was a definite odour of alcohol in the air. The dance started to resemble a punk rock bash; there was more bumping and tripping than anything. Finally, Marc pulled her to the sidelines. They were both out of breath.

"Wild." Marc wiped the perspiration from his forehead.

"I didn't know Iowa had it in her," she agreed.

"Hey, you guys," Susan called, hurrying towards them without Jeramie.

"Having fun?" Melanie asked.

"Not now." Susan was worried. "We've got to get out of here. The teachers are looking for Jeramie."

"Why?" Marc asked.

"They think he spiked the punch."

"The punch is *spiked*?" Melanie asked. She tried to remember how many glasses she had drunk and couldn't; that probably meant she had downed quite a few.

"Did he spike it?" Marc asked. "I didn't see him bring any booze in."

"I don't know," Susan said. "But with him anything's possible. Marc, I'm afraid they'll suspend him and won't let him be in the play."

"Where is he?" Marc asked.

"He told me he'd wait in the truck," Susan said.

Marc turned to her. "Do you mind cutting the night short?"

It was the biggest night of her life. "Not at all."

Jeramie was not in the truck but on top of the cab. Melanie supposed she should be furious with him, but he wasn't the sort it was easy to blame. Besides, he denied any knowledge of how the alcohol got in the punch.

"I would never stoop to such an old stunt," he said. Then he rubbed his long fingers together like a wicked cartoon character and grinned fiendishly. "Did I miss any behavioural deviations while waiting out here in the lonely night?"

"As we were leaving, Steve vomited on the dance floor," Susan said.

"I knew he'd be a credit to Tracy!" Jeramie said.

Marc was not amused. "You know, the girls had to pay for these tickets. It's still early. What are we going to do now?"

Jeramie began to weep pitifully. "I'm sorry."

Susan pointed to a group of horn-tooting cars leaving the lot. "I bet they're going to the reservoir."

Melanie had heard of the spot but had never been there. The night was warm. It sounded romantic. "Is there a lake and dam there and everything?'' she asked.

Marc was staring at Susan. "Yes, there's a lake," he said quietly.

"It was just an idea," Susan said defensively. Jeramie stopped crying and leapt off the truck top.

"It's a splendid idea," he said. "The water will feel great."

"Do people swim in this lake?" Melanie asked.

"Naked," Jeramie said, savouring the word.

Melanie had never been skinny-dipping before. A first date didn't feel like the best time to start. Then again, if it was dark enough . . .

"It's your decision, Marc," Susan said.

"Melanie?" he said, his reluctance showing.

"I'm the newcomer here. The reservoir sounds fun, but it's up to you guys." She just didn't want to go home.

"I want to visit the ducks," Jeramie said.

"What time do you have to be in?" Marc asked her.

"No particular time," Melanie said. "But if it's far, we can go somewhere else."

"It's not that far," Susan said. "About eight miles."

Marc took a deep breath. "All right, let's go."

They jammed into the front again: Marc driving, her in the middle, Susan sitting on Jeramie's bony lap. They left town on a road she had never used before. The countryside was rolling, covered with cornfields and grass. Trees were few and far between. The occasional farmhouse was dark. People went to bed early in these parts. But far out in front and not far behind, were other cars—other kids heading for the reservoir.

"I wish I had some bread to feed the ducks," Jeramie said.

"I'll be surprised if any of those birds come near you after what you did last year," Susan said. "Melanie, you won't believe what he did."

"I believe it already," she said. A car pulled up close behind them. Marc waved him around. He was driving slowly. The other car raced away.

"It was for charity," Jeramie said.

"They were having one of those drives at school to raise food for people in the area who couldn't afford a Thanksgiving feast," Susan said. "People were mainly donating canned goods. But this fellow here, he got it in his head he had to give a *fresh* bird. He went up to the reservoir and bagged one of the ducks. Broke its neck and plucked it himself."

"I didn't break its neck," Jeramie said defensively.

"Well, you cut its head off, then," Susan said. "What's the difference?"

It was a touchy subject for Jeramie. "Of course I cut off its head. But only after it was dead."

"And how did it die?" Susan insisted.

"I shot it in the head," he admitted.

"With what?" Melanie asked, half expecting the answer she got.

"With the gun you're using in the play."

Another car pulled up behind them. This one honked. Marc did not speed up. The car eventually went around. "Are you sure you want to go here?" Melanie asked.

"I'm just being careful," Marc said.

Twenty minutes later they entered a cluster of trees. For half a mile the ground rose steadily, then it fell again in tight curves. Several times branches of dried leaves brushed the windshield. Twice more they got passed by kids from school. As they rounded one particularly tight corner and a flat body of water became visible through the trees, Marc slowed to a crawl.

He doesn't like this place.

They parked a few minutes later, pulling off the road into a pile of crunching leaves. The other cars had stopped closer to the water. Melanie could hear laughter and splashing. They climbed out of the truck. The air was heavy with the sweet smell of damp grass.

"This is going to be wonderful," Jeramie said, bouncing up and down as they walked towards the water.

"We're not going swimming," Susan said. "I'm not taking off my clothes in front of all these creeps from school."

"But the ducks," Jeramie began.

"Shut up about those damn ducks, would you," Marc interrupted. His mood had changed. Melanie regretted having voted for the reservoir. He lagged behind the three of them, his hands in his pockets. Someone farther up the beach howled. "Sounds like all the animals from the dance are here," he growled.

"We could go for a walk in the other direction," Melanie suggested, gesturing towards a pale shadow on the other side of the lake she believed to be the dam. The size of the reservoir surprised her; it was at least a quarter mile across, and a deep ominous grey. She didn't see any ducks.

"But I want to see my fellow classmates and enjoy stimulating conversation and nocturnal aquatic sports," Jeramie protested.

Susan glanced at Marc, spoke to her. "Melanie, why don't you two do that—go for a walk. I'll let Jeramie play with the ducks for a while and then we'll try to find you."

Marc was agreeable to the plan. Susan and Jeramie disappeared in the direction of the noise. Melanie turned to walk in the other direction, towards the dam. Marc's reluctance remained.

"You want to go that way?" he asked.

"I thought— Do you want to join the others after all?"

"No, I was just thinking— " He shrugged. "Either way is fine."

There was no clear path. The foot-high grass went right to the water. Although she could hear other kids far behind them, they weren't visible, and silence seemed to hang heavy in the air. They walked for a while without speaking. Daydreaming about this date for the past couple of weeks, she hadn't imagined a more perfect setting in which to finish the evening: the two of them strolling alone in the dark beside fragrant trees and a quiet lake. Marc's hands were still jammed into his pockets, however, and the fun they'd had on the dance floor seemed a memory of something long ago. Finally, she felt she had to speak up.

"Marc, is something wrong?"

He stopped, looking away from the water into the trees, whose top branches hid the curving road they'd arrived on.

White light flashed through the leaves. More people coming. "I thought I saw a spark," he said.

"That was a car."

"Before that, I mean."

She came up by his side. "I don't see anything."

"If a fire started here, this place would never be the same." He continued to peer into the dense foliage—shadows wrapped in shadows. Then suddenly he relaxed. "I must be imagining things." He looked at her. "What did you ask?"

"Nothing important."

He took his hands from his pockets. "I'm sorry, Melanie. Nothing's wrong. I just wander off sometimes. I'm like that."

She smiled. "I'd noticed."

"Had you really?"

"Oh, yeah."

His tone lightened. "So you've got me figured out?"

"No, I don't know where you go when you wander."

He let the remark pass. "Do you want to sit down?"

"Is the grass wet?"

He dropped to the ground. "A little."

She knelt by his side. Just when he appeared to be relaxing, she was getting nervous. You could do a lot of things on the ground you couldn't do standing up. No, she didn't have Marc figured out at all. She didn't know what he expected of her. Worse, she didn't know what she expected of herself.

"Nice weather we've been having," she said.

That amused him. "Did you like the dance?"

"Oh, yeah. Did you?"

"A lot more than last year." He leaned back on his elbows.

"I'm glad."

"Were you afraid I wouldn't?"

"Actually, yeah. Thanks, you know, for going with me."

He patted her knee, spoke seriously. "You don't have to thank me, Melanie."

A mosquito landed on her hand. She waved it away. Tilting her head back, she could find few stars through the night-time haze. A light breeze had been blowing, but now

69

even that had stopped. "I guess I feel I didn't give you much choice in the pizza parlour."

"I never go out with a girl unless I want to."

There was no arrogance in his voice. He must like her. His hand continued to rest on her knee. "Marc, would you think I was nosy if I asked a personal question?"

"Ask, and I'll tell you."

"Did you ever have a steady girlfriend at school?"

"No."

"Really? That's strange."

"How so?"

She smiled. "You're handsome. You could have just about any girl, I'd think."

He sat up, moved closer. "I don't put much stock in appearance."

"That's good for me."

"Why do you say that? You're nice looking."

Nice looking? As opposed to bad looking?

Pretty, or even cute, would have been better. Still, she was flattered and felt herself blushing. "I'm all right, I guess."

"You shouldn't worry about the way you look."

"Oh, I don't. Not since the last operation."

"What?"

She cleared her throat. "That was a joke. A small joke."

Marc took his hand from her knee and brushed something from her hair. His fingers lingered, gently tugging on individual strands. It felt very nice. She supposed she should respond in some way. She started trembling.

"There's a lot of prettier girls at school," she mumbled.

He began to rub the base of her neck. She must be putty in his hands. "Yeah?"

He isn't interested in other girls! Why don't you just shut up?

"There's Rindy," she suggested.

"Rindy is pretty," he agreed. He was sitting on her right. He put his left hand on her left shoulder blade. Later, she was sure, she would remember the exact spot. The pressure he was exerting was not enough to tell her that he absolutely definitely wanted her to fall into his arms. She didn't know

70

what to do. So she opened her mouth again.

"Oh, she's beautiful. Her eyes are like emeralds."

Marc began to massage her left shoulder. "You have pretty eyes."

"Nah. I bet you don't even know what colour they are."

"You're right, I don't." His mouth was just inches away. She could see it out of the corner of her eye. She was not looking at him, but at the reservoir. A safe place to look. His breath smelled like the punch from the dance.

"They're hazel," she said.

"Hmmm." He touched her chin with his right hand.

"Rindy's are green."

"Emeralds usually are."

"Oh, you think her eyes look like emeralds?"

He turned her face slowly towards his. "Melanie?"

"What? Did you ever go out with her?"

"Once."

She knew it! "Oh."

"I took her to a dance and then to this spot." He leaned closer. "And then I had my way with her."

She went to speak. He closed the words off with a kiss. His arms slipped around her body. They felt strong, and she felt weak, and it wasn't such a bad way to feel, not for a little while, at least. Something inside her let go. She was kissing him back, but mainly he was holding her, and that was good—to be held.

Unfortunately, the sensation lasted only as long as the kiss. When he let go, she stiffened and immediately asked, "So you went out with Rindy only once?"

Marc didn't respond for a moment. Then he burst out laughing. He laughed so hard he fell back on the grass. She had never heard him laugh before. She couldn't honestly say she was enjoying it, not when it was her he was laughing at.

"Melanie," he gasped, trying to catch his breath.

"Well, I was curious! I don't know." That was right. She knew nothing. Not even how to let the cutest guy in the school kiss her. Marc sat up. He had grass in his hair.

"You really want to know about Rindy and me?" he panted.

71

"No!"

"There's nothing to tell."

"Then don't tell me."

"Then why did you ask me?" He was enjoying himself.

She sniffed. "You took her here?"

The question quieted him. "I took her nowhere. Rindy was my best friend's girlfriend."

She should have been relieved. Yet something in the admission troubled her. Why, she didn't know. Nor did she understand why a faint crackle of dried leaves at their backs made Marc suddenly move away from her and stare once again into the trees. Following his gaze, she noticed an orange spark dimming and then brightening in the sheltered black space, exactly as a cigarette would when being smoked by someone who had a lot on their mind.

"Is someone there?" she whispered.

"Yes," he said flatly.

"Who? Should we shout for help?"

He got up on his knees. "She won't bother us. Let's just go."

"You know who it is?"

Marc stood and offered his hand, pulling her up as if she weighed a ton. He appeared suddenly weary. "Let's go," he repeated.

They headed in the direction of the other kids, sounds of laughter echoing across the still waters. Marc held her hand loosely, his palm sweaty.

When they were a quarter mile from where they'd kissed, he said, "It was Rindy."

"How can you be sure?"

"I'm sure."

He refused to explain further.

Jeramie had gone swimming with the ducks. He had forgotten to take off his clothes. They made him sit in the truck bed on the drive home. Susan said one of the ducks had tried to bite Jeramie. He said ducks were not to be trusted.

Marc drove back to Careville at sixty miles an hour. He

dropped Melanie off first. That hurt. She'd been hoping to invite him in for coffee. It hurt a lot. When she got out of the truck after only a pat on the shoulder from Marc, she had a baseball-size lump in her throat. She managed, however, a carefree good night. Susan gave her a quick hug and handed her a manila envelope. "Start memorizing," Susan said. It was the last act.

Her dad was already in bed. She made herself coffee. She hadn't drunk coffee in years. Then she began to read.

A month had passed since Melissa murdered Ronda. So far, no one knew who the villain was. Charles had reconvened his welcome-home party. Robert, Mary, and Melissa were present. Charles wanted to reenact the night of the murder. Was it one of us? Someone from the outside? Or did she kill herself? Charles asks all these questions.

Of course, the audience already know the answer.

When Melanie finished reading, Melissa, her character, was dead. Charles, Marc's character, had tricked her into telling the truth. And in disgrace she had blown her brains out with a gun that wasn't even loaded with real bullets.

FIVE

Opening night, Melanie thought. Now it was too late for further preparation. Curtain was in half an hour. Strange how her nervousness seemed unconnected with the play. Her imagination was not rushing through stage-disaster scenarios. She was simply worried.

About being alive, maybe.

"You look beautiful," Rindy said at her back. They were alone in the dressing room. Melanie was standing before a full-length mirror, admiring her white knee-length pleated skirt and reddish brown silk blouse—which complemented the colour of her hair. Rindy had surprised her with the outfit the past week. With the addition of a proper pink hat and heavy lipstick, Melanie thought she could pass comfortably as a postwar young lady.

"I can't thank you enough for these clothes," Melanie said, turning to face Rindy, who was sitting at a cluttered makeup table in front of another, shorter mirror, her curly black hair rebounding in the reflections of the overlapped mirrors into a deep blurred tunnel. Rindy wore a longish tan skirt and a short-sleeved green sweater that drew attention to her green eyes. As always, she was stunning.

"Thank you father's fat credit cards."

"You charged the clothes?"

"I charge everything. That way, especially when your family's loaded, you can pretend everything's free."

Three weeks had passed since the night at the reservoir. Rindy hadn't mentioned it and Melanie hadn't had the nerve to bring it up. Melanie still wasn't sure how Marc could have identified the person in the trees. It had been so dark. Relying on the fact that Rindy occasionally smoked seemed illogical. Lots of people smoked. It depressed Melanie to believe Care High's beauty had been sitting all alone in a lonely spot on the biggest social night of the young school year.

The past few days Rindy had begun to liven up. They couldn't be called friends yet, but at least Melanie could foresee the day when they would be. Rindy had admitted how much she was looking forward to performing in front of an audience again.

"Are you scared?" Melanie asked.

Rindy smiled faintly. "I feel like the hard part is behind me. I've climbed the mountain, and now all I've got to do is jump off. When I'm onstage, I feel that way—like I'm falling through the air. I like it."

Rindy picked up two plastic Baggies of red liquid, beginning to roll up her sweater. "I'd better tape the blood on my chest. I won't have time later."

"Does that gook stain?" They had practised the blood only once. Rindy had had to hit herself hard to get the juice out.

"It's a formula Jeramie dug up. He says it'll never come out."

"You'll have your nightgown on then. It's a shame you'll be ruining it."

"I have a lot of clothes I've worn only once." Rindy cut a piece of grey duct tape. "Did I tell you my parents are here?"

"How nice for you!" She felt a pang, as her dad was still in Chicago. She wanted him here tonight after all.

"I'll introduce you to them after the play. My mother's real caste conscious. She'll want to know if your family has 'old money' or 'eastern money' or 'land money'. Tell her your parents are into oil and she'll love you."

Someone knocked at the door. Rindy rolled down her sweater. "Come in," Rindy said.

Carl poked his head inside. "Tell our mom, Melanie, that your dad 'favours' silver over gold. She just bought fifty grand in silver futures. 'Favours' is her favourite word."

"Eavesdropping, brother?" Rindy asked sweetly.

"With ears like mine, sister, it's hard not to," he replied, opening the door farther. In his left hand he carried a thick extension cable, and in his right a bouquet of long-stem red roses. He held up the flowers. "These are for you."

Rindy's face brightened. It was a delight to see her happy, for even in her lighter spells her melancholy was usually close at hand. "They're so pretty! Carl, you shouldn't have. I haven't even performed yet."

He set down his cable and presented the roses to Rindy with a kiss on the cheek. "I don't have a vase of water for them. I thought if I waited, they'd dry out."

"There's an empty bottle in the girls' room," Melanie said. "That might hold them for now."

Carl looked at her. "Feels a long way from audition day, huh?"

"Sure does," Melanie said.

Carl spoke to his sister. "Would you think less of me if I gave you eleven flowers instead of a dozen?" Rindy shook her head, and Carl plucked a rose from the bundle, handing it to Melanie. "Good luck, Melissa," he said.

"Melissa doesn't need it, but Melanie does." She smelled the flower. "Thank you, Carl." His politeness never ceased to impress her. He gathered his extension cord from the floor.

"Got to get back to work," he said.

"Isn't everything with the lights already set?" Melanie asked, surprised.

"The lights are fine. But the icebox under the bar uses more electricity than we planned. We keep tripping circuit breakers."

Carl again wished them good luck, then left. He was gone less than ten seconds, when Heidi entered without knocking. Melanie had not spoken to her since the audition.

"Am I invited to opening night? . . . I'll be there. You can bet I'll be there."

Rindy had pulled her sweater up again and was still fooling with the Baggies and tape. Heidi scowled at her. "What are you doing?"

"Getting ready to bleed," Rindy said simply.

"How about you?" Heidi asked Melanie. "Do you bleed in this play?"

76

"Only at the end." Marc would touch her head after she committed suicide, and draw away a bloody hand. But the gook would actually come from his own pocket. "How are you doing?"

"Glad I'm sitting in the audience, thank you." Heidi wasn't exactly the forgive-and-forget type. "Where's your pal Susan?"

"Suzy's around," Rindy said. She was the only one who called Susan that.

"Suzy's behind you," Susan said appearing in the doorway, dressed entirely in black, holding a small red box with white lettering on the sides. "What can I do for you, Heidi?"

"Don't you remember your promise?"

"My very own play is about to start in twenty minutes. I've a million things on my mind. What promise are you talking about?"

"That I could have all the free tickets I wanted to opening night."

"I never said any such thing," Susan said.

"Yes, you did," Melanie said. Her memory could be a pain in the ass, especially when it automatically connected with her mouth.

"Melanie! You look perfect," Susan said. "Keep quiet."

"I want ten tickets," Heidi said.

"Ten? You don't have ten friends. What do you want them for?"

"Shut the door, please," Rindy said, her bra showing. Without turning, Susan tried to shut the door with her foot. By chance—if the word could be applied to anything that happened around him—Jeramie was entering at that moment. The door smacked him neatly on the nose.

"Oh, dear," he said, putting his hand to his face. He had on an army fatigue jacket over a thick sweater and looked about twenty pounds heavier. "Stiff upward blows to the nasal cartilage have been known to cause brain damage."

Rindy glanced over her shoulder, not bothering to pull down her sweater. "Are you OK?"

Jeramie sniffed. "Yes. Nice breasts you have there, my love."

Heidi scowled again. "You promised me ten tickets," she insisted.

"You can have four," Susan said firmly.

"But—"

"Take it or leave it," Susan said. "In fact"—she reached into her back pocket and withdrew four green slips— "take them now and leave. These people have got to get ready."

Heidi took the tickets. "Bitch," she said softly.

"What did you call me?" Susan asked, her tone deadly.

"A bitch," Jeramie said matter-of-factly. "Few people realise that *bitch* refers not only to a female dog, but to a female wolf, a female fox, a—"

"Shut up, Jeramie," Susan said. "Get the hell out of here, Heidi."

Melanie wasn't exactly sure what happened next. As Heidi stepped towards the door, she seemed to brush against Susan. The small red box Susan was holding dropped to the floor. Brass cartridges spilled over the tiles, a few rolling towards Melanie's feet.

Susan sighed impatiently. "Now look what you've done."

Heidi knelt to examine the shells. "What are these?"

Susan went to stop her. "No, don't help me pick them up. Just leave. Please?"

Heidi already had a couple of cartridges in hand. With feigned casualness she flipped Susan off with the other hand. "Since you said please," she said, standing back up, exiting quickly.

Did she take the bullets with her?

"Melanie, give me a hand with these, would ya?" Susan said, down on her knees. "No, Jeramie, leave them alone. You might accidentally put one in your mouth and swallow it."

Melanie did as requested, saying, "I already bought my own blanks." These shells were the same as the ones Steve had sold her.

Susan was surprised. "Where?"

"At Arnie's Arsenal, in Barters."

"That's where I got these. Didn't know you knew the place. You brought them?"

78

"They're in my bag."

"Just use yours, then."

"OK," Melanie said.

"The Baggies would stick better if you removed your bra," Jeramie told Rindy. She laughed at his suggestion. She didn't seem to mind his staring at her chest.

"Another thing," Susan told Melanie, "I want you to take full responsibility for the gun. The PTA has got wind of the fact that we're not using a cap gun. I don't know who told them. Don't load the revolver until after the first act."

"Why? I'll be pressed for time during the break."

"Because I don't want someone dropping the blasted thing during the first act and have it accidentally going off. Don't worry, you'll have time to load it. It'll take only a minute."

They finished collecting the shells, and Rindy finally succeeded in securing the red dye to her chest. With her sweater rolled down, the Baggies weren't noticeable.

Susan gritted her teeth. "Jeramie, I've got some bad news for you. When Carl came in earlier, he found the mirror in your china cabinet cracked. We had to remove it. Will your mother be upset?"

"You can count on it."

"Damn. I don't know how or when it happened. Tell her we'll replace it."

"All right." And he added as thought it were related, "Ken knows how to work the video camera."

"Who's Ken?" Susan asked. "I thought we agreed not to tape tonight."

"Yeah," Melanie said. Two days before they had recorded a dress rehearsal, and the camera intimidated her more than any audience she could remember.

Jeramie looked unhappy. "I'd like a recording of tonight. There will never be another tonight."

"Well, I don't care, I'm not the one onstage," Susan said. "What do you think, Rindy?"

"I'd rather not have the video on."

"Melanie?" Susan asked.

"The show will be smoother a couple of weeks from now.

79

Let's wait till then.''

Jeramie dropped the issue. He noticed the roses. ''A special delivery from a secret admirer?'' he asked Rindy.

''Carl brought them.''

''How nice,'' Jeramie said, adding, ''Are you looking forward to getting shot tonight?''

Rindy stared at him a moment. ''Why don't you ask Melanie? She gets to shoot herself.''

Jeramie did not ask. Had he, Melanie would have told him she wasn't crazy about the idea. In the scene—as in really life—the gun was only loaded with blanks. The trick was to have the audience believe she had the nozzle pressed to her temple when, in fact, she had it pointed towards the ceiling. Melissa was to die from the force of the exploding air. If Melanie was not careful with her aim, it was conceivable she would end up like Melissa. Also, to save her hearing, Melanie had to slip drugstore wax into her ears just before the climactic shot.

The last act was complicated.

Jeramie left all of a sudden. Gathering up her roses, Rindy stood and muttered something about finding a vase. Melanie suspected she was going after him. Jeramie's last question had been weird even for Jeramie. Rindy paused as she stepped past Susan.

''I'm happy you started all this,'' Rindy said.

Susan was perplexed. ''What? Jeramie's always—''

''No, the play.'' Rindy smiled. That was twice in two minutes. ''I'm happy I'm here.'' She hugged Susan quickly. ''Thank you.''

Susan was momentarily at a loss for words. ''I should thank you,'' she said. Then she snickered. ''Just be fantastic, Rindy, that's all I ask.''

Rindy left in the direction Jeramie had taken, down the hall, away from the stage. Faintly, Melanie could hear the audience settling. Her tension, which all the coming and going had overshadowed, returned sharply.

''A nice crowd?'' she asked.

''Should be a full house,'' Susan replied, her expression thoughtful.

"Mad you're not getting a slice of the profits?"

Susan glanced up. She had not heard the question. "How do you feel?"

"Like I'm waiting to get shot. No pun intended."

"I'd tell you to relax, but I don't seem to be able to relax myself."

Melanie had noticed. Heidi had barely touched Susan, and the box of shells had jumped from her hands. Of course the circumstances made the nervousness understandable. Everyone in school knew this was *Susan's* play. "Did you ever get hold of the author?"

"No. But maybe he'll be here in spirit." Susan turned to leave.

"Susan? Have you seen Marc?"

Her big romance had fizzled. Marc hadn't actually been avoiding her the past few weeks. Three times he had given her a ride home from rehearsal. But he hadn't asked her out, and he certainly hadn't tried to kiss her again. It was weird, but it was as if he no longer trusted her. Perhaps Charles's suspicions of Melissa were carrying over into daily life. The situation was wearing on her. She'd had so much hope.

"He told me he was going to watch the first act from Carl's lighting board in the back," Susan said.

"Has he said anything to you?"

"About what?"

Melanie hesitated. "About me?"

Susan was sympathetic. "Marc's a complicated guy. Give him time."

Melanie forced a smile. "Maybe when we get this show under our belt, we'll be friends again."

"I'm sure everything will work out." Susan paused in the doorway. "I have a lot of faith in you, Melanie."

Melanie was touched. Susan really had put a lot on the line, giving her this chance. "Thank you," she said.

Susan left, and Melanie sat down to wait, frequently glancing at her watch. Tracy entered a few minutes later. For once she wasn't chewing gum. She'd put on several layers of makeup and pinned her hair up. She looked better than usual, Melanie thought.

"How are you doing?" Melanie asked.

"Lousy. I feel like throwing up," she said, setting down a grocery bag on the chair Rindy had been using. "I just bought a punch from the machine in the courtyard. You know those filthy metal machines? I bet that junk has been sitting in there for months. Curdled my stomach."

"Maybe your stomach is upset because of the play."

Tracy snorted. "This small-time stuff doesn't make me nervous. You scared? You look scared. I'll give you some advice. Just think who's in the audience—the same dips we see every day at school. No way we got to worry about impressing them. That's the way I see it." She pulled two quart bottles of Seagram's 7 out of her bag.

"What's that for?"

"What else? It's for Rindy, or Ronda. Don't you remember? She's a boozer."

"Ronda drinks gin."

"What's the difference? Whisky, gin—who gives a damn?"

"Twice in the play we refer to her gin drinking. We use the word *gin*."

"So use the word *whisky*."

"Why don't we just stick with water and call it gin?"

Tracy was exasperated. It didn't take much. "Water and gin look like nothing. There's no impact. You've got to have impact."

"Have you told Rindy about this change?"

"I told Susan. She's in charge."

"But Rindy is the one who has to drink the stuff."

Tracy's eyes blazed. "Why are you hassling me? I've got to go onstage in a few minutes!"

"You just said you weren't nervous. You also just said there's no difference between whisky and gin. I don't think it's wise to make a change at this point."

Tracy fought to control her fury. "I went to a lot of trouble to get these bottles. We're using them. And I'd like to know where you get off on giving me orders?"

"Save it, Tracy," Melanie said, her patience running out

"Save it for Mary. She'll need all your asinine antics to get by tonight." And with that she left the dressing room, slamming the door.

She found Rindy in the bathroom, smelling her flowers. She mentioned the liquor switch—Rindy simply nodded—and they went on to talk about roses and roles, killing time. Actually, Melanie found herself doing most of the talking. Telling Tracy off had not soothed her nerves.

As the minutes ticked down, they left the rest room for the stage. With the curtains down and the lights off, the living room was like a cave. They peeked at the audience. Every seat was taken. There were as many adults as teenagers. The programmes passed out at the door were being rolled into telescopes. It was time.

Susan grabbed Melanie and Rindy and handed them their grocery bags. Tracy, doing her best to look bored, hurriedly placed the whisky bottles on the bar. Jeramie and Marc were nowhere around. Susan whispered last-minute instructions.

"If you can't remember a line, say anything appropriate. On opening night an actor can't speak too slowly. Take your time. Try to have fun." She raised a kid's walkie-talkie to her mouth. "Carl?"

There was a burst of static. "Ready. Everyone's seated."

"And my stars?" Susan asked, looking at the three girls.

"Yeah," Melanie said. Rindy nodded. Tracy shrugged.

"Then let the show begin," Susan said.

Melanie started off with a mistake. When she walked onto the stage, Rindy at her back, she was in view of the audience a couple of seconds before she began to speak; she should have had her first line out before anyone saw her. It wasn't a major error and fortunately it didn't throw her off stride.

Immediately, she felt the influence of the crowd. There was a spontaneous energy in her words, and she knew instinctively that everyone could hear her. But Susan had made an excellent point. She found herself talking rapidly. She would have to watch it.

"He might have thought the whole arrangement too expensive. You know how Charles is when you take him

83

shopping.''

"Yes," Rindy replied, sitting on the couch. "I suppose I should have offered something of my own." She put a hand to her heart. "Sometimes, I think maybe I did."

Melanie wasn't exactly sure when she became Melissa. The transformation occurred near the beginning. The character didn't overshadow her personality so much as it— or *she*—took a part of her and moved a discreet mental distance away. The schizophrenia wasn't uncomfortable. In fact, they *both* began to relax. And Rindy was in her own groove also.

"So you took Robert to the fair last Sunday?" Melissa asked, thinking Ronda was seeing too much of Robert while her husband was away. "How sweet of you."

"He enjoyed himself." Ronda smiled. "He won a giant duck in an archery contest. I have it in the other room."

"Oh, that fellow—he always was handy with the bow," Melissa said, thinking Robert was still itching to shoot something. "He gave it to you, then?"

The banter, filled with sentences that had double meanings, flowed easily. The only hitch came when Melanie discovered the gun in the cabinet under the bar. Even then the disruption was purely internal. Melanie doubted the audience noticed a thing. Yet for a moment Melissa ceased to exist inside her. As it had during the first rehearsal, the weight of the gun filled her with misgivings. The thought of pointing such a leaden instrument near her head made her shiver. Thankfully, the sensation didn't last.

The audience heard of Robert's psychological troubles on the battlefields of Europe and of Charles's subsequent reporting of Robert to their superior officers. The crowd also learned of the doubt surrounding the extent of Charles's injury, and watched as Ronda frequently sipped her drink. Eventually, the ladies returned to discussing the party, and the subject of wine was brought up. Melissa left to check the cellar. Melanie exited by the right living room door.

"May I have your autograph, little girl?" Jeramie whispered, his pale face suddenly materializing out of the backstage shadows, making her jump. They were in one of the peculiar cul-de-sacs created by the oversize set. A door leading out of the theatre lay cracked, letting in a chilly draught.

"God, you scared me," she said quietly.

"You're doing well," Jeramie said. "But you're still going to get caught."

Melanie could hear Tracy knocking on the front door. Rindy went to let her in.

"What are you doing here?" Melanie asked Jeramie.

"I like to watch actors from behind. If their illusion is one-dimensional, they're easy to spot from this angle."

She smiled. "As usual, I don't know what you're talking about."

"Be careful, Melissa," he said seriously. "I feel reality closing in on Melanie."

Without another word, silent as a mouse, he left through the back door. He was always speaking in riddles, she told herself. There was no reason for this one to hang heavy in her mind. No reason at all.

The final portion of Act I went relatively smoothly. The single sticky part came when Melanie went to sneak the revolver into her purse; she found Ronda's bag where Melissa's should have been. Probably Tracy had purposely rearranged the bags to make life difficult. Melanie simply used Ronda's. She'd buy anyone who'd caught the inconsistency an ice cream.

As the three ladies left for more late-afternoon shopping, the stage lights dimmed and the curtain fell. The intermission was to last fifteen minutes. Charles and Robert would be home twenty minutes before the ladies returned. Melanie, therefore, had over half an hour to relax. She'd be lucky if she could sit down though. Her adrenaline was pumping furiously.

Susan was talking in the hallway with Marc as Melanie walked by. Susan smiled and briefly clasped her hand, and Marc nodded, muttering a word of encouragement. They were discussing Act II and Melanie was reluctant to interrupt, though a big pat on the back, especially from

Marc, would have been nice. Because Tracy had followed Rindy into the Green Room, Melanie returned to the dressing room.

She spent the next several minutes staring at herself in the mirror, wondering why she was thinking about Marc instead of the show.

I'm jealous of Ronda. And she doesn't even exist.

She remembered the gun. Pulling it out, she reached for the box of shells All-American Beef Steve had sold her, sprinkling several of the cartridges into her palm, the polished brass glittering in the glare of the naked bulbs that circled the mirror. She ran her finger over the flat tip of one, pressed her nail into the semi-hard wax that held the powder in place. Blanks. Definitely.

Someone knocked. "Yes?"

The door opened. "Are you busy?" Marc asked.

She didn't turn. She could see him in the mirror. In the movies the heroine seldom turned when she could see her lover in the mirror. A grey sports jacket was draped over his right arm. He'd cut his hair. He looked like Charles, and she felt like Melissa—as if her darling had been away too long.

"No," she said.

He came in and sat down. "You were great."

"I was OK." It had been easier to talk onstage. When had her girlish crush changed into—whatever this was? She couldn't remember; it seemed she had always felt this way.

"Loading the gun?"

"Yeah." She deposited the shells on the desk, picked up the revolver, snapped out the chambers. Her hands were shaking.

"Want me to help you?"

"That's all right, I can manage."

"Did Steve get you these blanks?"

"Yeah, I got them from him."

Marc nodded, glanced around. He was uncomfortable. Was it because of her or the play?

"The audience liked you," he said.

"How could you tell?"

"It's not hard." He stood. "I must be bothering you."

"No!" She put down the gun, turned. "I'm sorry. Stay a few minutes. If you can?"

He checked his watch. "I better not sit back down."

She smiled. "You'll have fun out there with Jeramie."

He nodded. "Yeah. How's Rindy?"

"She's—uh, fine." She forced a laugh. "Were you watching me so closely, you didn't see her?"

"I saw her." He consulted his watch again. There was an undecisiveness about him. "I'd better go."

"OK," she said softly. Did she sound so heartbroken? What he did next caught her completely unawares. He took a step closer to her, leaned over, and kissed her. It was not a casual peck. His lips pressed against hers. This time he didn't enfold her in his arms—how could he, as Charles, he had only one arm. And perhaps that was why she felt as though she were falling rather than being held. She fell quite a way before he broke away.

"Melanie," he said, staring at her.

"Yeah?"

He thought for a moment, shrugged. "I've got to go."

Watching him leave, she remembered Rodney Rosenberg's line.

"You're a nice kid, even though you don't know what the hell's going on."

How true. She loaded the gun. Three blanks.

Alone on the dark stage, Melanie waited. The curtain was down. In a moment it would rise. Charles's welcome-home party was over. Everyone was in bed except Melissa. She was waiting up for Ronda. The gun was in a drawer in a cabinet on the back wall. Melissa had placed it there during the party. Melanie had rechecked it a moment ago with the aid of a flashlight.

Paranoia.

Where was Rindy? The murder scene was supposed to follow the party scene. Just a quick drop of the curtain to imply the passage of a couple of hours—enough of a break to allow the actors to jump into their pyjamas. Melanie looked down at Melissa's gloved hands. Rindy and Ronda both must have had to use the bathroom.

Melanie felt surrounded. Immediately after the shooting, the others in the make-believe house, sleeping in widely separate rooms, would awaken and call out. Jeramie was in the right—stage right—cul-de-sac, Tracy was in the left one, and Marc was behind the curtain on the far left of the stage, close to but invisible to the audience. Melissa's bedroom was in the direction of the hallway that led to the dressing room. The setup would become critical in the last act, when the crime was reenacted.

Finally.

Rindy appeared in the hallway. She had changed into a green nightgown. Slowly, the hallway light was being dimmed, until it went out altogether. The curtain rustled softly, being pulled upward. They opened the curtain before Rindy made it onstage. A sigh went through the audience. They were tense. Every light in the theatre was off.

Melanie could hear Rindy's footsteps. She could not see her. Rindy was taking an inordinate amount of time. Her steps sounded timid. Melanie found herself listening so closely that she was forgetting to breathe. Her head shook minutely every time her heart pounded.

Finally, the icebox opened, its white light cutting Rindy in two. She was bent over, searching for a midnight snack, or perhaps some ice for another drink. Maybe it was the colour of the light; she looked very pale, scared even. And Melissa had still to draw her gun.

Rindy saw her. "Can't sleep, dear?" she asked, stepping towards the couch, leaving the fridge door ajar.

"I'll sleep later," she answered, her words drowsy.

Rindy sat beside her on the sofa. "Did you have a bad dream?"

She told her old friend about the last five years of her life, and it sounded like a nightmare. You don't deserve Charles. You're always messing with Robert. You could've talked Charles out of enlisting. If not for you, he would still have his arm. If not for you, he would have been mine. . . ."

Rindy was listening quietly, as she was supposed to. The only thing different from rehearsal was her distressed expression. Rindy looked as if she wanted to get up and run away.

Melissa's ramblings did not last long.

Melanie stood, casually strode to the back door, and opened it.

"Why are you doing that?" Rindy asked, her voice trembling.

"Fresh air." Melanie pulled open the drawer.

"You're wearing gloves, Mellie?"

Melanie lifted the gun. "It's a cold night."

"No, it's not that cold."

"Yes, it's very cold." Melanie showed her the gun. "And I'm worried about fingerprints."

Rindy stood suddenly, backing towards the bar. She tried to shout for help. The cry choked in her throat. In quick steps, discarding Melissa's drowsiness, Melanie rounded the couch.

Where am I?

Melanie could not find her reflection, which always jumped out at her at this point. Of course, the mirror in the cabinet was gone. There was just Rindy—one target.

"You'll also learn it's never good to play a part you wouldn't want to be."

Rindy's breath came in agonized gasps. Her face was ashen. Melanie stalked her as if she were a cornered animal.

"Wh-why?" Rindy whimpered.

"Are you looking forward to getting shot tonight?"

Rindy suddenly doubled up as though she were in terrible pain, clutching her abdomen. This was a new twist on her part. Melanie raised the gun, cocked the hammer.

"Come on, make me immortal. Kill me."

"You're a thorn," Melanie said. "I have to pull you out. And throw you away."

Now? No?

Melanie hesitated, momentarily confused, unaware of the source of her confusion. For an instant the whole play seemed to falter, and Melissa was a nonperson. Then Rindy stood suddenly upright in the harsh lifeless light thrown off by the half-open refrigerator. Her body shuddered. Her mouth opened wide. Her beautiful green eyes flashed. "Don't!" she screamed.

Melanie shot her. Three times. In the chest. Rindy clutched her heart as she fell, red blossoming across her nightgown. She did not land on her side, as she usually did in rehearsal, but on her back, her head rolling lazily beside the door of the icebox. Quickly, smoothly, Melanie crossed the stage, setting the revolver beside Rindy's messy hand. Melanie looked down into her face. Rindy's lips were slightly parted, her eyes shut. She could have been asleep. Melanie closed the icebox. The dark was deep.

Now Melissa was supposed to dash to her room and tear off her gloves. With her arms out in front, Melanie groped towards the hallway. The others started to shout. In the pitch-black, they all sounded as if they were shouting in her ear.

Melanie had grabbed hold of the hallway door when Jeramie, dressed in long johns, turned on a lamp onstage. Naturally, the curtain was still up. Marc appeared beside Melanie, then Tracy, both wearing pyjamas. Their eyes made contact. Then they moved past her. Melanie glanced at her gloves. The right one was splotched red.

Susan was also in the hallway, gesturing for her to hurry. Melanie ripped off the gloves and threw them on the floor. She had to return to the scene of the crime and plead her ignorance.

A moment later the four of them stood silently beside the body. The red dye had seeped across the wooden floor almost to the edge of the stage. There was a lot of the gook, Melanie noted, more than could have been in the Baggies Rindy had taped to her chest. Yet the observation sounded no internal alarms.

Charles knelt by the body of his wife. He touched her neck, his face grave. "She's dead," he said.

Then Charles frowned. Or was it Mark? The expression was quite out of character, as was his suddenly ripping his right arm free. He cupped Rindy's white face in both his hands. Marc had definitely taken over.

So had reality.

He looked up at Melanie. "She *is* dead."

SIX

The jail cell was hot and bright. Melanie lay sweating on the rumpled cot, staring up at the fluorescent lights whose switch couldn't be reached through the grey bars. She had to go to the bathroom but was afraid to call for the night officer on duty at the front desk. She was afraid he'd ignore her, or worse, humiliate her by following her into the ladies' room to be sure she didn't slit her wrists. But there was no danger of her trying to cut herself. She had seen enough blood that night to last her for the rest of her life.

"Does that gook stain?"

"It's a formula Jeramie dug up. He says it'll never come out."

She had the cell to herself, and an empty one on either side to make her feel properly isolated. The company of a car thief or a child molester probably wouldn't have buoyed her spirits; she supposed she should be thankful for small favours. Yet her loneliness was almost unbearable. If there had only been a drunk to plead her innocence to, she might have felt better.

Melanie sat up, her head swaying. Blood dripped from her nose onto the lap of her nightgown. For a moment the memory she had in her mind seemed impossible, the imaginings of a mind divorced from reality. There appeared no relationship between cause and effect. Everything that had happened had happened because of her. And yet she had had nothing to do with it.

I couldn't have been there. It was someone else—Melissa.

But as she looked around for something to wipe her nose with, her hand fell on the glove that had held the gun. Splotched red. Real blood, Rindy's blood.

Melanie wept.

*

That the audience continued to enjoy the play was an unintentional blasphemy. So the girl was dead. She was supposed to be dead. It took Susan, running onstage and screaming for a doctor, to ruffle the crowd. Then there was all kinds of noise.

There was no doctor in the house. There was, however, a deputy sheriff—one of Careville's finest. Tall, blond, and approximately thirty years old, he had a commanding voice. He was out of uniform, but when he identified himself and ordered everyone to remain seated, his order was obeyed. His examination of Rindy lasted only ten seconds, long enough. He spoke to a man Melanie didn't know, giving him a number to call. Then he took Melanie by the arm and led her to the dressing room. She did not really look at *the body*, not after Marc had told her the news. All she remembered was Susan crying. None of the others were crying. And then there was the blood. The stuff was everywhere. She wasn't going to forget that. The deputy sheriff told her to stay in the dressing room and not to move an inch.

Twenty-one minutes went by. She timed it. The deputy sheriff finally returned. "What is your name?" he asked.

"Melissa. Is Rindy dead?"

"Yes. What is your last name, Melissa?"

"What?"

"Your last name?"

"Martin. Melanie Martin."

"You just said your name is Melissa?"

"I did?"

He grew impatient. "You realise I can easily verify your correct name." He didn't like her.

"I'm Melanie." Nausea twisted her guts. "Can I go home? I don't feel so good."

"I'm afraid not, young lady. I'm placing you under arrest." He pulled a pair of handcuffs from his back pocket. "You have the right to remain silent. If you give up the right to remain silent, anything you say can and will be used against you in a court of law. You have the right to speak with an attorney and to have the attorney present during questioning. If you so desire, and cannot afford one, an attorney will be appointed for you without charge prior to questioning. Do you understand each of these rights that I've explained to you?''

"Yes."

"Put out your hands, please." She did so. He clamped the handcuffs around her wrists. "Stand and follow me."

"Can I get dressed?"

"No."

He led her into the hallway and stood her against the wall and told her not to move. Then he strode to the end of the hall, where he spoke to a fat, elderly, cigar-smoking man in a police uniform. Beyond them she could see the brightly lit stage, and had she looked hard, she suspected she would've caught a glimpse of *the body*. Marc, Susan, and the others were not visible. The fat man glanced at her a couple of times. He appeared confused by the whole affair. He kept shaking his head. She doubted he would have handcuffed her.

While she was waiting, an exquisitely dressed middle-aged couple approached the two officers. The clear green eyes in her pale pretty face left no doubt in Melanie's mind whose mother she was. Melanie looked at the floor. Consequently, she did not see how the lady slipped past the officers; why they didn't stop her.

"Do you know what you've done?" the woman hissed. *"Tell her your parents are into oil and she'll love you."*

Melanie coughed, looked up. The combination of grief and bitterness in the woman's face was difficult to take. "No."

Melanie did not see the blow coming. She hardly even felt it. There was simply a fuzzy spell where everything jumped wildly in the air. Then the fat policeman was hanging on to Rindy's screaming mother, and the deputy sheriff was dragging Melanie outside, her nose bleeding freely. She didn't even remember having picked up the gloves Melissa had worn.

The deputy sheriff drove her to Barters in a police car. She had to sit in the back behind a wire grille. He didn't speak a single word to her. The car was cold and she shook the entire trip.

At the station, a second clean-cut young man booked

her. She was the most excitement he'd seen in a while. He took great pleasure in snapping her mug shot and pressing out her fingerprints.

"You can make one call," he said, handing her a quarter.

Her father was God-knew-where in Chicago. She had the operator place a collect call to her mother in San Francisco. There was no answer. There was no one else to call. The night officer said it would be morning before the judge could set bail. He took her in the back, removed her handcuffs, and locked her behind bars.

"You look like a nice girl, Melanie," he said by way of good night. "I don't know what the hell got into you."

A hand was gently shaking her. "Melanie? Melanie?"

She opened her eyes. A sad black face stared down at her. The man wore a yellow, long-sleeve shirt and a green tie. His frizzy hair was white in spots. He looked as if he had recently stood too close to a Christmas tree that was being flocked.

"What time is it?" she croaked, her throat dry.

"Nine-fifteen."

She sat up. Everything came back to her in a flash. "Is Rindy still dead?"

"I'm afraid so." He sat beside her on the cot. "I'm Captain Michael Crosser. I'm the detective in charge of this case."

"A captain," she muttered. "Who assigned you?"

"I assigned myself."

Michael Crosser had brought the blouse and jeans she had worn to the theatre. He led her out of the cell to an upstairs bathroom. Changing out of the nightgown, she noticed a tear on the upper right arm, and she couldn't think how it had happened. Her nose and upper lip were swollen from Mrs. Carpenter's blow. The caked blood was difficult to wash off. She couldn't believe she had slept through the whole night. And Rindy was dead. That's how it would be from now on. *Oh, I went to the store today. And Rindy is dead. That's a nice dress. Rindy used to love those colours. Before she was dead.*

Her tears were easier to wash off than the blood.

The captain took her to his office and shut the door. The furnishings were stylish: lots of lacquered wood on the walls and soft leather on the chairs. Pictures of two pretty, black teenagers in cheerleader uniforms hung on the walls.

"My daughters," he explained, noticing her attention. He leaned against the edge of his desk and indicated for her to take a seat. "Linda and Pat. They're about your age: a senior and junior."

"They go to school around here?"

He shook his head. "In L.A. They live with their mother."

"Oh, I see."

He smiled. Somehow, his face looked sadder when he smiled. Like her, his bottom teeth were crooked. "Their mother is not the reason I work in Iowa."

"You didn't like L.A.?"

"I loved it as much as you must have loved San Francisco. But circumstances beyond my control—departmental politics—inspired me to leave."

He must have already checked up on her. "What do you think of Iowa?" she asked.

"I'm still getting used to the weather, the people. I hardly know anyone here. How about you?"

"The same, I guess. Do you miss your daughters?"

"When I see their pictures." He paused. "Are you hungry?"

"No. I didn't kill Rindy."

He didn't blink. "Who did?"

"I don't know."

He sighed, glanced out of the window. The police station was located at the edge of Barters. Rolling farm fields stretched as far as the eye could see. "You understand you don't have to talk to me?"

"Yes. But I didn't kill her."

"Before we talk, you might want to discuss your situation with an attorney."

"Can't I just tell you what happened?" she asked desperately.

"How old are you, Melanie?"

"Eighteen." She'd caught chicken pox and the measles, one after another, in first grade, and had been held back.

96

"You're legally an adult. If this goes to trial, you'll be tried as an adult."

She hesitated. But he seemed like a good man. She had to trust somebody. "I want to talk."

He moved behind his desk. "I'll be taping our conversation. OK?" He wanted her to talk too.

"Fine."

He pressed a button on a cassette player, gave his name and the date and time, then had her state her name and that she was speaking freely and understood her rights. "Tell me what happened," he said finally.

Where to begin? Wherever it was, it was important she got her facts straight the first time. A jury wouldn't execute a confused teenager, but they could put one away for a long time.

"In the play, at the end of Act Two, the scene called for me to shoot Rindy Carpenter's character. We'd practised this scene many times in rehearsal, using a gun and blanks belonging to Jeramie Waters. A few days before opening night I ran out of blanks. I bought more at Arnie's Arsenal in Barters, from All-American Beef—from Steve Fisher. The box he sold me was unopened. The night of the play, between Acts One and Two, I loaded the gun with these blanks. And they *were* blanks. I checked them out myself. Before the murder scene, minutes before, I rechecked them."

"Are you taking full responsibility for what was loaded into the gun?"

"I—yes."

He took a flat-topped shell from his pocket and placed it on the desktop within her reach. "This is a thirty-eight shell. It fits in the revolver you used in the play. Take it. Examine it."

Melanie did so. It appeared identical to the ones Steve had sold her. She told the captain as much.

"Are you sure?" he asked.

"Yes."

"You would say this is a blank?"

"Yes."

"Melanie, have you ever heard the expression 'wad cutter'?"

97

"No."

"You are holding a wad cutter. They are used in target practice. The flat shape of the slug cuts neat holes in cardboard. This is why they're preferred in practice shooting over ordinary shells. They resemble blanks but they are very real. They can kill. Rindy Carpenter was killed by a wad cutter."

"How do you know?"

"An autopsy was performed earlier this morning and a wad cutter was removed from her chest."

She grimaced. *Autopsy*. They'd already cut Rindy open like a side of beef. And she had been so beautiful. . . . "I see," she whispered.

He spoke gently. "It's possible, likely, in fact, you loaded a wad cutter into the gun without knowing it."

"No." She re-examined the strange cartridge. "This is not the same as the shells Steve sold me. Those were plugged with wax, not lead."

"But you just said they were the same."

"I was wrong. I didn't look at this bullet close enough."

"Did you look at the bullet last night close enough?"

"Yes. Real close."

"Why?"

"What?"

"Why did you examine the bullets Steve Fisher had sold you so closely?"

"To make sure they were blanks."

"What made you suspect they wouldn't be?"

The question sliced through her, disturbing what she was trying to have remain undisturbed. "I was being cautious," she said quietly.

He thought about that a moment. "If a wad cutter had been placed accidentally or intentionally into the box of shells Steve Fisher sold you, then you would be, for all legal purposes, off the hook."

He hung the possibility out like a rope to safety. "They were blanks," she said stubbornly.

"All right, let's accept for a moment the possibility that when you loaded the gun between Acts One and Two, you

98

did so with blanks. Was the gun out of your sight from *that* point to the actual instant you shot it?''

"Not really. I slipped it in the drawer during the welcome-home party. I was onstage the whole time.''

"Yet you left the stage before the murder scene?''

"Are you familiar with *Final Chance*?''

"I read the script last night.''

"You've been up all night?''

"Yes.''

He might know details she didn't. "Yes, I left the stage. We all did. The curtain had fallen. We all had to change into nightclothes.''

"At this time was the stage dark?''

"Very dark.''

"Then you returned to perform the scene. But before you did, you rechecked the gun?''

"Yes. I used a flashlight.''

"A flashlight?''

"I had placed it in the drawer earlier. The gun was still loaded with blanks.''

"You went to the trouble to plant a flashlight so you would be able to reverify that the gun still contained blanks?''

Her paranoia was transparent. "I was being cautious,'' she repeated.

"Hmm. Tell me, when you rechecked the shells, could a wad cutter, *at this point*, have escaped your notice?''

He'd had her examine a wad cutter in broad daylight and she'd failed at first to distinguish it from a blank. "I just glanced at the shells to make sure they were flat-headed,'' she admitted.

"Was the gun lying in the drawer in the same position you had left it?''

"I think so. Do you think someone sneaked onstage during the blackout?''

"The possibility seems unlikely. At this point in the show, where was the cast?''

"After the party Tracy, Rindy, and I changed in the dressing room. Marc and Jeramie changed in the Green Room. Then we met in the hallway. Tracy and Jeramie each went into one of the corner cul-de-sacs: Jeramie into the right, Tracy into the left.''

"They were totally isolated from each other?"

"Yes. The scene painting hanging outside the set back door blocks the passageway between the cul-de-sacs.''

"Go on."

"Marc hid behind the curtain near the audience on the left side of the stage. I'm talking about stage left and right. I went onto the stage, rechecked the gun in the drawer, then sat on the couch and waited for Rindy. I had to wait a long time.''

"Why?"

"I think Rindy had to go to the bathroom."

"Who else was around?"

"Susan."

"Where was she?"

"I don't know exactly."

"Then why did you say she was around?"

"Because after I shot Rindy, I saw Susan in the hallway."

"But *during* the actual scene you couldn't say with certainty where she was?"

"No." She stopped, asking suspiciously, "Have you already spoken to Susan and the others?"

"All last night. But I want your point of view." He consulted a notepad on his desk. "So far your account agrees with the others. Susan says she was in the back with Carl. But when the murder scene started, she began to circle around outside to the hallway. It was her job, she said, to clean up the red dye while the rest of you were changing back into your street clothes for the last act.''

"That's correct."

"With all these people coming and going, you can see why I think it's unlikely someone could have slipped a wad cutter into the revolver while it was in the drawer onstage.''

"Someone from the cast, maybe. But both back doors were unlocked. When the rest of us were changing into our nightclothes, someone could have come in from the outside.''

"That's unlikely."

"Why?"

"I'll tell you in a moment. But first, did the gun kick when you shot it?"

"I don't understand?"

"Was there a recoil?"

"None that I noticed."

"How about on the second shot? Try to remember that one in particular."

"It was the same as rehearsal." She paused, frowned.

"What is it?"

"The gun was the same. But Rindy was different. She was so nervous. She—"

"What?"

"I can't remember. Why are you asking about the second shot?"

"It was the one that killed Rindy. Our people have examined the used cartridges." He leaned forward, clasped his hands on top of his desk, and looked her straight in the eye. "Your fingerprints, Melanie, were on all the shells, including the wad cutter."

"That's impossible! How come you didn't tell me this to start with?"

"I told you, I wanted your point of view."

She was upset. "But I'm telling you what I know. You should tell me what you know."

"Melanie, I'm trying to help you."

She was close to crying. "I don't believe that! If you'd told me at the beginning my fingerprints were on the real bullet, I would have—I—I don't know." Closing her eyes briefly, she took a deep breath, fighting to calm herself. "All right, then, what are you saying? That I murdered Rindy?"

His voice was reasonable. "Not at all. I'm merely trying to eliminate the possibility that the shells were changed after you loaded the gun. Since your fingerprints were on the wad cutter, you must have put it in the gun. Agreed?"

"I suppose," she mumbled.

"Let's go on to—"

"Wait!" *"Melanie, give me a hand with these, would ya?"* "I touched other bullets last night besides the ones Steve sold me." She briefly described Susan's extra box of blanks,

Susan's run-in with Heidi, and how the box fell to the floor. The captain listened closely. This was obviously new to him.

"This Heidi left with two of Susan's blanks?" he asked when she was done.

"Yes."

"Were they ones you had touched?"

"I don't think so. I'm pretty sure they weren't."

"Interesting. And yet Susan couldn't have switched the bullets before the murder scene. She was with Carl up until the scene started."

"I wasn't trying to implicate Susan." She coughed dryly. Her face ached. "How was Carl when you spoke to him?"

"Not good. Would you like to take a break?"

"No. He was real upset?"

"I had to repeat each question to him a couple of times. It's a terrible tragedy." The captain again looked out of the window. Clouds were moving in. A black storm. "So now we have a second box of bullets to chase. Hmmm— Did Susan's blanks get mixed up with yours?"

"Definitely not. Susan told me to use my own."

"Susan didn't mention her blanks to me," he said. "Of course, there was no obvious reason to do so."

"Were mine the only fingerprints on the wad cutter?"

"Yes. You mentioned Jeramie was in the room when Susan dropped her blanks. Did he touch any of them?"

"He might have. I'm not sure."

"Why were Susan and Heidi fighting?"

"Susan picked me over Heidi for the part of Melissa. Heidi still seems to resent us both."

He made a note on his pad. "I'll have to have a talk with this girl. Tell me, did Rindy touch any of Susan's blanks?"

"Maybe. They scattered all over the dressing room. Why?"

"Just wondering." She could practically hear his mental gears turning. None of his questions were frivolous. He was a shrewd man. "Let's return to when you loaded the gun, between Acts One and Two. What makes you so certain they were blanks? Tell me specifically?"

"I stuck my nail in the wax at the end of them."

"In all three?"

"Just one," she said reluctantly.

"And you were alone in the dressing room at this time?"

"Yes. Well, most of the time."

"Who else entered?"

"Marc."

"Marc Hall?"

"Yes."

"Did he touch your bullets?"

"No."

"Did you check your bullets before or after he entered?"

"Before."

"Did he get *near* your bullets?"

"What do you mean?"

"What I said. Why are you blushing?"

"I'm not." She stuttered. "Y-yes, he did."

"He got close to them?"

"Yes."

"Were you watching him the whole time?"

"Yes. Well, I knew where he was the whole time."

"But you took your eyes off him?"

"Not exactly. I—closed my eyes for a moment."

The captain considered that. "Did he kiss you in the dressing room?"

"Did he tell you that?"

Her reaction surprised the captain. Despite the grave nature of the situation, he laughed. "Marc kept your confidences," he reassured her. "He's an interesting young man."

"I like him." She sighed, feeling terribly exposed. It was as though this man had been there. His seriousness returned.

"Could Marc have replaced one of your blanks with a wad cutter?"

"No! What kind of question is that?"

"A logical one. Marc was close to the blanks and, for a moment at least, he had your attention elsewhere."

"He wouldn't have done that."

"But *could* he have, had he wanted to?"

"I don't know. I suppose so. You don't think Marc wanted to kill Rindy?"

Captain Crosser stood and stepped behind her chair,

beginning to pace, his arms folded across his chest. She turned, following his thoughtful expression. His clothes were pressed and his shoes shined; nevertheless, he looked like a man who lived without a woman. He was too thin; he probably ate on the run. Initially, when he had awakened her, she had thought his face sad; and it was true, there was a long, hard life behind his tired eyes. Probably a lonely life.

"The temptation for any investigator in a situation such as this is to invent a complex explanation when a simple one will do as well or better," he said. "No, I don't think Marc killed Rindy. Or that Susan did. Or Jeramie. Or a stranger. I believe, as I have already suggested, that a wad cutter was accidentally placed in your box of blanks. And that you loaded it without realising it."

"But the gun didn't kick."

"This was a climactic moment in the play. Would you have noticed a recoil?"

"I think so."

"I wonder." He glanced at his daughters, continued his pacing. "On the other hand, the reverse of what I just said is equally true. Do you want to delve into the complex?"

"I want to know what happened."

"So far, I've thought of two alternative explanations. Both of them would require a brilliant villain who would almost certainly have had to be directly involved with the play. First, there is the possibility Rindy did not die when you shot her."

"You've lost me already."

"The most brilliant crime is the one that didn't occur when everyone thought it did, but rather, a few minutes before, or a few minutes after. Let's say you shot Rindy with your three blanks. She falls down and plays dead. You go over, drop the gun next to her, shut the icebox, and plunge the stage into darkness. While you're stumbling towards the hallway, our imaginary villain emerges from somewhere behind the stage. He dashes to Rindy and, using a silencer, puts a bullet in her chest. He then removes the silencer from the gun and replaces your gun with his. Naturally, he would have to be wearing gloves."

"Maybe that's what happened," she said, excited at the idea.

The captain shook his head. "This scenario has its problems. Number one: a Smith and Wesson thirty-eight revolver doesn't take a silencer, not ordinarily. Sure, somewhere, a weapons expert could design one for the barrel, but where are you going to find such an expert at Care High? Number two: a silencer still makes a noise. You've heard silencers used on TV?"

"Yes."

"Did you hear such a noise while groping for the hallway?"

"No."

"I didn't think so. To complicate things further, you would have had to have handled our villain's gun and bullet to have gotten your fingerprints all over them."

"Huh. What's the other alternative?"

"The oldest trick in the book. The simultaneous shot. I even explored this possibility last night when I interviewed members of the audience."

"You did all this last night?"

"I wanted fresh memories. The scene calls for three shots, right?"

"Yes."

"I asked those I spoke to how many shots they heard. Some said four."

"Really?"

"Some said two. There was a couple who said they heard five. The majority said three, but the point is, these people were there to relax and enjoy the show. They weren't counting. The deputy who brought you in swears there were only two shots, when we know how unlikely that is."

Melanie scowled. "Him."

The captain stopped pacing. "He wasn't very nice to you, was he?"

"He treated me like I was filth."

"Don't feel bad. He treats me that way, and I'm his boss."

"Let's not talk about him."

"Agreed. Now, we've established the audience can't count. Testimony from them in this regard can't be trusted.

Fortunately, we don't need it to all but eliminate the possibility of a simultaneous shot. First, from the autopsy, we know Rindy was hit from the same angle you shot her from.''

''What if someone had been standing behind me?''

''*Was* someone standing behind you?''

''I don't think so. But I wasn't looking.''

''This person would have had to have materialized out of thin air. The only way he could have gotten onstage was to have entered through the fire-escape door. Had he done that, the alarm would have gone off. We checked it thoroughly.''

''But what if he had tampered with the alarm? And then quickly fixed it?''

''An expert checked that alarm. It hadn't been touched in years.''

''When Rindy was backing away from me, she was moving this way and that. How can you be so sure what angle she was shot from?''

The captain leaned against the wall. ''You're sharp, Melanie. The answer is, we can't be a hundred percent sure. It's feasible someone in the right cul-de-sac could have done it.''

''Jeramie,'' she whispered.

''Feasible, but very unlikely. He was at least thirty degrees off the coroner's calculated angle. Then we have the same problems we had with the other alternative. You would have had to have handled both the villain's gun and bullet. Not to mention that after our Mr. X did all these amazing things, he would have had to have disappeared.''

Melanie rested her head in her hands. She had been hoping this close scrutiny would uncover an explanation that would clear her of any responsibility. Was she that selfish? Rindy was dead and she was worried about herself. Yet nothing could be done for her friend.

I would have been your friend. Can you hear me?

The tears were there before she realised it. The captain waited patiently while she wept them. He *was* a good man. She had been wrong to snap at him. ''So I guess it was my fault, then?'' she said finally.

''This was opening night. You were excited, and having

fun. How could you expect to notice the difference in shells?''

"I should have noticed," she said, her voice cracking. "If I had, Rindy would be alive now."

"We don't know that for sure. Even if we did, you can't blame yourself. Guilt is a wicked thing. Once it gets into you it's harder to get rid of than a cancer."

True and kind words. She doubted she could follow them. He offered her a box of tissues and she blew her nose. Looking up at him as he stood over her, she asked pitifully, "But you believe I didn't do it on purpose, don't you?"

He turned off the tape recorder. "Yes."

She nodded to herself, sniffed. "That's good."

He knelt beside her, took her hands. "You've been through a terrible ordeal. The worst is over. You'll be out of here soon."

"Do I have to post bail and stuff?"

"It's already been done."

"How?"

"Your mother is an excitable woman."

"*You* called her?"

He smiled. "Like I said, it was a long night. Yes, I spoke to her. And I'm sure she'll want to speak to you later on." He added, "I explained it was an accident."

"Does my father know?"

"Your mother said she would try to track him down."

"So what happens next?"

"Now you go home. In a week or so there will be a hearing to see if there should be a trial. Between now and then you'll have to see a lawyer."

"But I won't be tried, will I?"

He hesitated. "You should really speak to a lawyer."

"But you know it was an accident."

"I *think* it was an accident. There are still loose ends that need to be tied up. My investigation has only begun."

"We're going to talk again?"

"Yes. Unless your lawyer gets in the way."

"What haven't we covered?"

He stood and again leaned back on the edge of his desk, his expression strange, impossible to read. "Melanie," he said carefully, "all last night you were waiting for something terrible to happen?"

She nodded. "I know."

He glanced at the recorder, left it off. "Why?"

"I was scared."

"Why?"

"I don't know."

"Was there anything that happened, last night or in the last year, that made you think someone wanted Rindy dead?"

Clyde.

The name just popped in her head. She didn't know from where.

"I'll have to think about it."

SEVEN

There were papers to sign: those from the bondsman and the police station. She put her name to them only after a thorough reading. From now on she was going to be more careful. The captain offered to give her a ride home. He was returning to Careville to ask more questions. Do you always work this hard, she asked? No, he replied, policing this part of the state is as exciting as guarding a cornfield.

Apparently, there had *never* been a murder in Careville.

When she entered her house, the phone was ringing. The captain had already pulled away. The last person in the world she would have expected was calling.

"Melanie, this is Dave. How are you?"

"I'm OK. How are you?"

"I heard about what happened in the play."

"What? Who told you? My mom?"

"No, it was on TV, and in the morning paper."

"In *San Francisco*?"

"Yeah, it's big news out here. So what happened? Did you really kill the girl?"

Her nerves were frayed. She almost hung up then and there. "What do the papers say?" she asked coldly.

He noted her tone. "That the police are still investigating. Melanie, I didn't call to hassle you."

"Then why did you call? And how's Judy? Is she impressed that you used to neck with a celebrity?"

He didn't answer immediately. "Melanie, I can't believe this is you talking. I called because I was concerned about you."

"OK. I'm sorry. I don't feel so hot. I spent the night in jail. What do you want to know? It was an accident. I thought I put blanks in the gun, but I guess I didn't, because one of the

109

blanks killed her.''

"Did you know her?"

"Of course I knew her. We were in the play together. Her name was Rindy Carpenter."

"Was that the same girl who ran into you last spring?"

"Yeah. Right. It was her. She hit my car and I was still pissed off so I killed her."

"Melanie—"

She slammed the phone down. Almost instantly, it rang again. David didn't know when to quit. She snapped it up. "And tell your jerkoff Judy I might take care of her next!"

"Melanie!"

Damn. "Hello, Mom," she said quietly. "What's new?"

"What's new? I get a call in the middle of the night from a policeman who says my daughter's in jail for killing someone and you ask me what's new? Melanie, what have you done this time?"

Melanie sat on the floor. "It was an accident," she said and sighed. How many times would she have to repeat that for the rest of her life? "My blanks got mixed up with something called a wad cutter. That's what killed the girl."

At least that's what they keep telling me. . . .

"How could you be so stupid as to get them mixed up?"

"Bad genes, I guess." Her mother always inspired sarcasm.

"Don't get smart. I've gone to a lot of trouble and expense on your part. Do you know how much it cost to meet your bail?"

"I have no idea," she lied. It had been ten grand.

"More than your father makes on half a dozen of his business trips, that's how much. By the way, I got hold of him early this morning. He's driving back from Chicago. He should be there soon."

"How did he take the news?" Dumb question.

"Better than I did. Listen, do you have a pencil? The captain said you need a lawyer. This lady works in Des Moines."

She reached for a pen and an old newspaper. "I'm ready."

"Her name's Claudia Schaefer. Her number is five-one-five-five-five-five-five-five-four-zero-eight. My lawyer recommends her highly. I've already sent her a deposit. She'll be expecting you to call her today.''

"I will." She added, "Thanks."

"The captain told me it looks like it wasn't intentional."

"Intentional? Mom, do you think I would kill somebody on purpose?''

"Don't put words in my mouth. What I mean is, even if it's an accident, this girl's family can still sue. Thank God, your father wanted complete custody. He doesn't have anything they could take.''

Melanie was having trouble breathing. "Mom, this girl was my friend. How can you talk about money right now?''

"All right, don't get upset. I was just thinking ahead. I'm sorry about what happened to her. She had her whole life in front of her. And I'm sorry you're having to shoulder the blame.''

"Maybe that will change," she said, thinking.

Her father arrived home an hour later, at two in the afternoon. He told her if she wanted to talk, he would listen, but if she wasn't up to it, that was fine. He was great. Briefly, she repeated what she had told Captain Crosser. When she was done, he told her they could move if she wanted. No, she said, we're staying right here.

Three times reporters came to the door. One brought a cameraman. Her father politely sent them away.

It was Saturday. They called the lawyer and made an appointment for a consultation Monday morning. She spent the rest of Saturday and all day Sunday reading and cleaning the house. Sunday evening Marc and Susan called, about an hour apart. She had her father tell them she would return their calls in a few days. She also told Sam at the diner she wouldn't be in for a while. She was still contemplating the captain's last question. Carl Carpenter would be the place to start answering it.

At odd moments she considered calling Rindy's parents. A look in the mirror always stopped her. Her swollen lip was going down slowly.

Early Monday found Melanie and her father sitting in

111

Claudia Schaefer's office. *Ms.* Schaefer—as she introduced herself—was a big, strong, chain-smoking, no-nonsense brunette. She was from New York and spoke so rapidly Melanie could hardly keep up. Ms. Schaefer did not drill her as the captain had. The woman appeared to have decided on a course of action a few minutes into Melanie's tale.

"For the sake of the preliminary hearing," she said, "we cannot present the judge with all the details. The hearing is merely to see if there's sufficient evidence to indicate you *could* have purposely killed Rindy Carpenter. It's the reverse of a trial. During the hearing the burden of proof lies with you, not with the district attorney. I'll have to study up on wad cutters, but from what you've said, it's clear they could be mistaken for blanks. We'll tell the judge what the captain told you, that a wad cutter was probably accidentally packaged into the box of shells you bought."

"But I'm not sure if that's what happened," Melanie said.

"It doesn't matter. At this point it's better to keep things simple. Understand, we're not committing ourselves to a particular defence."

"The captain didn't seem to think I would be tried."

Ms Schaefer ground out a cigarette, sipped her coffee. "Did he tell you that?"

"Not exactly."

"I'm sure he didn't say anything of the kind. If you'd wanted to kill Rindy, and if you'd had any brains, a wad cutter is exactly what you would've used. You can bet that will occur to the judge."

"Are you saying my daughter will be tried?" Mr. Martin asked.

Ms Schaefer reached for another smoke. "It could go either way."

"When is the hearing?" Mr. Martin said.

"Next Monday."

"Shouldn't we be planning some sort of strategy?" Melanie asked.

"No. We don't want to show the district attorney what we've got. Likewise, he'll present the minimum evidence necessary to gain a trial. One thing, don't talk to Captain

Crosser again, at least not until after the hearing.''

"But he's trying to help me,'' Melanie protested.

Ms Schaefer struck a match. "No, he's trying to find out if you murdered Rindy Carpenter.'' She puffed on her cigarette. "It's not necessarily the same thing.''

When they were back in their pinto, heading for Careville, Melanie turned to her father and said, "My lawyer thinks I'm guilty.''

Tuesday was the day of the funeral. Melanie learned the time and location from the *Careville Star*, which would never be mistaken for *The New York Times*. The local paper had obtained a picture of her that had been taken as part of a press release to advertise the play. Blowing the shot up, the creative editors had superimposed her sweet innocent smile above a photo of the type of revolver used in "the moment of terror''. She was certainly no longer a nobody.

Melanie wanted to observe the funeral. The desire did not spring out of morbid curiosity. She believed the old adage that the villain was often drawn back to the scene of the crime, and the real scene of injustice was Rindy's lifeless body, and not the stage. And if there was no villain, then she would at least get to pay her final respects, even if it was from a distance. The careless remarks of her mom and her attorney were having their effect. Her feelings of guilt were like a knife in her heart.

Maple Lawns Memorial was located on the south-west corner of Careville, next to the town park. Here the landscape was pretty, with sculpted bluffs and dales and an abundance of trees that shaded large patches of well-tended lawn. Melanie parked behind a row of hedges on a narrow dirt road that wound along behind the cemetery. Standing up on the hill, she commanded a good view. She had not waited long, before a train of cars, led by a silver hearse, began to wend its way towards a freshly dug plot. She had brought binoculars.

Most of those assembled beside the grave were adults. The minister was old and solemn. Mr. Carpenter looked bent and weary, and his wife, in a long black coat, was a mess. Melanie recognized only three young people: Marc, Susan, and Carl.

Had Rindy been that unpopular? Where was Jeramie?

Marc and Susan had arrived together in Marc's truck. They stood close to the coffin; Marc's face drawn; Susan making no effort to hold back her tears; Carl watching the proceeding from a discreet distance. The minister's words seemed of no interest to him. He held a single red rose, perhaps thinking of the delight his sister had taken in the dozen roses he had given her before the play.

Melanie couldn't hear the ceremony. But it was brief, and when it was done, she wondered what she had accomplished in coming. When the final farewells were complete, however, and the mourners were leaving in their cars, she noticed Carl, alone and on foot, heading in the direction of the park. With the binoculars she was able to follow him and saw that he'd stopped to sit on a boulder in a children's sandlot. Obviously, he wanted to be alone.

But when will I be able to get him alone again?

She took one last long look at the coffin—it seemed all wrong for Rindy to be lying out there in a cedar box with all those dead people—then left the cemetery grounds.

Carl didn't appear surprised to see her. He wore a navy blue suit and a red tie. The granite rock he was sitting on was huge, riddled with spray-painted masterpieces. The cold wind ruffled his short black hair. He had lost weight.

"Do you want to be by yourself?" she asked quickly, approaching him.

"You're not intruding," he said, gesturing to a clay animal, polite as always. "Pull up a giraffe. How are you doing, Melanie?"

She sat on a lion instead. "Not so good."

"Yeah, I don't feel so hot myself." He glanced at the dreary sky. Rain could fall any moment. He sighed. "What a day to be buried on."

"She was a beautiful person."

Carl smiled suddenly. "Around here everybody knew Rindy. But if I were somewhere else, in another city, and I had to pay for something, I would always slyly display the picture I had of her in my wallet. And usually the clerk, or whoever it was, would notice, and say, 'God, she's beautiful!

114

Is that your girlfriend?' I used to love saying, 'No, that's my sister.' I always thought, girlfriends can come and go, but your sister—she's there for life.''

Her eyes burned. ''I wish I'd known her better.''

''Not many people did know her,'' he said wistfully. ''Not the way I did.'' He paused. ''How's your lip?''

''Fine. Carl, don't you blame me at all?'' The question came out almost as a plea.

''No. It was an accident.''

She wiped her eyes, hesitated. ''What if it wasn't?''

He looked at her strangely. ''It had to be.''

''Maybe it was. But since I've been around the people in the play, I've been hearing bits and snatches of stuff that scares me.''

He didn't want to encourage her. ''Don't believe everything you hear.''

''Carl, who's Clyde?''

He winced. ''Why do you bring him up?''

''It's too confusing to explain. When someone mentions his name, other people act weird. I have this feeling— Does Clyde live around here?''

Carl started scratching at the boulder on which he sat. ''Clyde was always doing stuff with his hands. He had great hands. That's what made him a great quarterback. He carved a heart with Rindy's and his initials somewhere on this rock.''

''Carl—''

''No, he's not in Careville. He lives in Des Moines.''

''What does he do?''

''He was never into books. I guess he watches a lot of TV.''

''I don't understand?''

''He's in the Teller Home,'' Carl said reluctantly. ''It's a kind of hospital.''

''What's he doing there?''

Carl suddenly loosened his tie, began to tug at it angrily, as if it were a garrotte. ''Most people would say Rindy put him there,'' he said bitterly.

The change in him was dramatic. ''What?''

''Those are the same people who will say you murdered Rindy.'' He gestured towards the town. ''All those jerks at

115

school. Their lives are so boring that they wait for something bad to happen. Then they get off on pointing their self-righteous fingers.''

''Tell me what happened? From the beginning? Please?''

''The beginning?'' Carl asked, his tone returning to normal. ''I don't know when that would be. Maybe when Rindy was a sophomore and Clyde was a junior. Yeah, I guess that's when they met. I wasn't even in high school then. God, that seems like ages ago.'' He relaxed his grip on his tie, laid it, wrinkled, beside him on the boulder. ''Clyde was the school quarterback. He led the team to a league championship. He was phenomenal. Marc was his top receiver. Everybody loved Clyde. He was real funny, easygoing. He didn't have a big head. And Rindy was as pretty then as—as when you knew her. It was natural they'd get together, you know? The school prince and the school princess. They dated all through that school year, and the beginning of the next. They were really in love. You couldn't pull them apart.

''Rindy wasn't as well-liked as Clyde. Everyone thought she was stuck-up—which was a bunch of crap. She was just quiet, or, rather, she was just too pretty, too rich, too lucky to have Clyde as a boyfriend. The girls envied her and the guys resented her because they couldn't have her. She couldn't win. It's weird how no one was jealous of Clyde. People are weird.''

Carl returned to picking at the stone. ''Have you ever read *Catcher in the Rye*?'' he asked.

''Twice.''

''Do you remember the part when Holden asks the New York cabdriver where the ducks go in the winter when the lake in the park freezes?''

''Yeah, that was a funny part.''

''There was this party,'' Carl went on. ''It was near the end of the football season, after a game we'd won. There were a couple of games left to go. We were in first place, thanks to Clyde and Marc. The party was at Steve Fisher's house. There was a lot of beer and loud music; it was a rowdy time. Practically the whole team was there, and the cheerleaders and song girls and baton twirlers—the whole social clique.

"Anyway, during a break in the dancing and carrying on, Rindy started talking about that part in *Catcher in the Rye*. And she was wondering about the ducks up at our reservoir. This was the beginning of November. Winter started early last year. There was already snow on the ground. My sister really loved animals: horses, dogs, cats—it didn't matter what. She was worried the ducks up at the lake might be freezing. Everybody thought she was off her rocker. Especially when she started on Clyde to drive her to the reservoir that night. OK, she wasn't perfect. She could be stubborn when she got something in her mind. Of course no one believed he had changed his *own* mind. After the accident, everyone thought Rindy had dragged Clyde up there."

Carl stopped. Melanie had to ask, "What happened?"

"There's a sharp turn just before you get to the water. There was ice on the road." He shrugged. "She drove over the edge."

So that was how Marc knew it was Rindy sitting in the dark trees beneath the road. Poor Rindy—the place must have had a sick hold on her. "Rindy was driving?" she asked.

"Yeah, she was driving Clyde's car. It was a fifty-foot drop. Clyde didn't have his seat belt on. His head hit the roof hard. Broke his neck. Rindy walked away from it with a few scratches and bruises. I remember thinking my sister must have had her guardian angel with her that night."

"What happened next?"

"Another car came by. Someone called an ambulance. Clyde had a long operation. He never walked again. And no one ever spoke to Rindy again. Oh, and the football team lost their last two games. What a tragedy, huh?"

"But how could anyone hold it against her? It was an accident."

"The accident was just an excuse to jump all over her." Carl shook his head. "Clyde's family is poor. He didn't have any medical insurance. His parents were going to sue our parents. It was in the local papers. Then my dad set up a trust fund for Clyde with some huge amount and the suit was dropped. But there was all this publicity. All this bitterness in the air over what Rindy had done. And what had she done

117

really? Nothing. I'm surprised you never heard about it.''

''Is Clyde paralyzed? Is that why he doesn't live at home?''

''His legs are wasted, but he has some use of his arms. It's been almost a year; I hear he's well enough to leave the hospital. He stays, I think, because he doesn't want to have to deal with everyone's sympathy.''

''What happened to Rindy and Clyde as a couple?''

''As far as I know, they never saw each other after the night of the accident.''

''Who didn't want to see whom?''

''Everyone said it was Clyde who didn't want to have anything to do with Rindy.'' Carl was puzzled. ''But Clyde was all heart. He would have forgiven Rindy. And my sister wouldn't have dumped Clyde just like that. To tell you the truth, she wouldn't tell me why things were the way they were. She just said, 'It's over.' I never visited him myself. She asked me not to.''

Melanie thought for a moment. The main difficulty she'd had in believing someone had purposely killed Rindy had been motive. Now Clyde's accident gave her a classic motive. *If* she could tie Clyde and Rindy together through a Mr. or Miss X.

''It was an accident,'' Carl repeated, reading her mind.

''If it wasn't, wouldn't you want to know who did it?''

''No.'' He bowed his head. ''I know enough already about how much my sister was hated.'' The wind whipped his pale face. His colouring had faded since last Friday.

''But what about me? I'm in a lot of trouble.''

He looked in the direction of the cemetery. ''I know,'' he said. ''What do you want to know?''

Leave him alone. For goodness' sake, he just buried his sister!

Yet she was doing this for his sister as much as for herself.

''I'll tell you a name. You tell me the person's relationship to Clyde and Rindy. OK?''

He nodded.

''Tracy.''

He frowned. ''Tracy's Clyde's sister. She despised Rindy.''

''*His sister?* Why were they working together on the play?''

''You'd have to ask Susan.''

''Did Tracy despise Rindy before the accident?''

"She didn't like her."

"How about Jeramie?"

"Jeramie and Clyde grew up together. But I don't know if you could call them friends. They didn't talk a lot. They were two different kinds of people. But Jeramie loved Rindy. That's for sure."

"Did Jeramie and Rindy often dance together?"

"Oh, yeah."

"Before Clyde's injury?"

"Yeah."

"Didn't this bother Clyde?"

"He was cool. I'd say no."

"Would you say Jeramie was obsessed with Rindy?"

"That's a good choice of words."

"What would you think if I told you Jeramie knew something bad was going to happen last Friday?"

"What did he tell you?"

"He was worried. Real worried."

"Jeramie couldn't hurt a fly."

"He killed a duck once." *Oh! What a coincidence.*

"That's just a rumour."

"How about Heidi?"

"Heidi's a bitch. She hated Rindy more than anybody did. She asked Clyde to Sadie Hawkins last year. It was a stupid thing to do. Everyone knew he was Rindy's guy."

"So Heidi liked Clyde?"

"All the girls liked Clyde."

She'd heard the same about Marc. "But she went so far as to ask him out. That's interesting."

"The interesting thing is that Clyde went with Heidi."

"What?"

"Rindy had flu. She didn't want Clyde to miss out."

"Rindy wasn't jealous?"

"No."

"Did Heidi and Clyde have fun?"

"I heard Heidi paraded him around all night like a trophy. Oh, this is another thing you might want to know. Heidi and Susan have always been rivals, for parts in plays and stuff. Though Susan usually wins out over her."

119

Susan wasn't on her suspect list. Susan had been in the hallway when Rindy had died. Besides, Susan was her friend. . . .

She was also the director of the play, idiot!

Lightning flashed—always strange when it struck in the daylight—and thunder rolled. It would rain any second.

"Would you say Susan has frustrated Heidi year after year?"

"Yeah," Carl said.

Another motive. What better way to ruin Susan's directorial debut than to kill one of her leads in the middle of the play?

"Did Rindy ever take an important role away from Susan?"

"No," he said.

"How did they get along before Clyde's accident?"

"Pretty good. Susan was one of the few girls that wasn't jealous of Rindy."

"How about after?"

Carl considered for a moment. "Susan seemed cooler towards her."

"Was Susan another of Clyde's adoring fans?"

"Not in a romantic way. But they were close, like brother and sister. They'd known each other since kindergarten. Still, in a way they were opposites. Clyde wasn't into much besides sports and having a good time. Susan's more artistic."

"Like Jeramie?"

"Yeah."

"Did Susan blame Rindy for what happened to Clyde?"

"I'm not sure. Ask her."

"I will." Melanie climbed off her lion. "I really appreciate this, Carl."

"Don't you want to know about Marc?"

She stopped. Had she forgotten about Marc on purpose? "Is there something I should know?"

"You decide. Marc was Clyde's best friend. When Clyde got paralyzed, Marc immediately quit the football team, even with two games left to play. He got real quiet, real introspective. He's still that way."

120

"Did he blame Rindy?"

"He never said anything."

"Does Marc visit Clyde?"

"I hear Tracy and Marc are practically the only ones that do go to the hospital."

The next question was the last one she wanted to ask. "Did Marc love Rindy?" she whispered.

Carl was watching her. "Marc's not the type to go after a friend's girl."

"Did he?" she insisted.

"Before the accident—maybe. Afterwards—they avoided each other."

"Except to do the play," she said.

Carl nodded. "I wish Stan Russel had never written that damn script."

Lightning cracked inside a fist of thunder. This time the rain must have been waiting in buckets over their heads. They were soaked in a second. Carl slid slowly off the boulder, looked around as if he didn't know which direction to take.

"I'll give you a ride," she said turning towards the parking lot.

"Thanks." He made no move to follow her. As the downpour washed over the boulder, he suddenly began to rub vigorously at a spot on it. "Melanie?" he called. She came up beside him, wet sand clinging to her tennis shoes. "See," he said, pointing.

Etched in the rock was a heart. The dirt had covered it. "C.P. luvs R.C." Romeo and Juliet. Oh, happy dagger . . .

"I feel I'm a year late," she said.

He picked up his soggy tie, touched the engraving lovingly. "I'm glad I gave her the flowers when I did."

"Could I see her picture in your wallet?"

He protected it with his suit coat as he showed it to her. Rindy was smiling. There was a flower in her hair. The sun was shining. Clyde was probably still throwing perfect passes. Melanie put her arm around Carl's waist. "She's still yours for life," she said.

They held on to each other as they walked to the car.

121

EIGHT

The rain was still coming down the following Monday morning when Melanie's preliminary hearing took place. Sitting beside her father and attorney on the wooden benches of the courtroom, waiting for the judge to appear, she longed to be back in San Francisco. A storm in the Bay area had been a reason to pick up an umbrella and go for a walk in the park or along the beach. Here it was just an excuse to catch pneumonia. It was cold. Pulling a tissue from a box resting on her lap, she blew her nose. She had been ill since the day of the funeral.

Captain Michael Crosser was outside in the hallway. Claudia Schaefer had hurried her past him, whispering in her tobacco breath not to talk to him. Melanie felt bad about that. The captain had waved to her.

The reporters had all gone away days before. Apparently, news was news only when it was brand-new.

"Am I going to get sworn in and all that?" Melanie asked her lawyer, who was observing the No Smoking signs and not liking it.

"You won't be taking the stand. I'll do all the talking. You have nothing to worry about."

How about I do the talking and you be Melanie Martin, and we'll see what there is to worry about.

The judge entered. They all rose. He was fat and ruddy and wore his gold-rimmed glasses down near the tip of his big nose. Yet somehow he projected dignity and fairness.

Procedures were observed. The stenographer was given the names of the involved parties. Melanie didn't know Rindy's middle name had been Ann.

The district attorney was built like Jeramie, tall and thin. But there was nothing wild in his demeanour. He appeared to be one serious dude.

The hearing started predictably enough. The D.A. briefly sketched how a certain Melanie Martin had fired a Smith & Wesson .38 at Rindy Carpenter during the course of a school play, and how the said Miss Carpenter had died. He then stated that Miss Martin's fingerprints had been found on the used shell of the wad cutter that had killed the aforementioned Miss Carpenter. The gentleman had a way with words.

Claudia Schaefer's statement was equally brief. In essence, she said it was an accident, and that Miss Martin was a sweet young lady with an excellent grade point average and no criminal record of any kind. Melanie wondered how much her mother was paying Ms. Schaefer. On the other hand, the woman probably knew her business. The judge immediately started to give the D.A. a bad time.

"Has the state any significant proof to contest the defendant's claim that she accidentally placed the wad cutter into the gun?" he asked, glancing at the star suspect. Melanie tried to look sweet and innocent for his benefit.

"Your Honour, there are still many questions regarding this whole affair," the D.A. replied. "Not only has the defendant gone on record as saying she loaded the gun, she has emphasized that she could tell the difference between a blank and a wad cutter."

"Did you do that?" Ms. Schaefer hissed in Melanie's ear.

"I guess," she whispered.

The judge was not impressed. "Before the State of Iowa can take on the cost of prosecuting a teenage girl for the murder of Rindy Carpenter, a girl who from all appearances was a friend of Miss Carpenter's, it will need a strong basis from which to build a motive."

Her father squeezed her hand. So far so good.

The D.A. retreated to his desk, whispered in an assistant's ear. The assistant nodded. Glancing at her, the D.A. pulled a sheet of notebook paper covered with handwriting from a manila envelope in his briefcase. He approached the bench and gave it to the judge.

What the hell?

"Your Honour, this is the beginning of a letter we believe to have been written by the defendant. Note the last paragraph where it says, 'I'm in a play. It's called *Final Chance*, by Stan Russel. In it I get to kill that awful girl who whacked my car last spring. I can hardly wait.' "

Melanie went very still. For a moment she could hear nothing. Only the sounds of the storm whirling around outside her. The letter she had written but never mailed to David had been found. Only the letter hadn't been simply found. That would have been too much of a coincidence. It had been stolen—and she had thought she had lost it.

Someone wanted her in jail, out of the way.

Rindy *had* been murdered!

"Melanie!" Ms. Schaefer was shaking her.

"I didn't do it," she breathed.

"Is that your letter?" Ms. Schaefer asked.

Melanie nodded.

"What does this mean?" her father asked.

Ms. Schaefer stood. The judge was waiting for the defendant's counsel to respond. "It means Melanie's going to be tried for first degree murder," she said.

Captain Michael Crosser was waiting in the hall as they left the courtroom. Her father and attorney tried to stop her, but Melanie broke free of them and strode towards the detective. He'd been putting in long hours. His eyes were red, tired.

"Did you read the letter?" she asked coolly.

"Yes."

"Are you the one who found it?"

He spread his hands. "I had to turn it over."

All the past week, despite Ms. Schaefer's advice, she had been aching to call him. In this whole mess he had seemed the single someone who could make everything make sense. Now he was working for the hangman.

"I guess this messes up your neat and clean scenario," she said, her voice trembling.

He shook his head sadly. "This business was never neat or clean." He added, "I'm still trying to help you, Melanie."

"Thank you, but I think from now on I should help myself."

Proud words. She cried on the way home.

NINE

Melanie went to school the next day. Her cold had left her nose for her chest, and although the sun was beginning to show its face, the temperature was stuck in the low forties. Still, she figured she might as well get out and enjoy her freedom—while she had it. Ms. Schaefer said the trial could start in as little as a month.

She was a celebrity. Everyone looked at her. And no one talked to her. The treatment didn't bother her. In a way, it made her feel closer to Rindy.

In Mr. Golden's trig class she saw Susan for the first time since opening night. They exchanged brief nods—the setting was not ideal to discuss a murder. Mr. Golden handed out an exam. It could have been in Arabic. She doubted she answered a single problem correctly, and she couldn't care less.

Susan caught up with her in the corridor as she walked towards her locker. Melanie was reminded of the day they had met. Marvellous Martin had been looking for some excitement in her life back then.

"Do you want to talk?" Susan asked.

"Yes," Melanie replied, not looking at her.

"When and where?"

"Now. Out in your car."

Minutes later, after having paid visits to their respective lockers, they were seated in the front seat of Susan's yellow Volkswagen, their breath fogging the windows.

"You sound like you're sick," Susan said. She was wearing what looked like a new outfit, heavy brown corduroy trousers with a matching jacket. There were circles under her eyes that hadn't been there a couple of weeks before.

"It's not fatal."

"Are we going to fight?"

Melanie sneezed. "Let's try not to." She opened her notepad, showed the first page to Susan.

" 'Number one—Heidi,' " Susan read. " 'Two—Jeramie. Three—Marc. Four—Steve. Five—Susan. Six—Tracy.' "

"They're listed alphabetically," Melanie explained, pulling out a pen and taking back the pad, turning to the next page, which was blank.

Susan frowned. "What's this?"

"Suspects."

"You really don't believe it was an accident?"

"Not when I might be getting five to ten years."

"That's nonsense! No jury would find you guilty."

She had already decided to tell no one about David's letter. From now on she was going to absorb information, not talk and incriminate herself. "That's not what my lawyer says."

"You're serious?" Susan said in disbelief.

She nodded, took the cap off her pen. "I have some questions."

"OK," Susan said softly. "You know, I can't believe this is you talking, Melanie. You've changed."

"I've adapted." Melanie looked her in the eye. "Did you kill Rindy?"

"No. Do you think I did?"

"You're on my list."

"Then I should be at the top of your list," Susan said, raising her voice. "I approached you to be in the play. I practically twisted your arm to audition. And I picked the play knowing full well there was a murder scene. I even picked Rindy to be the victim. I organized this thing from start to finish. I'm the only real suspect you have."

"But you say you didn't do it?"

"No! Why would I kill Rindy?"

"I don't know. Maybe revenge." She added, "Carl told me about Clyde."

Susan shuddered, looked down. "Clyde shouldn't be brought into this."

"He's Tracy's brother. Marc's best friend. And he was

126

Steve's teammate, Jeramie's rival, and Rindy's boyfriend. What was he to you?"

She met her gaze. "What he still is. A close friend."

"You lied to me about his condition the day I met you."

"I didn't want to talk about it. I don't want to talk about it now. Not again."

"Has Captain Crosser been after you?"

"He's been calling, asking questions."

"Did he ask about Clyde?"

"Yes."

"Did the captain check *your* box of blanks?"

"Yes, a few days ago. There wasn't a wad cutter in it."

"So you know about wad cutters?"

"Jeramie told me about them."

"How is Jeramie?"

"He hasn't been back to school. I talked to his mom, and she says he stays in his room practically all day. The only time he goes out is to go to the cemetery. I'm worried about him."

She softened. "He means a lot to you, doesn't he?"

Susan nodded, whispered, "So does Clyde. So did Rindy."

Melanie had previously steeled herself not to be thrown off by her suspects' pains; the intention had been excellent in theory. No wonder the captain had such sad eyes, doing this year after year. "I'm sorry," she said.

Susan touched her arm. "I understand your predicament. It's just that—God, the funeral was awful."

"I can imagine." She glanced out the clouded window. A few students had gathered on the steps leading to the parking lot. Were they watching them?

Number seven—an outsider?

"I shouldn't have listened to the others," Susan said suddenly.

"What do you mean?"

"I told you once you weren't my first choice for Melissa. Actually, I wanted to play the part. But the others said I couldn't direct and act at the same time."

"Did the others want Rindy in the play?"

"Yes."

127

"Tracy did?"

"Yes. But I had the final say. Rindy was a perfect Ronda."

Déjà-vu brushed Melanie. Jerk Tracy had been a perfect Jerk Mary. Crazy Jeramie had been a perfect Crazy Robert. Yet the pattern faltered with Charles and Melissa, Marc and herself.

"Why did you bring in Tracy? You must have known, with what happened to Clyde, that she hated Rindy."

"I was trying to mend old wounds."

"Really?"

Susan was hurt. "Don't you believe me?"

The Melanie of old would have trusted her without a thought. "I want to."

Susan accepted that. "Anything I can do to help, you know, just tell me." She nodded at her blank notepad page. "You didn't take many notes."

Melanie put her pen to the paper. "Tell me the name and address of the store in Kansas City where you found the play."

Melanie cornered Heidi after sixth period in the school gym. Heidi was a member of the cheerleading squad, her chunky hips and bad acne notwithstanding. Melanie did not wait for a break in the squad's workout. She interrupted Heidi right in the middle of a defence cheer.

"Could I talk to you, please?" she said politely.

Heidi was flexing into a standing bow. The other cheerleaders broke off suddenly, stared uneasily. "Bug off," Heidi said, not relaxing the pose.

"Talk to me now or be subpoenaed next month."

Heidi let go of her leg, stood normally. "What are you talking about?" she huffed, slightly out of breath.

Melanie looked about. "Want your friends to know?"

Heidi scowled, pointed towards the drinking fountain. "Let's go over there."

Leaving the rest of the squad behind, Melanie heard someone whisper, "Isn't she the one who—"

Like Tracy, Heidi was an ass. Yet she was more clever about it. She waited for Melanie to make the first move.

128

"Did you kill Rindy?" she asked, pulling no punches.

"No. Don't you remember, you did."

"I didn't do it."

"You won't convince me."

"Has Captain Crosser spoken to you?"

Heidi hesitated. "He called. He wants to see me tomorrow."

"He's going to ask you about the bullets you took from the dressing room before the play."

"What bullets?"

"I wasn't the only one who saw you take them."

"Oh, those. I've still got them."

"I'm sure he'll want to see them. Why did you take them in the first place?"

Heidi put on a bored expression. "Because Susan had just insulted me by ordering me to leave and I didn't feel like politely handing them over to her."

"Why did you pick them up at all?"

"I just wanted to see what they were, to look at them. I did it on the spur of the moment."

The excuse fitted well with Melanie's memory of the dropped blanks. When she came right down to it, she didn't have much on Heidi. "In the dressing room before the play you gave the impression you knew the story of *Final Chance*?"

"That's bullshit. All I knew of the script was what I'd read in the audition."

The statement had been bait—or a lie, depending on how you looked at it—and Heidi had not fallen for it. Melanie tried another angle. "The captain's going to ask you about Clyde."

Heidi's cheeks flushed. "Why should he?"

"Because you had a crush on him, and Rindy was his girlfriend."

Heidi laughed. "Are you saying I killed Rindy so I could have Clyde? That's absurd! He can't even walk! He's a basket case!"

What a compassionate young lady Heidi was. At least Melissa had still loved Charles even after the loss of his limb.

Two legs—one arm?

129

Odd how those two things sort of went together.

"Thank you for your time," Melanie said, turning away, thinking.

After rehearsals, before opening night, when Marc had given Melanie rides home he had occasionally dropped Tracy off at work first. Melanie therefore knew the video rental store where Tracy spent her evenings chewing gum and gossiping about all the "complete jerks" in Careville. Melanie even knew her schedule. She visited the store three hours after speaking with Heidi. By then it was dark, and the store was crowded. Heads turned as she entered. *Isn't she the one who . . . ?*

Tracy was working the floor, replacing movies that had been rented the previous day. She looked up as Melanie approached. "Hi, Melanie, what's new?"

Her mother would have loved that one. "Not much. Flunked a trig test today. Skipped lunch. Watched the cheerleaders work out."

"Huh," Tracy grunted, shelving *Halloween*.

"Oh, and I forgot. Rindy's dead and the judge is measuring my neck for the rope. What's new with you?"

"They still hassling you about that?" she mumbled, reaching for another title. Melanie grabbed her wrist.

"You're not that dumb, Tracy."

Tracy shook loose. "Hey! What do you want?"

"Let's go in the back."

"I got to work."

Melanie raised her voice. "So you're glad Rindy's dead, Tracy?"

There wasn't a pair of eyes not watching them. Tracy paled; she was more scared than angry. Melanie felt her heart quicken. "All right," Tracy said.

They ended up in a dingy storage space crammed with piles of boxes. Tracy was jumpy.

"I didn't appreciate you saying that in front of everybody," she complained. "It's not true."

"Get off it. You hated Rindy's guts."

Tracy's eyes widened. "I— That's not true!"

"Everybody else tells me different."

"Are you saying that I killed Rindy?"

"Maybe. Why did you insist on changing the gin to whisky?"

Tracy was perspiring visibly. "Rindy got shot; she didn't get poisoned."

Melanie turned her back on her, strolled casually around the tight space. "Have you ever thought of me as the nosy type, Tracy?"

"Huh?"

"Nosy. Would you say I'm nosy?"

Tracy would agree with any personal defect in another. "Sort of."

Melanie looked at her, smiled. "You're right. I have this thing about listening to what people are saying behind closed doors." She paused. "I was listening the first day of rehearsal when you were alone with Marc in the Green Room."

Tracy was long in responding. "So?"

"I just thought you'd want to know I told the police about your *arrangement*. Melanie let the remark hang. Tracy did not react. "By the way, has Captain Crosser called?"

Tracy was trying to think. It was hard. "Yeah. He wanted to talk to me tonight. I told him I had to work." She shifted uneasily. "I've got to get back to work now."

"All right. Go ahead. You've told me what I wanted to know." Of course she was bluffing.

Tracy stopped in the storeroom doorway. "What was that?"

"None of your business." She added, "Give Clyde my best."

Tracy practically tripped in midstride. "Clyde?" she whispered.

"I hear Rindy messed him up pretty bad. Tell him I hope he's feeling better."

Tracy's face fell, he eyes moistened. "He's paralyzed, you idiot! He's never going to get better. And that bitch—" Tracy caught herself.

"Deserved to die?" Melanie finished.

Tracy swallowed. "My brother was the best. If you think you can use him to get out of the mess you're in, you can

131

go to hell.''

The condemnation—coming as it did from someone who mouthed them regularly—didn't faze Melanie. As she strode past Tracy, she said cheerfully, "I always thought you were a pathetic actress.''

Outside was a phone booth. She shut herself inside, wishing the booth were heated. It was freezing and she was shivering under a layer of sweat. A fever couldn't be far away. Scanning the White Pages, she came up with five Fishers. Number three was answered by a lady who said Steve was at home. Waiting for All-American Beef to come to the phone, she could see Tracy through the video store window getting chewed out by her boss.

"This is Steve!''

"Hi, Steve, this is Melanie.''

"Melanie! I remember you!''

She moved the phone three inches away from her ear. "Great. Do you remember the bullets you sold me that killed Rindy Carpenter?''

"Hey, you sound mad.''

"I'm pissed off, Steve. I just spoke to Tracy. She told me you were in on it.''

"I was?''

"You put the wad cutter in the box of blanks I bought.''

"Man, I'm sorry.''

Wait a second. "Did you?'' she asked softly.

"I don't remember doing it. But like Coach always says, if you're going to play, you're going to make mistakes.''

"Steve.''

"Yeah?''

"Never mind.''

"You're not mad any more?''

"Not at you. Have a good night.''

When she had set down the phone, she noticed a familiar car pulling up at the video store. Captain Crosser had not been put off by Tracy's excuses. He climbed out of the front seat, stood in the cold night surveying the posters in the windows, the people inside. For a moment she wanted to run to him, confide in him. But her suspicions were too

132

confused in her own mind to be put into words. Besides, he was a public servant, and she was beginning to believe the public did not necessarily appreciate being served with the whole truth. When he entered the store, she hurried to her father's Pinto. Before driving away, however, she flipped open her notebook to her suspect page. Michael would have a similar list; it might even be longer.

She made an addition.

"7. All of them."

It was late. She was sick and she was tired. Driving to Barters was the last thing she wanted to do. She didn't even know if Marc was working that night. There were a dozen good reasons that she should call it a day. Except she was no closer to an answer. Barters it would have to be.

And maybe he'll be glad to see me.

She had never been to the terminal where he loaded freight, but he had told her about it, and once in the city she only had to ask at a gas station for its exact whereabouts. IME— Iowa Motor Express—was a greasy collection of oil-dripping semis and sweating dock workers. There was a guard at the gate. "Yeah, Marc Hall's working tonight," he said. "Should be finished in about twenty minutes." He let her in the lot, suggesting she wait by Marc's truck.

A half hour later, after most of the men had entered their cars and driven off, Marc appeared. By then she was a teeth-chattering Popsicle. He didn't notice her sitting nearby in her Pinto. She had to get out.

"Marc?"

The lot was dark. It was silly, while chasing this murderer she had not stopped to consider that he could murder her when she found him. Marc's face was part of the night, impossible to read.

"Melanie?"

She moved closer. "I just happened to be in the neighbourhood," she said gamely.

He put something down in his front seat, zipped up his sweatshirt. She waited near the truck's rear bumper. "You have a cold," he said. "You should be home."

"I didn't think you would visit me there." He hadn't been at school.

He shrugged. "I called."

"Once."

He nodded. "Yeah, just once." He gestured towards the passenger side. "Get in."

The front seat vinyl was icy. Mangled leather gloves rested between them. Marc started the engine.

"I've got my car," she said quickly.

"I wanted to turn on the heat."

"If you turn it on in my dad's car and just sit there, you'll die of carbon-monoxide poisoning."

He looked at her. His eyes were darker than she remembered. "You're safe," he said, seeing through her fears.

"What do you use the gloves for?"

"Blisters. You can get them when you load."

"I guess you're wondering what I'm doing here?"

"Not really. Susan called."

"Do you think I'm being stupid?"

He shook his head, then let it fall back on the seat top. He must have put in a hard shift. He was exhausted. "You're too smart to be stupid."

"I was sorry to hear about Clyde."

He had closed his eyes. "So was I."

The terminal lot would have been ugly in the day. Without light it was sinister. Marc's breathing was slow and deep, like someone asleep. She let him rest a minute before asking. "What do you know that I should know?"

"That I didn't kill Rindy."

"I know that."

"No, you don't."

He was right. There was nothing about him she could be sure of. Except that he was important to her. "Did you love Rindy?" she asked.

He yawned. "I told you, she was Clyde's girl."

"Did you hate her, then?" she asked, frustrated he had not really answered her question. He opened his eyes, and

134

again, he saw through her.

"You've always had this weird thing about Rindy, even before she died. You ask about her when you want me to talk about you."

He was right. "I'm in trouble. Can you help me?"

"What do you want me to do?"

"I don't know. That's why I'm here."

"Rindy liked you. All of us could see that. When your trial starts, we'll tell the judge that. You'll be all right."

"But what about Rindy? She's dead. Someone killed her. Am I the only one who cares?"

"No. You're just the only one who thinks someone killed her."

Logical enough. Except for the planted letter. Marc had looked away as he had spoken. "I think I may be the only one in the play who doesn't know who killed her," she said.

"What can I say, Melanie? That's ridiculous."

She coughed. The air from the heater had not started to warm. "I remember when we went for a pizza. You talked about Clyde. I should have noticed something was wrong. Your fingers were clenched around the table knife."

Marc nodded. "They operated on him for six hours."

"I'm sorry."

"It wasn't your fault."

"I was just thinking about myself then. When you said you'd go to the dance with me, that was probably the high point of my life." She chuckled, embarrassed she had made such an admission, yet not really caring either. "I've led a pretty small life, huh?"

He reached over, touched her arm. "We had fun."

"Yeah," she said, remembering Rindy's remark. "One fireball of fun."

And that was that. The conversation had nowhere to go. Marc wished her a safe drive home. He did not kiss her good-bye. Back in her freezing car, his truck already turning out of the lot, she wrote in her notepad, "Number 8."

She left it blank.

Jeramie's house was located across the street from the town

park. Unlike most of the residences in Careville, it was relatively new: three storeys of stained and lacquered timber. Jeramie's dad was also a salesman, she remembered. Her dad should work for his company.

Melanie sat down the street from the house in her Pinto—grey morning light soaking through the car's dusty windows—wrapped in a down comforter. From her long summer of reading, she knew Jeramie's mother worked in the local library. She was waiting for her to leave. Another school day missed. Many more, and she wouldn't even make the jail warden's honour roll. Her father had thought she was at the library the night before. Sam at the diner probably thought she had left the country.

Half an hour before the library opened, the garage door automatically swung up and Jeramie's mom backed into the street in a red Pontiac and drove away. Melanie climbed out of the Pinto.

"Looking forward to getting shot tonight?"

The sun was out, she told herself. She was safe.

At the front door no one answered her knock.

"Jeramie!" she called. "I know you're in there!"

Actually, she knew no such thing. Jeramie could very well have picked this day to return to school. Or he could simply be asleep.

"Jeramie!" she screamed.

He was not asleep. Standing on the porch, she made a quick visual search for a cracked window. What was a little forceful entry for the main suspect in a homicide? But the windows were latched shut. Then she remembered where she was—in a small middle-America town, where no one locked a door. She turned the knob. The door swung open.

Jeramie's house was tidy. The living room could have been pictured in *Home* magazine. The warmth of the house was a welcome relief after the shivers in her car. She recognized the china cabinet from the play. The mirror had been replaced.

"Jeramie?"

Silence. The house was empty. Still, perhaps there were questions it could answer. Jeramie had previously mentioned the view of the park from his bedroom. She headed for the

136

stairs.

What she found at the end of the third floor hallway surprised her. Melanie had expected his room to be like a cluttered corner of the twilight zone. But he had no desk or chest-of-drawers. No pictures or posters cluttered the plain white walls. The bed was a mat on the floor covered neatly with several blankets. A small wooden case sat at the end of the mat. The only extravagances were a couple of 35mm cameras sitting in the corner and *two* VCRs hooked up to a tiny TV. A row of VHS tapes rested on a shelf above the video equipment. Each was labelled on the side with white masking tape and black Cato.

Melanie stepped into the room, studied the selection. *Final Chance.*

The plastic container was empty. The tape was in the top VCR. Glancing out of the window, she turned on the power. A minute later her pulse speed doubled.

"I'd like a recording of tonight. There will never be another tonight."

The crowd. The curtain. Melissa and Ronda's entrance. Jeramie wanted a picture of everything.

He had recorded opening night!

Her pulse rate tripled.

"Hello, Melissa."

He was not standing in the doorway but sitting on the floor against an already closed door. Susan was right; he moved like a cat; perhaps a necessary prerequisite for someone bent on killing in front of an audience. His wild hair seemed to have grown since she'd seen him last. His usually bright eyes were flat.

"Let me guess," he said with forced cheerfulness, untying his damp sneakers. "You've brought me my homework?"

She sat and stared. The play continued.

Jeramie smiled, his right cheek twitching. "You shouldn't have bothered. As you can see, I've already got a black market copy of the final exam."

She remembered to breathe. "The police?"

Jeramie shook his head. "They don't know about the tape. Would you like to see it?"

"Who killed her?" she whispered.

He stood and went to the window, closing the blinds. "Watch," he said.

She took a seat on the floor, leaning against the wooden case at the foot of his bed. Jeramie returned to his previous spot, guarding the door. Her fear would have been greater had his own fears not been so obvious. This was not one of his finer performances. She suspected he had just returned from Rindy's grave.

Ordinarily, she would have sat and drunk up the first act. Both Rindy and herself were excellent (if she did think so herself). But anticipation did not make for pleasurable viewing. Jeramie sat with his eyes closed—listening, not watching. She reached for the control box, pushed Fast-Forward. He did not stir.

"Can't sleep, dear?" Ronda asked.

"I'll sleep later," Melissa said.

"Did you have a bad dream?"

Melissa's disparagement followed. Then she took the gun out of the drawer. Melanie began to squirm. She closed her eyes, forced them open. Even with them shut, though, she could feel Rindy's fear. But the terror was largely internal. *This* Rindy on *this* screen was not as horrified as the one in Melanie's memory.

"But we were friends," Ronda pleaded.

"I'm no one's friend," Melissa said.

Three shots. Melanie jerked with each one. Rindy hit the floor, rolled on her side. Melanie watched herself cross the stage, drop the gun, and shut the icebox. The screen went dark. There were shouts. Then, before Jeramie could turn the lamp on, the tape ran out.

"Where's the rest?" she asked.

Jeramie looked up. "You see, everything happened as it was supposed to."

"Where's the rest of the tape?" she repeated.

"You want to show it to the police, I don't care."

"Jeramie?"

"It's here she was shot," he replied impatiently. "The rest—what does it matter?"

"I still want to see it."

"I don't have it."

He had wanted her to view the tape, she realised, and then pass it on to the police. Leaning forward, she pressed Rewind.

"What are you doing?" he asked suddenly.

"I'm going to watch it again."

He jumped to his feet, crossed the room in two long strides, and shut off the VCR power. "No," he said firmly, positioning himself between her and the equipment.

"Why not?"

"Once was enough."

She sat back on her ankles. "I don't know who you're trying to fool with this charade."

"The tape speaks for itself."

"Just now, Rindy did not really die."

His face fell for a moment, then brightened. "Of course, it was just a play."

"Jeramie, it's real. Rindy's dead."

He was insulted. "You died in the play. What difference does it make?"

She understood in a flash. Denial—taken to the extreme Jeramie took everything. "What did you do to the tape?" she asked patiently.

His eyes moistened. "Everything went just as we rehearsed."

Rehearsed? That was it! The beginning of the tape had been from opening night. The murder scene was from their dress rehearsal. He had two VCRs. He had dubbed the one over the other. But why? Had he seen something in the real murder scene that no one else had that night?

Had he seen himself killing her?

"No," she insisted. "Something went wrong. What was it?"

He slipped past her, fell on the mat on the floor, throwing his arm over his face. "Leave me alone," he said.

"I wish I could," she said, moving beside him. "But you can't live in a fantasy world."

"Go away."

"I can't. Not until I get through to you."

"Melissa still doesn't know what the hell is going on."

"There is no Melissa."

He shifted his arm, cracked an eye her way. "There is now."

Cold touched the back of her neck. And the room was warm. "Is there a Ronda?" she asked.

He covered his eyes again. "No."

Who was trying to get through to whom? Suddenly, she wasn't so sure. "What did you edit out of the tape?"

No answer. But his fists clenched.

"All right, your name's really Robert. But you can't switch it back to Jeramie whenever you like." She grabbed his arm, pulled it away from his face. "Are you listening to me?"

He shook her off. "No."

"Where were you just now?"

"Talking with Rindy."

"You were at the cemetery."

"I was at the park."

"You were at the cemetery next to the park. And you were not talking to Rindy."

"I was."

"No."

He sat up. "Get out of here."

"Not till you face the truth!"

"I know the truth!"

"Rindy, Ronda—they're both dead!"

"But I saw her taping on the blood!"

"You also saw her bleeding real blood!"

"But I just talked to her!"

"All right, then! What did she say to you?"

His brow wrinkled in pain. "She said she loves me."

She was a devil whipping a child. "Jeramie, Rindy loved Clyde."

He closed his eyes again, buried his face in his knees. "I know," he whispered. He began to cry softly. She put her hand on his back. There was nothing she could do but wait.

After some time Jeramie sat up. Without looking at her,

140

he went to the VCR, removed the tape, and then left the room for a bathroom across the hall. She heard water running. Ten minutes later he reappeared without the tape. He had washed his face and combed his hair. He knelt at the foot of the bed beside her, opening the wooden case. He drew out a Smith & Wesson .38 revolver.

"Jeramie," she said quickly.

"It isn't loaded," he said in a calm voice.

She decided to believe him. "You have two of them?"

He looked her in the eye. "Lately, there's been two of everything." He weighed the weapon in his hand, a flicker of disgust touching his lips. "But you ruin one, you ruin the other." He added softly, "Yeah, I was talking to myself this morning."

"I'm sorry." She was saying that a lot these days.

He handed her the gun. "Take it."

"I don't want it."

"You'll need it."

"What for?"

"The last act."

He was serious. And as sane as he ever got. "What did you see in the tape?" she asked.

"Reflections."

"Whose?"

"Several people's." He pressed the gun on her. "You know what type of bullets it takes."

"No. Wait! Who killed Rindy?"

He looked out the window in the direction of the cemetery. "I know some of you think I'm not all here. I don't mind. It's true, and it's OK. I like to play many parts. As long as the part's a good one. Remember, I warned you at the beginning? Melissa was a bad part." He bowed his head. "For me, it's like Rindy died today. Please leave."

He would speak to her no more. Going down the stairs, carrying the gun, she passed a framed newspaper clipping about Jeramie. His mother had probably saved it. There was a photo adjoining an article telling of some acting award he had won. Beneath the picture was printed his full name.

Jeramie Robert Waters.

In her car, she opened her notepad and picked up her pen.

"8. Stan Russel."

Des Moines didn't lie in a straight line between Careville and Kansas City; the Teller Home was an hour out of the way. Speeding along the interstate, Melanie doubted Clyde would be thrilled about meeting his old love's executioner.

The hospital was tiny. The chipped single-storey building could have sheltered at most a couple of dozen patients. This is where Clyde had spent the better part of a year?

The reception area was small. A young nurse with kind eyes and a ghost of a moustache greeted her from behind a desk.

"Can I help you?"

"Yes. I'm here to see Clyde."

"Are you family?"

"A friend."

The nurse picked up a phone. "He doesn't get many visitors. What's your name?"

She should have realised his visitors would be screened. "Melanie Martin." She added hastily, "I'm not really a close friend."

"Clyde?" the nurse said. "There's a Melanie Martin here to see you." The young woman listened, glanced at her, frowning slightly. "He says he doesn't know you, Melanie."

"Tell him I'm a friend of Marc's."

The nurse did so, then said to her, "He wants to know what you want."

"I have to talk to him."

The nurse relayed this message also, then said, "He insists you state your business." The woman put her hand over the phone, added quietly, "In his condition, he's very sensitive about whom he sees. Perhaps you should talk to him here on the phone first."

That would have been fine except going through a list of suspects wasn't something she wanted to do in front of the nurse. "I'll write him a note," she said.

The nurse told Clyde to stand by. Melanie took a seat by the window and tore out a fresh sheet from her notepad.

Clyde,

I realise we've never met, but you must know who I am. I was

142

in the play with Rindy. I'm the one accused of having killed her.
Those who think I didn't do it say it was an accident. They're
wrong. I didn't kill her, but I know someone did. I need your
help to catch them.

Melanie

She folded the note and gave it to the nurse, who rose and disappeared through a door. While waiting, she wondered what he would look like.

The young nurse didn't return. Instead, a couple of minutes later an elderly woman in a starched white uniform burst through the door. Her expression was stern. "Who are you?" she demanded, shaking the note in her hand.

She gestured beyond the door. "Do you know what you've done?"

"No. Is something— Is Clyde all right?"

"He was. Until you showed up. His parents gave us strict instructions regarding this matter." The old nurse shook with disgust. "Now I don't know what we're going to tell them."

Melanie felt faint. Everything she touched ended up hurt. "He didn't know about Rindy?"

"Of course he didn't know."

"I'm sorry. I didn't realise. Is he upset?"

"Upset? The doctor may have to sedate him." The woman pointed to the exit. "Get out! You've a lot of nerve coming here."

"But—"

"Out! And leave good people alone."

In the car, through a blur of pain, she asked herself again and again: *Why?*

Kansas City was windy and wet. A sewer on the street outside the bookstore Poems & Pages had been plugged up, damming a river of rain over the sidewalk. Stepping out of her car, Melanie felt a gush of water spill over her boots, making her socks squish. She sneezed. Her only consolation was that the day couldn't possibly get any worse.

Poems & Pages appeared to be a browser's heaven. The rows

143

were narrow and tall, the shelves packed and disorganized. Boxes jammed with old paperbacks were stacked against the walls.

"May I help you?" a middle-aged man with a dark beard and rapidly blinking eyes asked. Glancing around, Melanie saw they were alone.

"Do you sell plays?" she asked.

"Were you looking for a particular title?"

He had a European accent—Slavic perhaps. With his thick glasses and intelligent face, he looked like a writer. "Yes. *Final Chance*, by Stan Russel."

He thought a moment. "I'm not sure we have that one." He turned, adding, "Back here is where we keep our plays. I'm afraid we haven't everything in alphabetical order."

She followed him past a science-fiction section thick with old pulp star adventures. Her dad would have loved this place.

"Are you an actress by chance?" he asked as they stopped before several waist-level shelves packed with plays. The majority were in book form, but there were a surprising number of stapled manuscripts.

"No, I go to high school," she said abruptly. The scolding by the prune at the clinic was still with her. She realised she was being rude. "Well, actually, I'm in drama at school." She smiled, trying to sound nice.

He was interested. "At which school?"

"Care High." She began to flip through the plays.

"Is that in Kansas City?"

"No. It's in Iowa."

"Then you've come a long way."

She stopped. "Have you seen any other kids in here from there?"

"Not today."

"How about in the last few months?"

He set his glasses back on his red nose. "None that I recollect. Did your friends tell you about my store?"

"Yes." She reached into her bag, removed a picture of the director and cast of *Final Chance* taken for the school newspaper. "Do you remember any of these people stopping by?"

144

"Now I do. These three were in a couple of months ago." He pointed to Susan, Jeramie, and Marc. "Delightful youngsters. They were looking for material to perform."

She returned to going through the plays, particularly the ones in manuscript form. "Do you remember what play they bought?"

"They purchased several. What was that title you mentioned?"

Just then her fingers stumbled onto a copy of *Final Chance*. The play was sticking out. She showed it to the man, saying, "Here it is."

He nodded. "I remember. They did buy a copy of this." He studied the title page. "Copyright 1949. I must say, it's in excellent shape."

"Is it? I mean, even though it was written a long time ago, couldn't it have been recently reissued?"

"I suppose," he replied doubtfully. "But it looks like something the author put together himself. And if he wrote it forty years ago, I doubt he waited all this time to have it printed." He paused. "Oh, I take that back."

"You think it was published?"

"No." He flipped it open. "But this is a photocopy. Xerox wasn't around in the forties."

"So this copy isn't that old?"

"It would have to be younger than Xerox."

"But it says it was copyrighted. Doesn't that mean it was published?"

"Not at all. Most authors put a copyright line on their work when they finish it. By doing so, even without registering the work with the Library of Congress, the author gains a degree of legal protection." He continued to leaf through the pages. "This is strange though."

"Why?"

"The copy your friends bought was old and dusty."

"You're sure?"

"Yes. I remember brushing it off. I'm surprised I didn't sell them this copy instead."

She rechecked the shelf. The manuscript they held was the last one. "Do you know where this copy and the other one came from?''

The man smiled. ''I'm afraid not. There are so many books and plays in this store, all the time coming and going—you understand?''

''Certainly. How much is it?''

He glanced at the cover. ''A lot of these works I never get around to pricing. Does two dollars sound reasonable?''

''Very reasonable.''

They returned to the front, by the cash register. ''Did your friends lose their copy?'' he asked as he rang up the bill.

''Ah, yeah. By the way, have any of them been back in?''

''Any of the three that were in before?''

''Yeah.''

''I don't think so. But I couldn't be sure.''

''I was just wondering.''

He put the manuscript into a plastic bag. ''What's it about?''

''What's what about?''

''The play.''

She accepted the bag, clasped it to her chest. ''It's a long story.''

In her car she quickly studied her purchase. It appeared to be, page for page, identical to her original copy.

Before getting on the road for the trip home, she stopped at a phone booth. The information operator provided her with the number for the office of the registrar of copyrights. It was located in Washington, D.C. She had to charge the call to her home phone. Her dad was going to wonder what was going on.

After speaking with three gruff people, she got a friendly young man who sounded as if he might be able to help.

''Yes,'' he said after she had explained her interest in *Final Chance*'s copyright. ''We have all that information in our computers. However, we're about to close for the day, and the normal procedure is to submit a form—which we'd be happy to mail you—when requesting such information.''

''But I need to know today if the play was ever registered.''

''Why?''

She had expected this question and had an excuse handy.

"This is sort of embarrassing. Can you keep a secret?"

"Sure."

"My boyfriend's a student at the University of Iowa. You know the big writer's programme they have there? Well, he wrote a play for a school contest that he's submitting today. And he's swiped portions of Stan Russel's work." She laughed. "I just want to know if he's going to get sued!"

The guy laughed with her. People liked to be let in on a secret. "I guess there would be no harm in having a quick look in our files. How did you spell the author's last name?"

She told him, listening as his fingers tapped on a keyboard. "That property must be currently in the public domain," he said a minute later.

"Does that mean it was never copyrighted?"

"No. The old copyrights lasted only twenty-eight years, unless they were renewed. Let me go back to the forties. Hold on a sec." Another couple of minutes went by. Finally he said, "As far as this office is concerned, your boyfriend is off the hook. *Final Chance* was never registered. In fact, Mr. Russel has no published works we're aware of."

"That's very interesting," she said.

That night, around ten o'clock, after a warm bath and a bowl of chicken soup, Melanie sat cross-legged on her bed, wrapped in a blanket, with her notes and the play resting on her knees. When she closed her eyes, her list of suspects and Mr. Russel's characters blurred together in her mind and became one.

They are connected. Somehow.

She picked up the phone, dialled the Barters police station. That Captain Crosser was still on duty didn't surprise her. In spite of her vow not to trust him, she was comforted by the sound of his voice.

"Melanie, I was just thinking of you. We seem to be just missing each other."

"Were you in Kansas City today?"

"No. What's in Kansas City?"

"A lot of rain. Do you have a suspect list?" she asked.

"Right in front of me."

"How many names are on it?"

"Eight."

"Who are they?"

"Clyde, Heidi, Jeramie, Marc, Susan, Steve, Tracy, and Mr. X," he replied.

"You have Clyde on your list?"

"Does that surprise you?"

"Not really. I'm surprised you didn't list me."

"Melanie, I couldn't keep that letter to myself."

"I suppose you couldn't," she admitted. "So who do you think it is?"

"I don't know. Who do you think?"

"I think Melissa did it."

The captain was silent a moment. "I don't understand."

"As soon as you heard what happened to Rindy, you went to the scene of the crime to gather as many clues as you could. Since then you've been trying to reconstruct what happened and why it happened. I've been trying to do the same thing. But I think we've been going at it backwards."

"What do you suggest?"

"That we reperform *Final Chance.*"

"Why?"

"The play will tell us why. Look, the story was about a murder. And someone *was* murdered. Haven't you noticed the similarities in the circumstances surrounding Rindy's and Ronda's deaths?"

"I'm not sure I know what you're saying."

"Someone used the story as a bloody blueprint!"

Captain Crosser chewed on that awhile. She suspected he'd had similar thoughts. "Let's say for the sake of argument someone did," he said cautiously. "Rindy's parents wouldn't allow the play to go on. And I doubt your friends would cooperate."

"Rindy's parents will go along if you tell them it might help get to the bottom of their daughter's death. As far as the others are concerned, tell them they have to do it."

"They can't be ordered about."

"*All* of them are hiding something. They'll be afraid to refuse."

"Exactly what do you expect another performance to show?"

148

"I expect it to fit all our clues together."

"You're forgetting something. Rindy's dead. You're one actor short."

"Susan can play my part. She knows all Melissa's lines."

"And you'll take Rindy's role?"

"Yes. This time I'll be the victim."

TEN

The stains came out, Melanie thought. *My blood must be thinner than Rindy's.*

Ten days had gone by. The captain had pulled all the right strings, and once again Stan Russel's world lived. Act I was over and Act II was coming to a close. The murder scene was next, and after that the last act. Melanie sat in the dressing room with Susan and Tracy, her nightgown in her hand. It was time for a quick costume change. Yet she stalled, examining the cotton fabric. This was the same nightgown she had worn as Melissa. An overnight soaking in powdered bleach had returned the material to a light pink. The floor where Rindy had fallen had been another matter. Scrubbing with industrial detergent had failed to erase the dried dark splashes of blood. They'd had to bring in a rug.

At least when I hit the floor it won't be so hard, Melanie thought.

She was tense. Melissa's gun—now Susan's gun—was waiting by the door. Between Acts I and II the entire cast had supervised its loading: three blanks—each with a flat head of harmless wax. This gun was new. Captain Crosser had purchased it. The revolver that had killed Rindy was locked in the D.A.'s office. But the untried gun was a Smith & Wesson .38 short barrel. It looked the same as the other one.

"What are you waiting for?" Tracy asked impatiently. Tracy had not wanted to revive her role as Mary. She had let Melanie know this every day for the last week and a half.

"I'm supposed to be slightly drunk, remember?" Melanie said, reminding Tracy that Ronda's poison had been switched from whisky back to gin. Actually, Melanie had not wanted the change. She wasn't sure how it had come about. The purpose of this run-through was to see everything exactly as Rindy had. It was another reason she was stalling. Rindy had been late coming back onto the stage.

"Maybe you should go wait where you're supposed to," Susan told Tracy, probably worried that the two of them were going to fight.

"Take care of yourself, Ronda," Tracy said sarcastically and left.

"I hope Clyde and Tracy have nothing in common except the same parents," Melanie said.

Susan was already in pyjamas, giving her hair a quick touch-up. "If you'd known Clyde, you'd swear they weren't even related." She put down her brush. "Are you scared?"

"No," she lied.

Susan leaned forward. "Have you learned anything?"

Susan and Jeramie had approved the idea of another performance. Susan had thought it was the logical thing to do. Jeramie had acted as if it were their destiny.

Marc had not wanted to re-enact the crime, the exact opposite reaction of his character in the play. Captain Crosser had had to apply pressure. Carl had not been enthusiastic either. Yet, at this very moment he was in the control booth.

Rehearsals—all two of them—had been a drag.

"Ask me later," she replied. What insights had come to her in Act I had belonged to Ronda. Charles's wife had known Melissa hated her. Had Stan Russel been available, she was sure he would have agreed with her. She was reading between the lines of the script.

"I will," Susan said, checking her watch. "Better change."

Melanie stood, loosening her skirt. A minute later she was down to her underwear, pulling her nightgown over her head. It was then she noticed the tear on the upper right sleeve. She remembered having made the same discovery in the police station bathroom the morning after opening night. She would have to sew the tear before it got bigger.

"Don't worry about it," Susan said, watching her. "In the dark no one will notice."

She nodded. "We have another full house. Isn't that odd?"

"Adolescence is a ghoulish age. I bet half those out there are hoping to see more blood."

"Yeah." They had decided to skip the Baggies filled with

red dye. Ronda would just fall down. That was one change Melanie had approved of. Susan started to leave. "Susan?" she said.

Susan stopped at the door. "What is it?"

We're not going to give them what they want, are we?

"Nothing." She coughed. Her cold was hanging on.

Susan was sympathetic. "You'll be all right. We know there are blanks in the gun. And the captain's in the crowd. That guy misses nothing."

Melanie was left to herself for a few minutes. Staring in the dressing room mirror, she hardly recognized the person staring back. Lately she'd played too many roles.

Out in the hall the light was still on. The stage was dark. Reaching for the dimmer switch, she glanced in the direction of the crowd hidden behind the grey and green drapes. Marc was there in the folded shadows, watching her. She raised her hand, waved once. He shook his head. He didn't like this.

The curtain rustled upwards as she knelt near the refrigerator—the audience opening before her like a grey lagoon of watchful eyes. Far in the back glowed a red dot; the video equipment was on and running. Earlier in the week Jeramie had admitted to her that he had destroyed the recording of opening night.

"I burned it, Melanie."

As she opened the icebox, the light dazzled her eyes. She lingered a moment, letting her pupils adjust. Jeramie's whispers had pursued her all week. Less than three hours before, when the set had been empty, she had hidden the gun he had given her beneath the sofa cushions. Why she had done so was a question she was still asking herself. For she had loaded it with blanks—her fingerprints must be all over them—and how could they possibly work to save her?

While Melanie mused, her character stood and noticed Melissa on the couch. Here was a critical point. Here is where Rindy had shown her first signs of fear. Before the script had called for such signs. What had Rindy seen that she was missing? She searched and found nothing. She moved towards Susan.

"Can't sleep, dear?" she asked.

152

"I'll sleep later," Susan said.

"Did you have a bad dream?"

Yes, I dreamed of you. The bitter tirade poured out evenly. Melanie listened, marvelling more at Susan's skill than at Melissa's accusations. Melanie was having difficulty staying in character. The drafts from the corner cul-de-sacs were distracting. Jeramie and Tracy had their doors to the outside open. She tried to remember if that was standard procedure.

Susan opened the back door of Stan Russel's living room.

"What are you doing that for?" Melanie asked.

"Fresh air," Susan said, reaching for the drawer.

"You're wearing gloves, Mellie?"

Susan lifted the gun. "It's a cold night."

"No, it's not that cold."

"Yes, it's very cold." Susan showed her the gun. "And I'm worried about fingerprints."

Melanie leapt to her feet, backing towards the bar. At the edge of her peripheral vision a figure jumped. She half turned. The china cabinet was behind her, to the side. The mirror within it danced with two ghosts in nightgowns. This was different from opening night. While pursuing Rindy, there had been only one of each of them.

"You ruin one, you ruin the other."

"Why?" she moaned.

Susan aimed the gun, her face wild. "You're a thorn. I have to pull you out. And throw you away."

The fear Melanie had waited for came then, in an avalanche, icy and irrational. The gun couldn't harm her, she tried to tell herself. Susan was just an actress. She was her friend.

"Don't!"

"But we were friends," she gasped, forcing out the plea, simultaneously realising that Rindy had never said that.

Susan cocked the revolver. "I'm no one's friend."

Suddenly Melanie's universe narrowed in upon three things: the gun, Susan's eyes, and the dark space beyond Susan. By a trick of reflection, the black barrel had caught a scattered ray of light from the icebox, and the weapon shone in Susan's hand like a silver knife. In a similar manner,

Susan's eyes glittered, not blue as they normally were, but with a pale sheen. Yet these things were not the focus of Melanie's fear. It was the space behind Susan, which refused to come into focus, that held her frozen. A hazy region out of which seemingly any number of horrors could spring, even though she knew there was only a door fitted with a fire alarm at the centre of it.

In the slow motion of the moment, sight was sharper than hearing. The firing of the blanks hit her as spits of fire rather than as cracks of thunder. At the first shot she clutched her chest. With the second shot she rocked backwards. The last one sent her to the floor, where the carpet absorbed her fall. She rolled on her back and stared at the ceiling, not blinking. Susan's grim face passed above. The icebox was shut, leaving her in a confining dark; she was not supposed to move an inch.

She lay alone onstage, waiting; no madman, with silencer or otherwise, jumped out of the corners.

The rest happened quickly. Shouts sounded. Jeramie turned on the lamp. The others gathered around. Marc knelt by her side, his face grim.

"She's dead," he said.

Melanie closed her eyes, his pronouncement going deep inside her. In a weird way she believed Marc.

I am dead.

She had wanted to see out of Rindy's eyes. And now— even if it all was just make-believe—they had shared the same death. How close could two people get? And with the morbid feeling of intimacy came a fresh viewpoint, a new understanding.

Number nine—Rindy?

Melanie watched the last act with a double-focused mind. Like so much else of the craziness that had started with the audition, her summing up of the real-life situation and her perception of the twists in the play were strangely in sync.

It was three weeks since Ronda's murder. And Charles was trying to identify the villain. His suspect list was as long as Melanie's. Soon, though, Charles would narrow his down to size with a lie.

Charles—Marc—brought out a facsimile of the murder weapon. ''This isn't the gun that killed my wife,'' he said. ''That's in the custody of the police. This one, however, will suffice for our purposes.'' He flashed the chambers, adding, ''I've taken the liberty of loading it.'' He placed the revolver on the table, within everyone's reach.

From her position in the hall, Melanie shifted her gaze four decades, peering at the audience through a crack in the curtains. Captain Crosser was sitting near the front. Was he thinking, as she now was, that they had examined everyone who had approached the gun except Rindy herself?

Charles began to list incriminating points that applied to Robert, Mary, and Melissa as Melanie had already done for Jeramie, Tracy, and Susan. Now she concentrated on applying the same evidence to Rindy.

Motive: Rindy had accidentally contributed to Clyde's paralysis. Everyone hated her. Had she simply committed suicide, they would have despised her more.

Opportunity: Rindy had been in the dressing room off and on all night with the gun and blanks. How she had slipped in the wad cutter was still not clear to Melanie. Yet, more than anyone else, Rindy had had the best chance.

Miscellaneous: All the time Melanie knew her, Rindy had been depressed. Then, all of a sudden, opening night, she was happy. But as the play had progressed, her joy had quickly changed to anxiety. Why? Melanie had previously read it wasn't unusual for suicide candidates to show signs of relief in the days before killing themselves. As the countdown had ticked away, however, second doubts must have plagued Rindy.

''Don't!''

Rindy had known the gun would kill her. That last cry had been a plea to stop what she herself had set in motion.

So I did kill her.

Melanie felt a hollowness that the rest of her life would not be able to remove. The discovery brought not even the bitter sweetness of revenge. Somehow, she should have heard what Rindy was trying to tell her. Not just in that last instant, but in the past month. Jeramie must have already guessed the truth.

No wonder he had hidden away his evidence. He didn't want Rindy remembered that way.

The play continued, the last act moving swiftly towards its climax. Acting as though he knew more than he did, Charles set the groundwork for his pivotal lie. Even those who were innocent were feeling guilty. But it was the power of Susan's portrayal that drew Melanie to watch. It was like watching herself. Hadn't she, as Melissa, rehearsed this scene a dozen times?

"There was so much blood," Charles said, pacing in front of the couch. "I checked and didn't feel a pulse. My hands were trembling, I realise now. I should have made sure."

"What are you saying?" Mary asked.

Charles smiled. "What I should have told you before. What the young man in the ambulance told me as we raced towards the hospital." Charles stopped, spread his hand. "She's alive."

"Ronda's alive?" Mary said, shocked.

"Impossible," Robert said.

"I don't believe it," Mary said.

Melissa stood near the table, and now, as if by magic, she was holding the gun, pointing it at Charles. "I believe you," she said.

Charles nodded, his face dark. "You shouldn't, my dear Melissa." He looked at the gun. "It's loaded with blanks."

Not a person in the audience breathed. Susan held them spellbound, allowing the realization to register in Melissa's face in halting steps, the last step breaking through to despair. "Then she is dead," she said finally, lowering her aim.

"Yes," Charles said.

"And all this?" Melissa asked. "It was just a show?"

"For Ronda," Charles said sadly. "It was very real."

Robert and Mary watched, unmoving. Melissa swallowed thickly. "I'm glad she's dead," she said.

"Tell the judge that," Charles said. "Maybe he'll let you join her."

"You don't understand!" Melissa cried. "I did it for you! She was no good! She didn't love you!"

Charles shook his head, stepped towards her, and held out

156

his only arm. "Give me the gun."

Melissa jumped back. "No!"

"It's over. You can't get away."

Melissa stopped, her shoulders sagging. "You hate me, don't you?" she asked pitifully.

"Yes," Charles said flatly.

"And you never loved me?"

Charles shrugged. "When we were young I cared for you."

Melissa bowed her head. "When we were young," she whispered. Then suddenly, unexpectedly, she raised the gun, pressing the barrel against her skull. "Good-bye."

"Don't!" Charles shouted.

Melissa pulled the trigger. Blanks could kill.

Melanie was still in her nightgown when Captain Crosser knocked on the dressing room door after the show. Susan was with her, but not Tracy, who had left immediately after the final curtain. Susan was rubbing off the thick lipstick she had worn as Melissa, and removing the wax from her ear. Dying onstage, she had remarked, was not so bad.

"Come in," Melanie called, expected the captain. He poked his head inside cautiously.

"My daughters used to scream at me when I went in their rooms," he said.

Susan turned, smiled. "Did you enjoy the show, Captain?"

"It scared me. You were very impressive."

"Thank you."

"Particularly at the end, when you fired the gun at your head."

Susan grinned. "It's all in the wrist."

"I bet." He looked at Melanie. "You're wearing the same clothes as when we met."

She blushed. "I was just about to change."

"What was it like playing Ronda?"

His question had an undertone of seriousness. Melanie glanced at Susan, who was pretending not to listen. "Very enlightening."

He nodded. "We'll have to talk about it."

157

"I can be ready in a few minutes."

"I could leave you two, if you'd like," Susan said.

"No, let's talk tomorrow," he said abruptly. "I want to sleep on it."

"You? Sleep?" Melanie said.

"It has been a while," the captain admitted. He squeezed her right shoulder. "What are you going to do now?"

"Go home and go to bed," Melanie said. His hand was warm.

"Your father's still in town, isn't he?"

"Yes. He's waiting now to give me a ride."

"Good." He let go of her shoulder, studied her up and down. "Is that the only nightgown you have?"

"I also have a green one."

He nodded. "I'll call you in the morning." He suddenly seemed in a hurry to leave.

"Fine."

He opened the door. "Take care of yourself, Melanie. You too, Susan."

"I will," Susan said. "Bye!"

When he was gone, Melanie said, "That was odd."

"How so?"

"I don't know, he just seemed different."

"Do you think watching the play taught him anything."

"I guess we'll find out tomorrow." Melanie went to the door, peeked outside. Now the captain was talking to Marc in the centre of the stage. She couldn't hear what was being said. Marc was nodding his head.

"Did it teach *you* anything?" Susan asked.

"I think I'll sleep on it too," she answered, watching as the captain and Marc ended their brief talk and exited out of separate doors.

ELEVEN

The colours were pretty. They sparkled before Melanie like living lights.

"Hello," someone said in a familiar voice. Turning, Melanie saw through the haze of shifting hues a girl of extraordinary beauty sitting on the floor before a board littered with faintly glowing chips. "I'm glad you could make it."

"Where am I?" Melanie asked.

The girl wore a silky orange gown that resembled a sari. The material hung easily from her arm as she gestured towards the low ceiling, the stone walls, and the vanilla carpet. "In my basement. I often come here to think." She nodded to the space in front of her. "Please, sit and be comfortable."

Melanie sat on her knees beside the board. Each chip was lit with a letter. The girl held several in her hands. "Is this a game?" Melanie asked.

"Yes. Would you like to play?"

"Is it Scrabble?"

The girl thought before answering. Her skin was creamy, deliciously smooth. When she moved her head, her shiny black curls caught the glittering colours that filled the room. She had clear green eyes. "Scrabble was one of my favourite games," she said.

"I'm afraid I'm not very good at it."

"But you enjoy it."

"Yeah."

"As I do." The girl nodded. "We'll play together." Setting ten of the chips before Melanie, she took ten for herself.

"Excuse me, shouldn't we get only seven letters each?"

"Not in this game."

"But isn't this Scrabble?"

"It's a bit different," the girl said, sorting her chips in a seemingly random fashion. "Let's begin."

Melanie glanced around the basement. She had been here before, she was sure. She just couldn't remember when. "You start. I'll watch until I catch on."

The girl stopped. "You already know how to play."

"But I usually begin with seven letters?"

The girl looked down. "I can't start until you start."

"Why not?"

"It's one of the rules." She pointed to the waiting chips. "If you begin, you'll be halfway home. Make a name out of the letters."

"A name?" Melanie touched the chips. "Can't I make up any kind of word?"

"No."

"Hey, you have the same letters I do. Won't we just end up making the same names?"

The girl nodded. She was such a solemn creature—Melanie wished she would smile. "Yes. We want to make the same names."

"But then neither of us will win?"

"We'll both win."

Melanie was losing enthusiasm for the game. The basement, with its shimmering fog, was more interesting. The girl noticed her attention wandering.

"Please, just play. The more questions you ask, the less you will learn. The less you will remember."

The walls in this basement were strange. When stared at, they began to blur and fade, as if they weren't really there at all. Paradoxically, the colours did not vanish when she closed her eyes. They appeared to move right into her head. "What's going on here? What is this place?"

"I told you. My basement."

"And who are you?"

The girl sighed. "You know who I am."

"No, I don't." Melanie paused, trying to get a better look at her. But like the walls, she blurred when closely scrutinized. "You're not— Who are you?"

"Questions won't help you. There is nothing I can tell you that you don't already know."

"Rindy," Melanie whispered, recognition coming sudden and sharp. "But you're dead."

Rindy's face darkened with the mention of the word. Again she pointed to the letters. "Please, we haven't much time."

Melanie could feel her heart beating. The sensation was disturbing

160

because it was the only part of her body she could feel. "Are you dead?"

Rindy bowed her head, her face almost disappearing in her long, hanging hair. "Yes."

"Did you kill yourself?"

She looked up. "You know I didn't."

"You keep saying I know this and that. Just tell me."

"I can't."

"Why not?"

"You know why."

Melanie sat back. "I'm dreaming." She went to pinch her arm. Rindy stopped her.

"The game," she insisted.

"I don't want to play any games! I'm tired of them!"

"The game will continue," Rindy said seriously. "Until we win. Or until you lose."

"But if I'm dreaming, I'm just talking to myself inside my brain." Yet how wonderful it was to see Rindy's face again! "Can I ask you what it's like being dead?"

"If you lose the game," Rindy said sadly, "you'll know that too."

Anguish filled Melanie's heart. She looked down at the letters. They said nothing to her. "This isn't fair. I don't know the rules."

"But you do. Remember the reflection. There are two of everything."

Melanie picked up a couple of the chips. "I'm to make two names? Out of the same letters?"

Rindy nodded. "Be quick."

She began to arrange and rearrange the letters. To form something sensible, she had to concentrate, and when she did so, the chips became as ill-defined as the walls had. The beating of her heart was getting louder, driving blood through returning limbs that were unconnected with those striving to complete the task. The colours began to dim along with the light, and soon she was labouring in a murky grey twilight. Worse, Rindy was now difficult to see.

"Don't leave me," Melanie said anxiously.

"Hurry," Rindy said.

This nightmare was twisted. There was no visible monster to flee from. There was no striving to wake up. Indeed, her anxiety came from the possibility that she would wake up. Before she could know the monster's name. "I need help," she pleaded.

Rindy was a ghost image, her voice a whisper from many miles *away. "Think who you know."*

"Rindy!"

Her friend vanished. Melanie grabbed the chips. Their weight was increasing. Her fingers were turning to smoke. The letters elongated and began to lose form. The pounding in her chest shook the room.

"But I don't know!" she cried.

Her imagination refused her the time. Nevertheless, in the last moments before the basement and its reality evaporated, she made a partial breakthrough. A name came to her, one she had exactly the right letters to form.

Stan Russel. . . .

Melanie sat upright in bed, going from sleep to waking in a jarring instant. The phone in the kitchen was ringing. Throwing her bare feet to the cold floor, she cursed the gas company for not letting them afford to keep the heat turned up all night.

"Did I wake you?" Captain Crosser asked after her mumbled hello.

She glanced at the clock: eight-fifty. "No, I was just dreaming. I mean, daydreaming—Yeah, you woke me. That's the second time. You must think I sleep all the time."

"That's fine, you're making up for people like me."

He sounded far away. There were street noises in the background. "Are you calling from a phone booth?"

"Yes."

"So you didn't go home and sleep on it?"

"I haven't been home," he said. Then his tone became serious. "Melanie, I can be at the station by one. Could you meet me there?"

"Yeah. I'm eager to see you. I think I've got this thing figured out." She hoped he would be able to keep Rindy's suicide confidential.

"That's good." He did not appear too interested. How strange! "Is your father there?"

She spotted a note on the counter. "Melon, gone grocery shopping."

"No. He's at the store."

"Do you expect him back soon?"

162

"Yeah. Should he come to Barters with me?"

"Yes. What are you going to do now?"

He had asked the identical question the night before. "Well, I'll make breakfast, take a shower, and maybe clean up the house." She was also supposed to call her lawyer. Ms. Schaefer was building a defence entirely around the "terrible accident" formula. The defence didn't require much research outside her office and away from her six ashtrays.

"That's good. Take care of yourself, then. Drive straight to the station."

Melanie chuckled. "You sound funny. What's up?"

"I'll explain when I see you. If you get to the station early, that would be all right."

"I'll be there by one," she promised. "See ya."

He hesitated. "Good-bye, Melanie."

She had spooned plain yogurt into a bowl and was dicing a banana over it, when the phone rang again.

"Hello?"

"Hi, Melanie, this is Susan. Did Marc call you?"

"No."

"He called me. Woke me up. He says Mr. Murphy wants the set dismantled by Monday. Marc was wondering if we could give him a hand tearing it down."

"The police are done studying the set and stuff?"

"I guess. Could you help us out?"

"For a couple of hours. I've got to go to Barters in the afternoon."

"Why?"

"To see Captain Crosser."

Susan paused. "Well, maybe you shouldn't bother, then. Marc and I can probably handle it."

Melanie laughed. "You know me better than that. I'll take any chance to see Marc. But I'll have to take the bike. Unless you can give me a ride?"

"I would, but I don't have the car. I'm going to walk. Call Marc. Maybe you can catch him before he leaves."

"How about Jeramie?"

"I'd leave him alone. When he left last night, he was in a weird mood. And I mean weird even for him."

163

"I guess Carl's out of the question," Melanie said.

"Let's not bother him."

"I think I'm going to enjoy ripping that living room apart."

"It'll be a relief to put it all behind us," Susan agreed.

Melanie said good-bye and then tried Marc. His uncle didn't know where he was. She didn't bother leaving a message.

She finished her yogurt and decided to skip her shower. Care High was fifteen minutes away by ten-speed, and she wanted to get there and see Marc before Susan arrived. Her enthusiasm for trying to rekindle his interest in her was greater now than she knew he wasn't a psycho.

Dressed and halfway out the the door, she remembered to leave her dad a note: "Pop—Went to school to help Susan tear down the set. Be back by twelve. And I am not ja melon!"

Swinging onto her bike, she vaguely recalled the dream the captain had interrupted. Something about a small party where they were all playing Scrabble.

Melanie passed the video rental store on the way to the campus. She didn't look too hard, but she didn't see Tracy inside; there was one person she didn't want helping with the set.

Twice she had to stop to catch her breath. Her lungs were still weak from her cold.

To her disappointment, Susan, and not Marc, was waiting on the stage when she arrived. Her friend was sitting cross-legged on the couch, working on her trig homework.

"You didn't get hold of him?" Susan asked, seeing her bike. Melanie parked it against the back wall and walked down the aisle.

"He had already split. You mean he's not here?"

Susan put aside her textbook, marking her place with a programme from opening night. "I can't believe that guy. He drags me out of bed and then he doesn't show. What do you want to do? Should we stay or go get some junk food?"

"I wouldn't mind working. What are we supposed to do anyway?"

Susan gestured behind her. "Everything! There's a list in

the Green Room that tells who is the rightful owner of each prop. We have boxes out back we can pack the stuff into. Then there's the set itself. The living room walls are put together in about a hundred places. Carl's got some tools lying around we can use. I guess we could start and do what we can while we're waiting for Marc.''

''You don't sound very enthusiastic.''

Susan yawned. ''I just don't like dirty work.'' She leaned forward. ''Speaking of which, I want to know about Miss Sherlock Holmes's latest discoveries.''

For the first time in a long while, Melanie noticed how silent the theatre was. Their voices carried easily, but nothing came back. The lighting had been turned down low: the auditorium was dark; a couple of lamps were all that lit the stage. In spite of the isolation, Melanie felt as if she were being watched. She moved closer to Susan before answering. Susan would have to know.

''Can you keep this a secret?''

Susan smiled. ''Cross my heart and hope to die.''

''I'm serious.''

Susan nodded. ''OK.''

''I think Rindy arranged things so she would be killed.''

''Come again?''

''She wanted to die. She put the wad cutter in the revolver.''

''Did you see her do it?''

''No. But it all fits. Rindy was depressed. She was an outcast. Then, I remember, just before I shot her she shouted, ''Don't!'' She was terrified. She knew she was going to die.''

''Don't, don't,'' Susan whispered to herself, then shook her head. ''I don't believe it.''

''Are you sure? I think you remember her deviating from the script.''

Susan looked uncomfortable. ''Now that you mention it, I do recall a change in the dialogue. But to say Rindy committed suicide based on that is—saying a lot.''

''Not if you saw her the way I saw her. When we were sitting on the couch you're sitting on now, she was trembling. I tell you, she knew what was coming.''

165

"But if she wanted to die, why was she scared?"

"Obviously, she must have had second thoughts."

Susan was thinking. "How did the captain respond to this idea?"

"I haven't told him yet."

"You're not going to tell everyone this, are you?"

"Then you *do* believe me?"

"I didn't say that." Susan turned away, grimaced slightly. "But it does bring back something she said when I first showed her the script."

"What was it?"

"Wait a second. I don't know if I want to contribute to this theory."

"Susan, I don't want to screw up Rindy's reputation any more than it already is. I'm going to talk to the captain and my lawyer to see if this information can be brought up discreetly before the trial. I'm going to try not to let the papers get ahold of it."

Susan put her hand to her head. "A couple of months ago, when we were discussing the roles, she told me she definitely wanted to be Ronda. When I asked why, she said, 'Because she gets shot.' " Susan reached out, took Melanie's hand. "The night Rindy died, I remembered that remark. It made me wonder."

"You should have told me."

"Yeah, I should have." She let go of her hand. "Let's not talk about this any more. Do what you have to do."

Melanie was thankful for the confirmation.

Matching every item on the list with the stuff on the set proved to be quite a task. After an hour and a half of steady labour, however, they had the majority of the small items packed. The heavy work was next. Susan brought out a toolbox complete with a ratchet set and crowbar. She handed Melanie gloves, slipping on a pair herself.

"Carl and I got splinters when we put up the walls," she explained, scooting a tall aluminium ladder in from the hallway.

"Do we get the hinges from behind?"

"Yeah. But first let's get down these cables Carl ran above the lights. You climb up here. I'll put a chair on the bar."

Melanie did as requested. Up in the rafters she had a simultaneous view of each of the spots where Jeramie, Tracy, and Marc had hidden isolated while Rindy lay dead. It was as if the set had been designed for a cat-and-mouse game. She had to take the thought away.

Carl was no electrician. The cables were secured with ordinary rope and Boy Scout knots. They had no trouble loosening them. Coming down the ladder slowly, Susan doing the same off her chair, Melanie set the thick black wires on the floor at the foot of the couch.

"I wish Marc would show soon," Melanie said, checking her watch.

"You know, maybe he meant tomorrow," Susan said, puzzled. "It's just not like Marc to say something and then not do it." Fitting a piece in the ratchet, she added, "If you have to leave, go ahead."

"I can stay another half hour." And that would be pushing it. She walked to far stage right, near the fire-escape door. "Want me to start dismantling the set at this end?"

"Yeah, it's a tight squeeze, perfect for someone your size." Susan moved to the bar, fiddling with her gloves. "Would you like a Coke?"

Melanie knelt by the escape door and its silver plate stamped with the red letters: EMERGENCY. The space between the theatre wall and the set wall was indeed narrow. "If you've got it."

Susan disappeared behind the bar. Melanie noticed the icebox light going on. "Where were you last night?" Susan asked. "We've had a six-pack of Coke in this refrigerator since Thursday."

Melanie slipped her body into the space, slipped back out again. There was just room enough for her. "Oh, yeah, I saw it."

Susan reappeared, a Coke in each of her gloved hands. "Did you hear there's another dance coming up? The big H—Homecoming."

"Who's supposed to ask who?" Melanie leaned back

against the theatre wall, sticking her gloves in her pocket, trying to decide where to start. Susan stepped from behind the bar, walking towards centre stage. It was then Melanie's attention was drawn to the china cabinet. They'd need Marc's truck to return that to Jeramie's mom. They would have to be especially careful with the mirror.

Reflections.

Seeing both Susan's front and back in the mirror at the same time had a curious effect on Melanie. She felt somehow split in two. The sensation was similar to acting, being inside a character's mind, only stronger. Much stronger.

"The guy asks the girl," Susan said, skirting the cables on the floor. "We're off the hook. There's not a guy in Careville who'd feel safe with either of us."

"How's that?" Melanie asked, hardly listening, absorbed in following Susan's reflection. Her own reflection was also visible in the mirror, tucked in the corner, watching.

Susan smiled. "Melissa has a bad reputation, if you hadn't noticed."

In a single move Melanie pulled herself off the wall and leaned on the emergency door handle with her right palm. Why she did so, she wasn't exactly sure. No profound insight had come to her. If anything, her brain suddenly seemed sunk in a fog. Unreasonable disquiet gnawed at her insides. The urge to press the handle had just hit her.

The door opened.

Nothing happened.

She let go. It closed.

"What's wrong?" Susan asked.

"The alarm," Melanie whispered.

"I definitely want the icebox open. . . ."

Melanie turned. The bar fridge lay open. Susan had forgotten to close it. Like Ronda had forgotten.

"That's right," Susan said quickly. "Don't touch that door again. You were lucky you didn't set off the alarm."

Melanie stared at her and didn't see her.

Susan smiled. "What's with you?"

"Nothing."

Susan held out the Coke. "Still thirsty?"

"Yeah." She accepted the cold can. She needed a drink. Her throat was bone dry. Except she had this fear, if she drank now, she would vomit.

"This person would have to have materialized out of thin air. The only way he could have got onstage was to have entered through the fire-escape door. Had he done that, the alarm would have gone off."

"Are you sure you're all right?" Susan asked, concerned.

Melanie nodded, shuffled towards the sofa, sat down. Susan's trig book lay beside her, and tucked inside it, the programme for the play: *Final Chance* by Stan Russel.

Stan Russel. Ten letters.

The dream! She had dreamed of ten letters!

"Susan?"

"What?" she asked, crossing back to the bar, finally closing the fridge door.

Melanie gripped the programme. "Do you play Scrabble?"

"No. It bores me. Rindy used to be a whiz at it."

"Rindy?" Melanie croaked.

"Think who you know."

The dream came back to her then. Complete with unfinished details. The play hadn't been used as a blueprint for murder. She'd had it backward. From the start the play had been designed *as* a blueprint.

Susan Trels walked towards her. "Melanie, you're white as a ghost."

Ghosts. Reflections. Mirrors. Someone had removed the mirror so there wouldn't be a reflection for poor innocent Melanie to see. But Rindy had seen. Rindy had been looking the wrong way into the wrong end of a gun. *"Don't!"*

"I'm fine," she said, keeping her eyes down.

Scrabble. Ten letters each. The same ten letters.

Susan Trels. Stan Russel.

"You're ruining my one and only programme," Susan scolded pleasantly.

She had squeezed the announcement into a ball. She was also squeezing the blood from her fingers. "I'm sorry."

Susan sat beside her, put a gloved hand on her back. "Why did you ask about Scrabble?"

169

Melanie jerked her head up, forced a smile. "I was just wondering if you played, that's all."

Susan had such pretty eyes. Besides her long legs, they were her best feature. Big and blue—they could stare at you and not blink and you would never guess what was going on behind them. "What's wrong, Melanie?"

She coughed. "It's this cold. I've still got it." She stood, feeling Susan's hand slip from her. "I probably should get home."

Susan rose quickly. "You poor dear. I'll give you a ride."

"No," she said suddenly. "I mean, you don't have to. I've got my bike." She pointed towards it, trying unsuccessfully to keep her arm from shaking. Her other hand refused to let go of the programme. "See."

"Nonsense. If you're sick. We can—"

"I thought you walked," Melanie interrupted, in spite of a supreme desire not to make waves, to get out of the theatre and to a phone as smoothly and quickly as possible.

Susan backed away slowly. "My mom showed up with the car before I left," she said evenly, watching her.

Melanie smiled again. "I think the exercise will do me good. The fresh air and all."

Susan stopped nearer the door that led to Stan Russel's upstate New York lake. Despite her masterful control, Melanie could sense her indecisive air. "And then you're going to see that detective?"

"He's expecting me," Melanie said, suddenly certain it would be better if she didn't move an inch. Susan was lingering near the desk—the desk drawer.

"At what time?"

"Soon."

"What are you going to talk about?"

"I told you, Suzy."

Susan jumped slightly. "What did you say?"

"Rindy's suicide. The captain and I—"

"You called me Suzy," Susan interrupted. "Rindy used to call me that." Her hand touched the drawer knob. "I hate being called that."

Melanie dropped the programme. It floated to the floor

like a balloon. She swallowed. "I'm going."

"No." Susan opened the drawer, took out a revolver, pointed it at her. "I don't think you're going anywhere."

TWELVE

The best actress in the school, Melanie thought. How many times had the others said that about Susan? As Melanie stood there staring into the hole at the end of the barrel, her anger was as great as her terror, anger at herself as well as Susan. She had been fooled by a performance. Even when she had read the script ahead of time.

"This one isn't loaded with blanks." Susan gestured with the gun. "Sit on the couch."

Melanie did so. Keeping her covered, Susan sat beside her. The arrangement was familiar: Ronda on the left, Melissa on the right. "You're Melissa," Melanie said.

Susan's face was calm. She nodded. "And Stan Russel. That was a mistake, Melanie, mentioning Scrabble."

"Why did you leave the clue?" Curiosity was a powerful thing. It could remain in the face of death. She had no illusions about the fact that Susan intended to kill her.

"An author's vanity, I suppose. Or maybe I did it to give Rindy and you a chance." Susan relaxed into the couch, lowering the gun an inch. "I'm an actress; I enjoy being other people."

"Even rotten ones?"

"No, I get other people to play those parts."

Melanie looked down at the discarded trig text. Susan's homework lay beside it, each of the assigned problems worked out correctly and without difficulty. "You didn't need my help in Golden's class. That day we met, you made me want to help you."

"When the deed is done, who approached who can become critical," Susan agreed, allowing a trace of a smile. "Ask what you want. I have all the answers."

How vain, Melanie thought. Perhaps the big ego could be

exploited. She would have to stall for time. And she would have to think about a way out instead of what it would feel like to have a bullet explode her brain into bloody grey pulp. Susan would shoot her there—she was sure—and try to make it look like a suicide.

"Did everybody in the play represent someone in real life?" she asked.

"Of course. Robert was Jeramie. Robert's habit of pointing unloaded guns is like Jeramie's habit of taking pictures without film. Mary was Tracy. Mary was Charles's sister. Tracy is Clyde's sister. You see the pattern? Marc took Clyde's role and you took mine."

"Did Rindy try to hide the seriousness of Clyde's injury from you?"

"Yeah, wasn't that a stupid thing to do?"

"What about the war?"

"Certain things are symbolic. Charles lost his arm in battle. Clyde lost the use of his legs in real life. It's the same difference. Don't you think?"

Bitterness welled up inside Melanie. "I think you're mad."

"I'm not," Susan said. "From the beginning I knew exactly what I was doing, and why."

Melanie glanced towards the bar. They had rolled up the rug. Rindy's bloodstains were again visible. Melanie's stomach turned. She had to think! "How did you do it?" she asked.

Susan brightened. "You really want to know?" She was proud of what she had done. It struck Melanie then that it must have driven her nuts not being able to share her brilliance with anyone.

"Sure." Had the situation been less dire, she would have laughed. As it was, she could feel her eyes watering.

"I wrote *Final Chance* over the summer. I had you in mind to play my part. That's why I called her Melissa. But you weren't my only candidate. Heidi would have done. She despised Rindy. You were my first choice though. I'd heard through the grapevine about your acting experience, and about your run-in with Rindy in the rain. The hard thing was making sure both you and Rindy would try out for the play. To do that, I had to turn to Tracy and Marc.''

"Marc was in on this?'' She was having trouble breathing.

"It's complicated. When I mentioned directing a play to Tracy, she wanted to use it as a way to humiliate Rindy. She wanted something embarrassing to happen to Rindy onstage. I went along with it. Tracy was the only one who could assure me Rindy would be in *Final Chance*. You see, she talks to Clyde a lot. Around him she'd always acted bitterly towards Rindy, even before the accident. But when I told her about the play, I suggested she put on an act for her brother about how nice it would be if Rindy and she could bury the axe, and maybe work together on something creative. Apparently, Clyde fell for it. He must have asked Rindy to forget the past.''

"How can you be sure?''

"She accepted the Ronda role the moment I offered it to her.''

"She wasn't interested in getting shot?''

"Oh, that. I was lying. I can lie as easily as I tell the truth.'' She shifted in the cushions, the gun shifting with her. The weight of the revolver did not appear to be tiring her hand. "Am I boring you?''

"You have me on the edge of my seat.''

Susan smiled. "Witty till the end. I admire that.''

She had to keep things moving. "So Clyde and Rindy did talk regularly?''

"Not regularly. But they kept in touch. Few people were aware of it. Marc didn't even know. Rindy always gave people the impression that Clyde hated her.''

"Why?''

"I don't know.''

"Did Tracy plan to humiliate Rindy by putting something in Ronda's booze?''

"I'm impressed. How did you figure that out?''

"A lucky guess.'' A bullet through the brain might not kill her immediately. When they used to guillotine people, she had read, the severed head would sometimes live long enough to look up and see the blood gushing from the pink arteries hanging outside the neck. Maybe it would be the same for her, and she would feel skull chips splintering into her nerves, and—

Stop it!

"You're right. Opening night Tracy put a combination of herbs—that makes you throw up—in the Seagram's Seven bottles. That was why Tracy needed whisky to be used in the play. The herbs showed up in the clear water that was used for gin. But in the 'whisky' you couldn't taste it or see it. That's why Rindy was so anxious when she was sitting on the couch with you. She had just vomited and she probably had to vomit again. It was tacky, I admit, but that's Tracy for you."

"Did Marc know about the herbs?"

"No. But I did tell him I wanted you in the play. Before we ate lunch together that Friday afternoon, I told him I'd be introducing you to him. I told him to be nice to you. He went along as a favour to me, but he had no knowledge of why I wanted you in particular for Melissa."

"He was bait? To catch me?" Nothing was sacred to this witch.

"Exactly."

"How could you possibly know I liked him?"

"I told you, all the girls like Marc. Even if you'd found out Rindy was to be in the play, I knew you'd audition if you thought you stood a chance with him."

"I didn't know I was so predictable," Melanie said miserably.

"You're easier to read than a book. But you've made me skip an important part of my story. In case there were questions after Rindy's death, I didn't want to be identified as the one who wrote the play, or even the one who bought it. I had it printed up out of town and then planted it in that store in Kansas City. I made sure Marc and Jeramie found it."

"I went there," she mumbled. The extent Susan had gone to boggled her mind.

"Did you find the other copy? I put it there after you asked me for Poems and Pages's address. I went in as a redhead. Clever, huh?"

"You left a photocopy. Not an aged and tattered printed manuscript. That wasn't so clever."

Susan's eyes narrowed. "Who knows that?"

"Worried?"

"Answer my question."

Melanie debated pushing Susan, trying to bluff her way out. Something told her to save it. That something was a deep-seated fear of holes in her body. "*I* know," she said.

Susan moved the gun closer. "Who else?"

"The store owner. That's it."

Susan appeared satisfied. "Good."

Keep the questions going. Let her brag. "Did you plant my letter?"

"Yes. I saw it in your notebook when I returned from my locker minutes before the first rehearsal. It looked so incriminating, I felt I just had to use it. That may have been a mistake."

"Did Jeramie have a role in all this?"

"Jeramie's as innocent as he appears."

"He knew nothing?"

"Nothing."

Susan was underestimating Jeramie. Melanie was somehow sure of that. "I've always wondered—what's he to you?"

"He's a friend. Like you."

Oh, swell, lucky Jeramie. Yet speaking of him stirred hope inside her. She strove to pinpoint why. She had not called to tell him to meet her at the school. The cavalry wasn't going to come over the hill.

How fitting it was that Susan herself reminded her of what she had forgotten.

"You're wondering why I used his gun?" Susan asked.

"You'll need it for the last act." The gun! Two of everything! Jeramie's revolver, with its six blanks, was right beneath her, under the cushion!

"Why?"

"Because it was easy to obtain another exactly like it."

"There were two guns, then?" she asked. *Fool, Suzy, there are at least three.* If she could get to the revolver and fire it into Susan's eyes, the ejected wax might momentarily blind her. The chance, slim as it was, gave Melanie a better grip on her fear.

"Naturally. Let me tell you about opening night. First, the mirror in the china cabinet had to go. I couldn't have you seeing me in it. I came in early that afternoon and broke it. Then, when Carl came in later, he took it out without my even having to ask. The next step was more difficult. I had to get you to touch the wad cutter."

"And the other gun?" Melanie asked, slipping her hand over the edge of the cushion. Now that she remembered the hidden revolver, she could feel it as a bump in the couch. Unfortunately, she was sitting on the wrong edge of the bump. Her exploring fingers confirmed this, finding the lower part of the cushion bent up approximately a foot closer to Susan. To get right on top of the gun she would have to move significantly closer to Susan.

"You had already handled the gun that killed Rindy. It was Jeramie's and it was the one you regularly used in rehearsals. But opening night, when you came in, I gave you *this* gun, the one I'm holding now, a gun you had never seen before and weren't supposed to see again. Do you understand?"

"Yeah. Where did you buy *your* gun?"

"At a swap meet in Des Moines. The guy who sold it to me would have sold me a flame thrower if I'd wanted it. Anyway, I had to get your fingerprints on the wad cutter. Before I visited you in the dressing room, I put a few of them in my box of blanks. I'm glad Heidi was there. She gave me an excuse to drop the box. I can't tell you how relieved I was to see the two bullets she happened to pick up were blanks. Do you remember how I held the box out to you when we were picking them up? How I didn't touch the ones you touched? Until later, of course, when I had gloves on."

"I remember," Melanie said. Susan had her finger on the trigger of her gun. A sudden grab for Jeramie's gun wouldn't work, she decided. She would have to have it already in hand—in her left hand, ideally—before she tried for Susan's eyes. To do that, she'd have to practically climb into Susan's lap. "Tell me more," she said, racking her brain for a safe angle of approach. A possible solution was not long in coming.

"You'll recall I wore black that night. When the murder

scene started, I was with Carl in the control booth behind the audience. As the scene moved towards its climax, I left Carl—as I was supposed to—to walk around the theatre. But rather than go straight to the door in the hallway, I took the long way around, where I passed the fire-escape door. I had already hidden Jeramie's revolver with a couple of used blanks, and a pair of gloves in a bush by the emergency exit. As Carl's probably told you, the wiring in the theatre's not set up to handle the load we put on it. When the icebox is open, the alarm doesn't work. I discovered that last year by accident when we used the refrigerator in another play.''

"But if the load on the line trips the circuit breaker, why didn't the light in the refrigerator go out during the play?''

"Obviously, the circuit breaker doesn't get tripped. The current to the alarm just gets lowered enough to stop it from working. The alarm must be a pretty sensitive piece of equipment. It's a fine point, but it was important enough that I structured the story of *Final Chance* entirely around it.'' Susan paused. "I suppose you can guess the rest.''

Melanie sniffed, fidgeted. "I'm going to sneeze. Don't kill me.''

The sneeze, phony as it was, lifted her backside off the cushion. When she landed, her ribs were practically touching the barrel of Susan's gun. And she could feel the bump under her left cheek rather than her right. Yeah, Suzy had such pretty blue eyes; she was going to enjoy putting them out. Susan reclined in the arm of the sofa and smiled.

"I almost hit you instead of Rindy,'' she said. "To get the right angle, I had to stand directly behind you. I put a hole in your nightgown. It was that close.''

"Rindy saw you?'' Melanie asked, inching her left hand back under the cushion. This move would have been obvious to Susan had Melanie not wisely chosen to arrange herself at the very edge of the sofa. Also, Susan's overwhelming confidence was making her careless. She was too caught up in telling what a genius she was.

Melanie's fingers touched the handle of Jeramie's revolver.

"Yes,'' Susan said. "I jumped the gun, so to speak. I came through the emergency door a couple of lines early. Rindy never got a chance to say, 'But we were friends.' It didn't matter. You covered for her. You shot her ahead of time. And, on the second round, I shot her with you.''

Melanie coughed, leaning forward slightly, taking her weight off the revolver so it could be moved easily. ''You must have practised, to get her in the heart with one bullet?''

''For hours. Then again, she wasn't all that far away from me.'' Susan's voice had slowed. She was getting ready to finish her.

''Then w-what?'' she stuttered.

''When you shut the icebox, I crossed the stage, switched guns, and went into the hallway, where I tossed my gloves and the other gun into the dressing room. With everyone shouting, you didn't hear me run by you. Then when you went back onto the stage, I hid the gun you had used in the dressing room in a wall space I'd prepared earlier.''

Melanie tugged at the handle of the revolver. The blasted thing was turned the wrong way! ''Go on.''

''That's everything,'' Susan said softly, staring, thinking of death. She raised the revolver.

''You've told me how,'' Melanie said quickly. ''You haven't told me why.''

''I didn't want to just bag her in some deserted field. Where's the drama in that?'' She added, ''I love drama.''

''No! Why did you kill her?''

Susan's voice took on a slightly dreamy tone. ''You played Melissa. You know why.''

''Clyde was your boyfriend who was 'away'?''

Susan nodded. Still staring.

Melanie began to rotate Jeramie's gun into a more favourable position. Yet suddenly she realised her scheme was not going to work. Only a weekly TV star could outdraw someone who had a gun to her head. The star had to be there for the next episode; she had no such life insurance contract. Somehow she had to throw Susan off balance to get an extra fraction of a second.

''Did you love Clyde?''

Susan nodded.

''Did he know?''

"I never told him."

"Never?"

"Rindy was always there."

"Were you jealous of her?"

Susan cocked her gun. "I hated her."

Melanie coughed again, bending her left wrist at a painful angle, closing all five of her fingers around the gun handle. "Did it bother you that Jeramie loved Rindy?"

"Everything about Rindy bothered me," Susan whispered.

"But what about me?" she protested and the anguish came of its own.

"I never intended for it to end this way. I like you, Melanie. I honestly do."

"But you brought me here today to kill me!"

Susan nodded faintly. "Then you told me about Rindy's suicide. I was going to let you go. But you had to open that door. You should never have opened that door."

Melanie began to tremble, a million tiny convulsions. Where was the trigger and where was her index finger? "But what made you call me this morning?" she asked.

"That black man. Because of you, he's getting too close." Susan stretched out her arm, pressed the tip of the revolver into Melanie's hair. "Too close," she repeated.

My hair, I should have washed it. The coroner will think I was a slob when he tries to dig the bullet out of my skull. . . . Her tears flooded out as though through a broken dam. "Close?" she cried. "You idiot. He's right on top of you!"

"Please don't cry, Melanie. You won't feel it."

"The captain will know I didn't kill myself. I talked to him this morning. He knows about you!"

"Had he known, he would have told you." Susan dug the gun into Melanie's scalp. "It will be better if you don't move."

"Go ahead, you bitch!" she swore, her finger finally snuggling up against the trigger of Jeramie's revolver. "And then let Jeramie show everyone his tape!"

Susan hesitated. "There is no tape."

"He recorded the whole damn play!"

Susan drew back her gun. "You lie."

Melanie laughed an ugly laugh. "Not only that, he gave

180

me something for the last act.''

A sliver of doubt, tiny but sharp, jagged Susan. ''There was never to be a last act,'' she said, frowning. And as she did so, she accidentally tilted the barrel in the direction of the empty seats.

Oh, yeah, Ms. Russel? This is it!

Melanie pulled out Jeramie's revolver, swinging it up towards Susan's face. Susan reacted instantly, twisting her head to the side, snapping back her own gun. Melanie didn't have a chance to aim directly into Susan's eyes. But the tip of Jeramie's revolver was not far from Susan's brow when she pulled the trigger. The bang of the blank was followed immediately by a second bang. A lick of fire crossed Melanie's left side. She had been hit. So had Susan. Letting out a cry, dropping her gun to the floor, Susan threw her hands to her face. Melanie released her own revolver and dove for Susan's. It was at the tip of her fingers when Susan's shin cracked the side of her head. For a moment Melanie's eyes went out of focus. Then Susan jumped on her, and it was like being tackled by a grizzly bear. In a ball of flaying limbs the two of them rolled away from the couch, away from the two revolvers lying together on the floor.

''You little pipsqueak!'' Susan cursed, grabbing Melanie by the hair, snapping her head back. Melanie returned the favour, throwing an elbow into Susan's jaw. Briefly stunned, Susan released her. On all fours, Melanie again scampered towards the gun with the real bullets, a sticky warmth spreading under her shirt. And again she had Susan's black-market piece within her grasp, when she was seized by the legs and hoisted backward, the cable they had removed earlier scraping against her belly. Melanie quickly realised the hopelessness of the situation. She was wounded—she didn't know how bad—and in either case she was not going to win a wrestling match with Susan, who easily had twenty pounds on her. Not under these conditions. Twisting on her bleeding side, seizing the cable, not even attempting to shake free of Susan's hold, she yanked with all her strength. Sparks jumped from the far wall.

The stage was plunged into total darkness.

Susan let go of her feet. "Damn you!" she swore. Rather than going straight for the guns, Melanie immediately rolled to the side. She had anticipated her foe well. Susan stomped the floor hard where Melanie's head had been only moments ago. Obviously, the coward would have preferred to shoot an unconscious target.

Melanie leapt to her feet, holding her breath in spite of a desperate need to fill her lungs. The black was eerie in its uniformness. She took a couple of steps forward, reaching for the lamp on the coffee table beside the sofa. Susan's panting was as good as a beacon. Melanie knew exactly where to attack. Ripping the shade off the lamp she grabbed it at the top and swung the weighted base in a hard wide arc. The sound and feel of it striking home, a dull mushy thud, actually brought a smile to her face. Susan gave a strangled groan and appeared to drop to the floor.

Tossing aside the lamp and feeling along the edge of the couch, Melanie went down on her knees where the guns should have been.

There was only *one* gun.

Susan had not been knocked out.

Melanie finally had to take a breath. She couldn't see an inch in front of her face. On her knees, she scurried around the couch, choking on the searing pain radiating from her side. For a moment she almost passed out. Only the sound of Susan's scratchy breathing, her staggering steps, made Melanie hold on to consciousness. Susan was making for the bar.

Fine, I'll go in the other direction.

Orienting herself with the help of the sofa, Melanie stood and stumbled towards the emergency exit, clutching her .38, trying to convince herself she wasn't bleeding to death. An assortment of boxes tried to trip her, but she kept going.

Her free hand hit the door handle. Sunlight squinted around the door's edges. The alarm didn't go off. A pale light shone at her back.

"Stay," Susan whispered.

Melanie let go of the door and turned. How fitting. The open icebox again. Its bleak light silhouetted Susan's tall, shaking form. Her blonde hair was filthy with blood, the left side of her face already puffing into a gruesome purple.

"You look like crap," Melanie said.

Susan raised her gun and took a feeble step forward. "You don't look so hot yourself."

Melanie glanced down. These stains definitely wouldn't be coming out. They were getting bigger and darker. The torment in her side burned. The sweat dripping from her face felt like ice.

She didn't bother raising her own gun. Susan could decide for them who had the real bullets. Susan would fire first. But Melanie was not so exhausted that she was ready to welcome death.

"You've already lost," she said as Susan slowly closed in on her. "After all this mess, no one will believe I killed myself."

"You're still the main suspect," Susan wheezed, limping on top of everything else. "I'll just say it was self-defence."

"I was telling the truth when I said the detective's on to you. Don't you remember how he complimented you last night on your acting? He knows everything you've said and done is an act!"

Susan flashed a smile that was close to a grimace. "He hasn't seen anything yet. When I'm through with my act, there isn't a jury in Iowa that will find me guilty." Stopping twenty feet away, she waved her gun. "Come on, let's shoot together."

"No."

"Why not? It makes for a great finish. Come on, be a sport."

"Like you? How did you feel when Rindy hugged and thanked you just before the play began?"

Susan's expression hardened. "I felt just like I do now. I felt *fine*." She shook her revolver again. "Draw, damn you."

"No. I saw your face then. You were having doubts. Like you are now."

Susan's aim wavered. "You are mistaken if you think I will be talked out of pulling this trigger."

Melanie dropped her gun at her feet, spread her arms,

much as it hurt her to do so. "Shoot me, then! Like you shot Rindy! In the heart! I'm sure Clyde will love you for it!"

Susan coughed, choking. Blood dripped from the side of her head, splattering the floor. "Clyde never loved me," she said softly. "Just like Charles never loved Melissa."

"Susan—"

"No." Susan stopped her. "Don't talk. Don't tell me who loves me." She shook her head. "I have no friends." Cocking her revolver, she locked her right arm. "Say good-bye, Melanie."

Melanie stood frozen. Listening to her heart. And to another sound that seemed to come out of nowhere; the electric hum of a motor. When she looked, though, she saw nothing. Only the dark rows of empty seats.

"Good-bye, Susan," she said, closing her eyes.

"Hello, Suzy," someone said.

Melanie opened her eyes.

THIRTEEN

The wheelchair came down the steep aisle slowly; the gears and motor working to keep it from gaining speed. As the light from the icebox was splashed mainly across the set, his dark form became visible to Melanie only in stages. He was not tall; though perhaps on two good legs, a football in his hand, he would have been striking enough. His blond hair was long and curly, resting atop wide shoulders. He appeared to have some control of his left arm; it was his left hand that was steering the wheelchair with the aid of a control knob. But his right arm lay useless in his lap. No more perfect passes to his friend Marc running downfield.

"Hello, Clyde," Susan said, lowering her gun.

Clyde's wheelchair reached the front row, emerging into the light. His lower body, as expected, was shrivelled, yet his face seemed to have escaped the trauma of the injury untouched. Unlike Marc, he did not look tough; he appeared, rather, like the person Carl had described to her after the funeral, someone who was popular, who was friendly to everyone. His brown eyes were big and warm. That Clyde had once been someone the girls had longed for, Melanie had no doubt.

"You know who I am?" he asked, looking at her.

"I do," she said. "I'm Melanie."

He nodded. "You were my surprise visitor. Too bad we didn't get to talk then. Had I seen you—" His eyes strayed to Susan, to the horrible gash in the side of her head, the weapon hanging in her right hand. "Maybe we could have avoided all this."

White as a bedsheet, Susan stared at Clyde. Melanie hardly recognized her. The act was over, finally. This was the real Susan; she seemed such a fragile creature. "You knew?" Susan whispered.

"That you murdered Rindy? No, I discovered that only today, when I finished reading your script. Your portrait of us was interesting."

"I'm glad you liked it," Susan said.

"I didn't say I liked it." His voice was firm. "None of those people were us."

Before this one person, crippled as he was, Susan was ashamed. "I wrote what I saw."

"You wrote garbage. Your Charles would have seen through your Melissa long ago."

Susan flinched. "You saw through me?"

"I knew what you were after."

"No." Susan put a hand to her ghastly hair. "I don't believe you. What I wrote was real."

"Garbage," Clyde repeated. He looked like a nice guy, but he was angry. "Your Ronda was always quietly putting down Melissa. When did Rindy ever do that to you?"

Susan regained a brief measure of her strength. "From the time we were kids. She always placed herself above me. She was always so sophisticated, so rich, so pretty." Susan winced, realising she was listing facts, not prejudices. "She was always so godawful pretty."

"Yeah, she was pretty," Clyde agreed. "And where did you get that junk about her being an alcoholic?"

"She used to smoke cigarettes," Susan said quickly.

"She smoked once or twice a day. And she started doing that only after the accident."

"Well, she used to get loaded."

"Rindy got loaded about as often as we lost a football game. I was the one who liked to drink."

"You drank only when you were around her!"

"Suzy, I was always around her."

So Rindy was not the only one who called her Suzy. The reminder struck Susan hard. The tears burst out. "She used you! She was no good!"

Clyde sharpened his tone. "You're a fine one to talk."

"I am!" Susan swore, and it would have been funny had it

186

not been so pathetic. "I knew her better than anybody! Better than you! She was trash! She didn't love you!"

Clyde glanced at the stains on the floor by the icebox. He knew where they were from. "Not like you, huh?"

Susan's whole face crumbled. "She deserved what she got. I'm glad I killed her."

"Why?" Clyde sat up as straight as he was able. "Why did you kill her? Because she was *so* pretty?"

"No!" Susan cried. "Because she ruined you!" Suddenly she lowered her head, wobbling on her feet, her condition catching up with her. "Just look at you," she moaned.

"Look at both of us." Clyde sighed, sitting back in his wheelchair. He was not the emotionally shattered invalid Melanie had imagined he would be when she had gone to visit him. That he was here, bringing to his knees a murderer who held a gun, said much of his inner strength.

Melanie realised she could check the gun at her feet to see if it held blanks. She decided the knowledge, one way or the other, would not change the situation. Also, she hesitated to move, afraid of starting up her own bleeding—which appeared to be slowing—and afraid of disturbing Susan further. It was Clyde's ball game now.

"I will tell you a secret," he said finally. "This is something Rindy made me swear never to talk about. It's also something I should have talked about a long time ago." He paused. "I was the one who insisted we go to the reservoir that night."

"No," Susan said.

"It's true."

"I don't believe it." Susan braced herself on the sofa arm. She was on the verge of collapse.

"Then I guess you won't believe it wasn't Rindy's fault, but mine, we went off the road."

The comment surprised Melanie. It stunned Susan. "But Rindy said . . ." Susan began, not knowing how to finish. They waited for Clyde to explain.

"It was cold that night," he said. "I remember how the frosty grass crunched under our feet when we left the party. Rindy was tired; she wanted to go home. But I used to get so jazzed up after winning a game—I had a lot of energy left.

I wanted to do something. You were at the party, you know how she brought up the ducks. Well, I said, let's go see them now. She told me I was nuts. It was two in the morning." Clyde shrugged, much as Marc often did. "But I talked her into it, and finally she said all right, as long as I'd let her drive my car. I'd had a couple of beers and she was afraid I was drunk. I wasn't, but I wanted to get going, so I let her have the keys. When we left Steve's house, Rindy was behind the wheel. A lot of people saw that. No one saw us stop halfway to the reservoir with a flat tyre. No one saw me get behind the wheel after I'd changed the tyre."

Susan was looking at her gun, just looking at it. "No," she said.

"Yes," Clyde said. "I was driving when we went over the edge. I'd like to say that I *was* drunk, that the alcohol had slowed down my reflexes. Then I'd have an excuse. I seemed to be driving fine, maybe a little fast, but I thought I was in control. The turn just popped out of nowhere. I'd been up there a dozen times. I could have sworn it was farther along. I hit the brakes. I must have locked them. The way we slid, it felt like forever till we went into the trees and started to fall. The last thing I remember was Rindy saying my name. She didn't scream, just said, "Clyde," like she'd always said it. I didn't even feel my neck snapping."

Susan nodded as he spoke, her head hanging, her fingers manually revolving the revolver's chambers. *Click*. Empty chamber. *Click*. Loaded chamber. *Click*. He loves me. *Click*. He loves me not. Melanie watched and waited. *Click*.

"When I woke up," Clyde went on, "it was a couple of days later. At least that's what they told me. I was out of it. I knew I was messed up, but I had no idea how bad. Actually, I don't think I asked about my condition. I was afraid to. I remember nurses and needles, and doctors and bandages. They came and went. A while passed, I don't know how long. Then Rindy visited. I saw her before I saw my parents, before anybody I knew. God knows how she arranged that. I was in intensive care, not in a private room, hooked up to all sorts of stuff. Rindy knelt near my head and talked to me in whispers. She was the one who told me I was paralyzed for life."

Clyde stopped to stretch his upper torso. It appeared a habit; he was probably always stiff.

"I got mad," he continued. "No one was going to tell me I couldn't play ball any more, not even my own girl. But you see, right from the moment of the accident, when she was squeezing her way out of my wrecked car and I was lying there unconscious, she was thinking I had no medical insurance, no money, and, that if I did survive, I was going to need plenty of both. The way I was sprawled across what was left of the front seat, I guess it was hard to tell where I'd been sitting. When she got hold of the paramedics and the police, she told them she'd been driving. They believed her. Who would lie about such a thing?

"She told me all this in intensive care. She insisted I play along. She said my parents could sue hers and I'd be taken care of for life. If I told the truth, she warned, I'd be a burden on my family till the day I died. From my side, I was having a hard enough time swallowing the fact I wasn't going to walk again. I didn't want to get into this lying. But what she said made sense. I agreed to let her take all the blame."

"Go on," Susan said. *Click.* Kill myself. *Click.* Kill Clyde. *Click.* Kill Melanie. *Click.* Melanie began to experience a strange certainty that Susan had the gun with the real bullets. There was something about the sound of a loaded revolver. *Click.*

"You know the rest better than I do," Clyde said. "I was in the hospital. All of you were at school with Rindy. You didn't give her much of a break, did you? Marc told me all the crap that was being said about her. Oh, I suppose she didn't give herself a break either. Looking back, I see she didn't accept the blame just so my bills would be covered. She actually did blame herself. Yeah, she was hard on herself. She believed she couldn't even visit because others might think it peculiar I would still see her after what she had done to me. It was part of her guilt complex. When she called, and had to go through the hospital switchboard, she used to disguise her voice. Imagine that? And me, I was a real star. I crawled into a hole and felt sorry for myself and let Rindy spend her life dying a little each day, until you got it into your head that she should die all at once." He paused. "Give me the gun, Suzy."

About time you asked her for it.

Susan slowly raised her head, raising the gun also, and pointed it at Clyde. Her left eye was now swollen entirely shut. Red drops, one by one, fell into a bloody mess at her feet. She turned the chambers a final time. *Click.*

"You made this up," Susan said softly.

Clyde wasn't frightened. "She saved my life. She didn't ruin it."

Susan began to shake, and tried to stop but was unable. "I don't believe you!"

"Sure you do."

"But if what you say is true, I shouldn't have killed her."

"That's putting it mildly." Clyde wheeled closer to the stage, to where his head was not far from Susan's feet. She stood above him like a disintegrating statue. "Give me the gun."

"You d-didn't," she stuttered, "come by yourself."

"No, I didn't," he admitted.

Susan tried to search the rear of the dark theatre; it was doubtful she could see anything through the glaze in her remaining eye. Melanie, however, saw no one either.

"I could kill you," Susan said.

"And put me out of my misery? Don't do me any favours."

"But I would be doing you a favour."

"You certainly didn't do Rindy any."

Susan slowly began to aim the gun towards her own face. "There was still a reason."

"There was none at all. What happened to me was an accident. And what you did to Rindy was just something sick."

Susan sniffed, swaying. "You don't understand. The script explained it all."

Clyde was watching the gun closely, beginning to show signs of nervousness. "Your script was overly melodramatic.

190

It lacked believability. Don't try to follow it."

Oh, God, she's playing Melissa.

Clyde sighed and looked down at his lap, squeezing his lifeless right hand with his left hand. "I can't feel these fingers," he said, his tone softening. "I can't feel anything from my chest down. It's all numb. It's like it's dead. It's awful, believe me." He looked up. "You're a crazy girl, Suzy, but you don't want to be dead."

"You don't understand," she repeated sadly, putting her finger on the trigger.

"I do."

"You don't. You hate me."

"No."

"You do. Yes."

"This is silly. Don't do this."

Susan cocked the revolver's hammer. "You're right, I am crazy. I love you."

"Wait!"

Susan closed her eyes. "Good-bye."

Clyde tried to get out of his chair, and, of course, failed. For an instant an expression of utter helplessness filled his face. Then he did a most remarkable thing, probably the only thing that could have saved Susan's life. He laughed. "Hey, Suzy, don't take it so hard. I love you too."

Susan opened her eyes. "You do?"

"Sure."

Susan pulled the trigger.

The bullet shattered an overhead light.

Susan had twisted her wrist.

"It's nice to pretend," she said and collapsed unconscious on the stage.

EPILOGUE

Melanie spent a week in the hospital. On the morning she was discharged, Marc picked her up outside the back door. It had snowed the previous night. Careville was covered in a fresh white blanket. As Marc helped her into the cab of his truck, Melanie took a deep drink of the brisk clean air. It tasted great; the hospital room had been unbearably stuffy. She couldn't remember when Iowa had ever looked so beautiful.

Marc jumped in the driver's side, saying, "I got you something."

She smiled. "Body armour?"

He wrapped an arm behind his seat, pulling down a bouquet of yellow roses from the ledge. "I meant to bring you some at the hospital, but I kept forgetting."

"These are wonderful." She loved it when boys gave her flowers, never mind that this was the first time. "I'm glad you waited to give them to me. I think they would have choked to death in the room I was in." She had shared a room with an elderly lady with pleurisy who coughed continuously. The two times Marc had visited, he didn't look particularly comfortable, and she hadn't blamed him. Consequently, they hadn't talked much about the big showdown. She had a lot of questions.

"They probably would have turned green," Marc agreed.

She leaned over and kissed his cheek. "Thanks."

He nodded. "Hey, you feel well enough to go somewhere?"

Being cooped up the last week had given her cabin fever. "As long as it's not dancing. Where do you want to go?"

"Jeramie wanted me to meet him at the reservoir."

"Now?"

192

"Yeah. He said if I came, I'd learn the answer to one of the world's greatest mysteries."

"I love a good mystery."

Me and Stan Russel.

Her remark stayed with her as they left Careville on the same road they had taken the night of the dance. Marc knew she was deep in thought and didn't interrupt. The white fields rolled by silently. The interior of the cab was warm and cosy, but suddenly there was gooseflesh on her arms. The ache in her side seemed to have worsened. For her dad's sake, she had made light of all that had happened. He didn't know about the nightmares she had had in the hospital.

"How is she?" Melanie asked finally.

"She was in a coma." Marc glanced over, added, "The doctor said he had never seen anyone with a skull fracture as severe as Susan's wake up."

"But she's going to be all right?"

"The doctor thinks so."

She nodded, chewing on her lip. "I'm glad."

"You've got a forgiving nature."

"Did you think I'd hate her?"

"I wouldn't have blamed you if you did."

"Good, because I do hate her. I mean, I hate her and I feel sorry for her. You had to have been there on the couch. She bragged how she had set everything up. She went into every detail. Then she put the barrel right to my head and said"—Melanie had to take a breath—"she said, 'Please don't cry Melanie. You won't feel it.' That's what she said to me."

"Let's not talk about it."

She could feel herself getting upset. "I want to talk about it. She was *so* cold. She was just going to blow me away. Just like she did Rindy. Just because the two of us had somehow gotten in her way. Just because"—Melanie felt her eyes water—"because she loved Clyde. That's what makes it so awful. All this pain coming out of love. That's why I feel sorry for her."

"I feel sorry for her too," Marc said quietly.

She hesitated. "But you don't blame her like I do?"

He shrugged. "When Clyde got hurt, I accepted that. I had to. When Rindy died, I had to accept that too. Dwelling on how or why these things happen doesn't help. You know what I mean?"

"I do. You miss Rindy, don't you? Oh, there I go again. Never mind."

"No, that's OK." He smiled, a sad sort of smile. "When we were in grade school, I had a crush on her. I always tried to impress her with how fast I could run or how far I could kick a ball. That crush never really went away. When we were older, I used to watch her hanging on to Clyde's arm and wish that—I don't know, she had a twin sister or something."

"Did you ever tell her this?"

"No."

His admission didn't sting as she would have imagined. "Did your feelings change after Clyde's accident?"

"Lots of things changed after the accident. But I didn't hold it against her."

"I didn't think so." She was quiet for a minute. "Susan told me that you talked to me at first only because *she* wanted you to?"

Marc looked over at her. "Susan gives herself more credit than she deserves. And you a lot less."

Melanie smiled faintly. "She is a genius, though, you've got to grant her that. She sure knew how to pull my strings. The stuff that was going through my head. I even suspected you!"

"Me? Why me?"

Because you are left-handed like Charles, and because you told me where to buy the bullets, and because—

"Because you kissed me in the dressing room!"

"Huh. How about Jeramie?"

"He didn't kiss me. But, looking back, even now, he did seem to know what was going on. Have you talked to him about it?"

"Yeah, and it was rough. This whole thing has hit him harder than anybody. When you see him, don't even bring it up."

"I won't."

194

"He was suspicious from the day he read the play. He noticed the character similarities. But I'm not sure he realised one of us wrote the thing and patterned it after our group. In a weird way—and you know how weird he is—he seemed to fear that because the plot ran parallel to all that had gone down in the last year, if he were to act it out, it would become real for us."

"That is weird."

"Not as weird as the fact that he ended up being right. He told me you found out about the tape. After opening night, when he was still trying to deny Rindy was dead, he studied the thing again and again. The tape showed the same view of the stage the audience had. Susan wasn't visible. Still, he was able to tell that Rindy must have seen someone in the direction of the emergency exit. Also, he noticed a faint orange flash coming from the escape door at precisely the moment you fired your second shot. It wasn't hard for him to figure there had been a simultaneous shot. And he knew Susan had been circling the theatre at that moment, and that she was like Melissa in so many ways."

"So he knew Susan killed Rindy?"

"Sort of. Rindy was his fantasy. Susan was his buddy. Think how he must have felt studying the tape. He refused to accept it. Emotionally, he couldn't handle losing both of them."

"But he gave me a gun to protect myself?"

"Yeah, he tried to block it out and couldn't. He's crazy but not that crazy. He likes you. He knew the danger was still free and walking around. He wanted you to be safe."

"Would he have turned Susan in?"

"I doubt it. He'd cry whenever I said her name."

"That's sad. But while we're on the subject, I want to ask what the captain talked to you about after we did the play the second time. And when exactly did you come into the theatre during my fight with Susan?"

"The captain told me he wanted Clyde brought to the Barters police station the next day. I told him I'd try. I called Clyde Saturday morning, early. I was surprised. He'd been planning to call to have me bring him to the police. Apparently,

195

the day before, he'd had Tracy get him a copy of the play. He's no dummy. He knew Susan better than anyone did. He suspected her. When I got to the Teller Home, he told me what was on his mind. I thought he must be kidding. Then, before we could leave for the police station, we got a call from the captain. He said that no one was answering at your house, and that he was concerned. That was about ten-thirty. I asked him what he was concerned about. ''Susan,'' he said.

''So he did know!''

''Don't ask me how. He told me to take Clyde and head to your house, and that he'd meet us there.''

''Where was he at this time?''

''I don't know. But he also said he was dispatching a deputy to check on you. I drove ninety all the way to Careville. When I got to your place, your dad was there. He probably told you—he'd had car trouble and walked home carrying three bags of groceries. He was confused. Someone had forced open the door—that must have been the deputy—but had taken nothing. He showed me the note you'd left about going to help Susan. I must have turned white when I read it. Your dad immediately asked what was the matter. Before I could explain, a lady at the police station in Barters called for me with a message from the captain. He wanted me to go directly to the school theatre. Of course, I was going there anyway.''

''What did you tell my dad?''

''I don't even remember. Something to put him at ease. I didn't want him coming to the school with us. I didn't know what we'd find.''

''Ain't that the truth,'' Melanie muttered, shivering.

''The second I got to the school, the captain pulled up. He took hold of the back of Clyde's wheelchair and we sprinted to the theatre. There we found the deputy who'd arrested you on opening night. He was sitting outside the place, waiting. He told us the doors were locked, that he couldn't get in.''

''They were locked? That's interesting. Susan must have locked them while we were packing the props. I bet she was thinking of killing me even before I opened the emergency exit. Go on.''

''The captain was furious. He called the deputy an idiot

196

for sitting and doing nothing, and he was through that door in two seconds. As we crept inside, we could hear talking. The captain had his gun out. When I saw Susan had a gun on you, I assumed he'd order Susan to freeze. But that dude must be some kind of psychologist. He knew Clyde was the one who could safely disarm Susan. He said to Clyde, 'Go talk to her.' That was it. Clyde understood. He knew what he had to do.''

"I hope I get a chance to thank them both soon.''

Marc eyed her. "You won't believe this.''

"Jeramie invited Clyde and the captain to see the answer to one of the world's greatest mysteries?''

"Right. I'm not sure about the captain, but Clyde should be at the reservoir.''

"First time since the accident?''

"Yeah. He's coming out of his shell. He's staying at his parents' house now. He says he's going to take a couple of classes at school.''

"That's wonderful.''

"By the way, Rindy's parents heard the real story, that Rindy hadn't been driving when Clyde's car went off the road. Clyde told them. They're letting him keep the money. They said if Clyde's security meant so much to their daughter, then it means a lot to them.''

"Clyde showed a lot of character telling the truth.''

"Yeah.''

They lapsed back into silence. She stared out of the window. The ground was beginning to rise. They were entering the trees. Marc was driving fast, unlike the last time they had come this way. Back then, Susan had been sitting beside them, chatting about things any other teenage girl would: dancing, late-night swims, who had a crush on whom. Again Melanie felt a tear in a corner of her eye.

"She's not eighteen yet, is she?'' she asked suddenly.

"I don't think so,'' Marc said, probably wishing she wouldn't keep mentioning Susan.

"She's not, I remember she told me her birthday's the day after Christmas. She'll be tried as a juvenile. Can you imagine her up on the stand? God knows who she'll choose to be.

But like she told me when she was trying to kill me, there isn't a jury in Iowa that will ever find *her* guilty. She's too smart for them.''

"The captain will get her behind bars."

"I wonder if even he can." Melanie resettled herself in her seat. The road was a bit bumpy.

"Sore?"

"A little."

"We can go back."

"No! I'm fine, really. Were you going to say something?"

"Yeah." He hesitated. "I saw her."

"When?"

"Yesterday. She asked to see me. She's in a room a floor above the room you were in. She looked awful. Her head was wrapped in bandages. They'd shaved off her hair. She asked about you. She wanted me to tell you that there were no hard feelings."

"That was generous of her. Anything else?"

"Yeah. She smiled when she said this. I don't even know what it means. She said, 'Tell Melanie, Reggie Jackson's got nothing on her.' "

Melanie laughed in spite of herself. It was a good laugh. It tugged at her side, and at the same time it felt like taking a big step away from waking in the middle of the night from a nightmare about dying. "She was referring to how I used the lamp as a baseball bat, and her head as a ball. So she compared me to Reggie Jackson? That's not bad company. At least she's still got her sense of humour."

The rest of the drive went quickly. Close to the tight turn that had caught Clyde looking, Marc slowed. The reservoir became visible through the snow-laden branches. A thin layer of fog hovered above the still water. The heavy grass odour she'd noted previously had been replaced by a crisp timber smell. They parked and got out.

As before, they walked along the shore. The clouds overhead were beginning to part, letting in the sky. The snow squished under their feet. At the corner of the lake near the dam, three people were gathered. Melanie recognized Clyde—in his chair—and Jeramie, but was uncertain about the third guy. Closer at hand, heading towards them, was another person. He was easy to recognize.

"Michael!" she called.

The captain smiled and waved. A minute later he was giving her a warm—though careful-hug. He had visited her at the hospital the day after the showdown, but she had been so doped up she kept calling him Bill Cosby.

"How's your side?" he asked her after shaking Marc's hand.

"I'm like those cardboard targets you talked about when we met," she said. "Bullets make neat holes when they go through me. It's great to see you. It's great to see you not working!"

"To tell you the truth, I was just getting some final facts for my written report."

"From Jeramie?" Marc asked.

The captain nodded. "I had a few questions to ask. Just a formality. He's completely in the clear."

"Did he share with you the answer to one of the world's greatest mysteries?" she asked, noticing a small boat ploughing through the mist at the end of the reservoir opposite the dam.

"Yes. But I won't spoil it for him by telling you."

"Then you've got to answer some other mysteries. When did you start to suspect Susan?"

"There was no single moment. But I think from the very beginning, when I questioned her an hour after Rindy had died, there was something about her that made me uneasy. Her responses were reasonable. Her grief appeared genuine. But I couldn't help feeling she was watching me. Then the night the play was reperformed, I noticed something quite remarkable. Susan held and fired the gun like an expert. This made me wonder again about the possibility of a simultaneous shot. I remembered how you'd had a hole in your nightgown sleeve when I'd awakened you in the jail cell. At the time I'd passed it off. Then I began to wonder if it had been a bullet hole. Fortunately, as Ronda, you were wearing the same nightgown. I decided I'd better have a look at it. Before I spoke to you in the dressing room, however, I checked the emergency exit on the left of the stage. I'd noticed that the icebox had been open during the scene when Rindy had died.''

"The icebox!" Melanie cheered. "That's what tipped me off!"

The captain nodded. "I went up onstage, reopened it, then opened the fire-escape door. And the alarm didn't go off. I was almost afraid to go in the dressing room with Susan in there. When I did, you may remember how I put my hand on your arm. The hole in your gown was clean and round.''

"Why didn't you arrest her then?" Melanie asked.

He looked embarrassed. "I should have. I considered it. But when I watched her sitting and taking off her makeup and smiling innocently, I said to myself, 'This can't be.' I was swayed by her charm.''

"You weren't the only one," Melanie said.

"But by hesitating to go out on a professional limb, I was risking you. That's why I asked if you were going straight home, if your father would be with you. I was trying to convince myself that nothing could possibly happen to you before I could obtain a final piece of evidence.''

"What more could you possibly learn in the middle of the night?" Melanie asked.

"During the week following Rindy's death I assigned an officer to visit every gun shop in Iowa that sells wad cutters. I had him call ahead to each store to make sure all the employees would be present when he visited. While making these rounds, the officer carried with him a picture of everyone in the play, plus photos of Heidi, Steve, Carl, Clyde, and Susan. It was a long shot, and I wasn't surprised when nothing came of it. No one recognized any of you. Fortunately, I instructed the officer to make a record of *anyone* on the youngish side who had bought wad cutters. All together, my man brought back a list of three places that had sold wad cutters to *young females*.''

"But all those people had already seen Susan's picture?" Melanie asked.

"Correct. And they hadn't recognized her. Then again, I thought to myself, would Susan have given them a chance to recognize her? She was obviously an extraordinary actress. In my office at Barters, I had a tape of Susan's voice I made while questioning her the night Rindy died. After speaking to you in the dressing room, I went to my office and began to call the three people. I woke up two of them, told them who I was, and played the tape over the phone. One said the young lady could have spoken Chinese for all he could remember. The other was sure Susan hadn't been in.''

"What about the third number?" Melanie asked.

"There was no answer. I kept trying it. At around six a lady finally answered. She was the owner of a sporting goods store in Kensen; that's over a hundred miles south of Barters. Her ears perked up when she heard Susan's voice. I jumped in my car and hit the road. I met her at her store and she listened to the tape all the way through without saying a word, all the while staring at Susan's photo. When the tape was done, she said to me, 'The chick that was here had I.D. She was old enough to buy whatever she wanted.'

"I assured her that her retain licence was not in danger.

" 'My girl was a redhead,' she said. 'Yours is a blonde and younger. How could they be the same person?'

"I suggested a wig and makeup. The woman chewed on that a minute. I knew the voice on the tape had struck a chord with her. But she was hesitant to commit herself. She was afraid she was going to have to testify in court. Then suddenly she slapped herself on the head.

" 'The girl who was in here was wearing a black top!' she said. 'I remember picking a hair off her shoulder. It was a blonde hair!'

"It was then," the captain said, "I knew without a shadow of a doubt who had killed Rindy. I called you, Melanie, a few minutes later. I debated telling you the truth over the phone. But because Susan was your friend, I feared you might have trouble accepting it. I preferred to go over everything in person at the station. Since your father was to be back soon, and you were going to be around the house until you left for the station, I again decided you would be safe enough. But as I drove back towards Barters, Susan's ingenuity kept preying on my mind! Something kept telling me not to underestimate that girl. An hour after speaking with you, I stopped and called again. I let the phone ring a long time. Then I called Susan's house. Her parents said she had gone out, they didn't know where. It was then I realised my terrible mistake. I contacted the station and ordered a deputy sent to your house. I also directed Marc to go there.

"Not long after, while I was on the road, the deputy came over the wire with the information about your note. Naturally, I sent him to the school, and headed there myself. Marc must have told you how we met in the parking lot." The captain paused. "You know the rest."

"Why did you want me to get Clyde?" Marc asked.

"In case my gun shop leads came to nothing," the captain said. "From questioning everyone connected with the play, I knew Clyde had been important to Susan. I believed he could throw light on the situation, and, if necessary, be used to squeeze the truth out of her."

"Sounds like you had a long night," Melanie said, grateful he took his job as seriously as he did.

The captain yawned. "It's been a long month. Time to take a few days off."

Melanie grinned. "And get away from us crazy kids?"

"Funny you should say that. I have a plane reservation leaving tomorrow for L.A. I'm going to see my daughters." He smiled. "They're lightweights next to you. The worst trouble they get into is staying out after curfew."

"Tell them I said hello," Melanie said.

"I will." He glanced in the direction of the road. "Well, I'd better be going."

How do I thank this man for my life?

Melanie reached up and kissed his cheek. "I won't forget you," she said. "Anytime I get in trouble, I'm calling you."

The captain was touched. "Anytime, Melanie," he said. "Anytime."

When the captain was gone, they resumed their walk along the lake. The distant boat had changed course; it was now steering in their direction. The guys by the shore had noticed their approach and were moving to meet them. Melanie was finally able to recognize the third person. It was Carl, and he was pushing Clyde's wheelchair. She went to ask Marc if the chair could handle the snowy grass, when she noticed him staring into the trees.

X marks the spot.

Here is where they had kissed. And fifty yards away, in the shadows beneath the road, was where the world had changed directions for a handful of people.

"Did I tell you I dreamed about her?" Melanie said.

"Recently?"

"The day Susan shot me. We were in her basement, playing Scrabble. Rindy was trying to get me to spell two different names with the same ten letters. I managed one: Stan Russel. If I'd had more time, if I hadn't wakened, I think I would have spelled Susan Trels."

"Interesting."

"Marc, do you think she was trying to warn me?"

"You mean her spirit?"

"Yeah."

He shrugged. "Who knows for sure? It's nice to think so."

"Did Rindy play Scrabble?"

"She loved it."

"I didn't know that. Rindy never told me. No one did, not until after the dream."

"Maybe she told you and you forgot."

"Do you think it was just my subconscious that saw the connection between the names? That it was trying to warn me using a dream?"

He stopped, looked again into the trees, then out over the water, where the fog was dispersing. "Was there a mist in your dream?" he asked.

"Yeah. How did you know?"

"Was it full of pretty lights?"

"Yeah!"

Marc nodded. "I dreamed about her too." He smiled. "Who knows?"

They reached the others a few minutes later. Carl had regained his colour since she had seen him last. Clyde, a blanket draped across his legs, was laughing over something Jeramie had said. And the court jester himself, sporting black leather pants and a brilliant orange shirt, was forming a snowball in his bare hands.

"I have to throw this at someone!" he shouted. "It's making my fingers cold. It has to be thrown!"

"Hit Melanie or me and you're going in the water." Marc warned.

Jeramie let go of the snowball and smacked Marc right in the face.

"Jeramie!" Marc yelled, disgusted, wiping the ice out of his collar.

Jeramie began to pull off his shirt. "I want to go in the water."

"Damn you," Marc swore, looking angrily from Jeramie to the water.

Clyde giggled. "Don't, Marc."

"He'll get pneumonia," Carl said. "Jeramie, put your shirt back on and apologize to Marc before he drowns you."

"But I want to go in the water," Jeramie said. "I want to play with the ducks before they're all gone."

"The ducks!" Melanie exclaimed, searching about. "Where are all the ducks?"

Jeramie's eyes lit up. "That's one of the world's greatest mysteries." He pointed a long bony finger towards the boat, now in the centre of the reservoir. "And *that's* the answer."

Although the boat was still far from shore, it was much closer than when they had arrived. Melanie was able to see two people—they appeared to be kids—leaning over the edge with nets in hand. They were catching ducks!

"Who the hell is that?" Marc asked.

"You know that guy who owns that diner out on Madison?" Clyde asked.

"Sam!" Melanie cried.

"Yeah, him," Clyde said. "That's his boat and his kids out there. He's inside the cabin, steering. We talked to him earlier. Apparently, he hauls his boat up here this time each year and collects all the ducks."

"What does he do with them?" Melanie asked, remembering all the turkey sandwiches—so called— she had eaten at the diner, feeling mildly sick.

"He keeps them in his barn and feeds them until spring comes," Clyde said. "He's been doing this year after year, and not a soul in town knows it. I think he was the one who originally brought the ducks here years ago."

"How did you learn this?" she asked.

Clyde glanced at Jeramie, who suddenly stopped his dancing about and stood quietly, his face relaxing. Looking at Clyde, Jeramie said softly, "Rindy told me."

When?

But she didn't ask. Maybe Jeramie had had a dream too.

Clyde reached under the blanket that covered his legs, and handed Jeramie a Polaroid camera. "Why don't you take our picture?"

Jeramie eyed the camera suspiciously. "Does this thing have film in it?"

"It's got a whole roll, Jeramie," Clyde said.

They gathered in a group, with the water and boat in the background. Jeramie took the first picture, let it develop in his hands, looked at it, then let out a horrific scream and ripped it in two. He let the next couple of pictures live, however, after which Carl volunteered to be the cameraman. When Jeramie joined them by the water, he sat in Clyde's lap.

"Isn't he hurting you?" she asked.

Clyde took her hand and pulled her closer to his chair. "After all we've been through, I don't think anything can hurt us." He caught her eye. "We're invincible, Melanie."

"I believe you," she said.

Carl took a couple of shots, then asked if he could have a picture of her standing alone. The sun was now bright. Kneeling in front of her, he framed her head with a patch of blue sky.

"Smile," Carl said.

She smiled.

The camera clicked. "Perfect," Carl said, getting back to his feet. She stood beside him while the developing process finished up, noting his eagerness. "I *hope* it's perfect," he added.

"Hey, I'm not that cute," she said.

The photo came out wonderfully. Her eyes, especially,

looked better than they really were, not an ordinary hazel, but a clear green.

"Can I keep it for my wallet?" Carl asked, staring at the picture. She remembered what he had told her by the boulder after the funeral.

"Oh, Carl," she said, hugging him.